ODETTE'S VOW

INSPIRED BY THE ILIAD AND ODYSSEY

VOWS OF THE LOST EPICS
BOOK ONE

GWYNETH LESLEY

OUTSPOKEN INK PRESS

OUTSPOKEN INK PRESS

First published in New Zealand in 2024 by Outspoken Ink Press

Text copyright © Gwyneth Lesley, 2024

Cover image copyright © Sarah Kil Creative Studio

Editor: Erin Driessen

The moral rights of the author and illustrators have been asserted.

A catalogue record for this book is available from the New Zealand Library.

HARDBACK ISBN: 978-0-473-73060-4

PRINT ISBN: 978-0-473-73059-8

EBOOK ISBN: 978-1-7385837-7-5

OTHER BOOKS BY GWYNETH LESLEY

The Femme Fatale Series

(Modern-day Greek mythology retellings with heartbreaking romances)

Prometheus' Priestess

A Lifetime Kind of Love

Madonna: Medusa's retelling

The Underworld Novellas

(Bite-sized cozy fantasies based in Greek mythology)

#1 *The Signature Dish of the Underworld*

#2 *Taking Orders in the Underworld*

#3 *Drinking Wine in the Underworld*

#4 *Let Them Eat Cake in the Underworld*

#5 *You Are What You Eat in the Underworld*

#6 *The Restaurateur in the Underworld*

Omnibus edition: *The Urban Underworld*

PRAISE FOR GWYNETH LESLEY

"Gwyneth Lesley is back with another heart-wrenching story (in a good way)! So well-written, so much raw emotion. I am in love with how the author can ... not 'retell' Greek myths ... but she 'continues' the classic stories in a modern-day setting. I cannot understand how she does this so well, but it works! Beautiful. Inspiring. Emotional. Challenging." – *Taylor*

"Continuously so impressed at the way that Gwyneth can make her books so relatable. So much sadness, hope, and inspiration in these pages. Beautifully written and a genius blending with the myths. It's truly amazing the way that the Femme Fatale series books have each taught me something about self-growth or acceptance." – *Monica*

"Gwyneth Lesley's writing and storytelling still leave me awed. Harrowing, passionate, vengeance, and the ultimate vindication." – *Steffy Smith, Historical Romance Author*

"The author has a wonderful way of building the story and the characters." – *Sandra*

"I always read her books so quickly because they're so easy to read and so captivating that I don't want to put them down. I love a myth-based retelling that doesn't feel like I'm reading something written hundreds of years ago." – *Rene*

For Aleena,

who was absolutely spot-on when she said,
"The moral imperative to condemn inhumanity supersedes
identity."

If only we would learn it.

"You already know the story. You will die. Everyone you love
will also die. You will lose them forever. You will be sad and
angry. You will weep. You will bargain. You will make
demands. You will beg. You will pray. It will make no
difference. Nothing you can do will bring them back. You
know this. Your knowing changes nothing."

– Emily Wilson, Introduction
to her translation of *The Iliad*, 2023

AUTHOR'S NOTE

Odette's Vow is a *loose* retelling that takes the backdrop of the ancient classics – *The Iliad* and *Odyssey* – and focuses on the fictional relationship between Odysseus and Odette during and after the Trojan War. Some scenes from the original epics have been rearranged through creative licence, to serve the plot. The dialogue is entirely new and aimed at readers in the twenty-first century.

Odette is not a character mentioned in the original work; no Trojan slave's perspective is included in *The Iliad*. The original story was told at a time when slaves were considered property and not people. Even translations of the original text today are all *slightly* different, as is the nature of translations.

In the time when *The Iliad* was told through oral tradition, Odysseus was considered true and faithful to his wife, Penelope. Sleeping with slaves 'didn't count' (as they were property), and coercion of a man by a goddess (even a minor witch-like one) into sexual intercourse was considered divine compulsion and therefore, whether or not he had been willing, could not be held against a man's honour.

Of the many reasons I love revisiting and reimagining ancient myths through modern retellings, one stands out: they remind us how far we've come as a society. Ideas that once shaped entire cultures now seem absurd, while others have endured through the ages, remaining just as relevant today as they were in the past.

I began writing this duet because I wanted to explore the other side of Odysseus. After all, he wasn't necessarily a reliable narrator when it came to *The Odyssey*. Everyone – even the hero – is the villain in someone else's story. While ancient Greeks often described Odysseus as suave and clever, the Romans called him cunning and manipulative.

That's really what I want to bring to light with this tale: the duality we all hold within us. Humans are ... complicated creatures. We are multi-faceted; what one person sees, the other cannot. Often, I've found that we are indeed our own worst enemies; the most scathing judges of our own characters.

War presents humans with a choice: to stay human, or to choose hatred towards your enemies who stripped away the life you once had and turn into someone who only follows their most primal, animalistic instinct. So, the midst of the Trojan War seemed the perfect place to explore these themes. War puts humans in desperate and extreme conditions and invites you to decide who you actually are and who you want to be, without the luxury of lying to yourself about either.

I highly recommend reading the original works (my favourite translations of *The Iliad* and *Odyssey* are by Emily Wilson), but I also know the classics can be daunting. This book is merely one reimagining – hopefully a fun one, despite the trigger warnings below. It's my wish that it convinces even one young reader that the original works are worth tackling.

TRIGGER WARNINGS: While I believe that exploring triggering themes in the safety of fiction is actually a positive way to practise exposure therapy within the pages of a book, I recognise that some readers prefer to be forewarned.

Given the subject matter and material, here is a list of triggering events in this book: graphic violence, infant death by poisoning, murder, war, slavery, rape (off-page), revenge, gory medical scenes, and betrayal.

Please note, this book is written in British English.

GLOSSARY OF GREEK DEITIES IT MAY HELP TO KNOW

Aphrodite – Goddess of Love and Fertility

Apollo – God of the Sun and Light, music and poetry, healing and plagues, prophecy and knowledge, order and beauty, archery and agriculture

Ares – God of War, violence, male virility, and Defender of the Weak

Artemis – Goddess of the Hunt and the Moon

Athena – Goddess of Wisdom and Warfare

Charon – the ferryman that takes Souls over the river Styx and into the Underworld

Eos – Goddess of the Dawn

Dionysus – God of Winemaking, orchards and fruit, vegetation, fertility, festivity, insanity, ritual madness, religious ecstasy, and theatre

Gaia – primordial deity who personifies the Earth

Hades – God of the Underworld

Hera – Goddess of Marriage, women, and family, protector of women during childbirth

Hypnos – the personification/God of Sleep

Morpheus – the personification/God of Dreams

Persephone – Goddess of Spring and Queen of the Underworld

Poseidon – God of the Sea (and water in general), Earthquakes, and Horses

Styx – The River of Hate, on which everyone travels from the mortal realms to the Underworld

Thanatos – God of Death

The Fates – the three sisters also known as the Moirai: the one who draws the thread of life (Clotho), the one who weaves it (Lachesis), and the one who cuts it (Atropos)

The Judges of the Dead – three figures tasked with determining the fate of Souls in the Underworld

Tyche – the Goddess of Fortune

Urania – Muse of Astronomy, known for her fortune-telling

Zeus – God of Thunder and Lightning (who likes to think of himself as the God of Gods)

I

ODETTE

The first murdered body I saw was my son's. The second was my husband's.

We had known they were coming, of course – the Greeks. Seven years ago, they had landed on Trojan shores, their approach signalled by rumours seeping through the citadel walls and whispers carried across the ocean. One of their kings, Agamemnon (a strange name), had done what no man before his people had. He'd united the fractured Greek kingdoms for one cause: her.

Well, that's what they said. But we all knew the truth. The Greeks wanted access to our trade route with the other countries. Helen was just a convenient excuse to go to war.

I had seen her only once. Helen of Sparta. I could see why they coveted her. Hair when lit by the sunset shone like woven gold. A rare sight, in these parts. Yes, I could see why the men fought over her like she was a bone.

Worse, too, she had been kind when she'd visited my village. Shy, but kind. Asking gentle questions of the other women in that higher-pitched, accented voice of hers.

Taking flower offerings from the children. Smiling demurely at the men. A people's princess.

Now, they whispered she was Helen of Troy. That one of our princes, Paris, had saved her from a fate no woman would wish for. Yes, poor Helen. A queen, then a treasured prize behind Troy's walls. Poor Helen, married to a rich king and in love with a richer prince. Poor Helen, safe behind those citadel walls while our men were slaughtered.

Those were my thoughts as I'd watched my husband Alcander die before dawn. When the soldiers arrived, they had barged through our door and dragged him away before I could reach for him. Another soldier came for me, hauling me into the chaos outside.

When I emerged, the wheat fields were on fire, but my eyes found Alcander, pinned to the ground by a different soldier again, this one a boar of a man, driving his spear into my husband. It seemed to pin his body to the ground as easily as my knife had speared boiled potatoes the night before. Alcander's face had been smashed into the dirt and rocks, and blood pooled around his head, dirtying that mop of light brown hair. Still, my loving husband had turned his face to me, his eyes bleak – as if the blade had bled all colour from them – pleading with me to *run*.

But, there was nowhere to go. Our lands were on the outskirts of the citadel, a small modest wheat farm my husband's family had run for generations. Acres of golden fields stretched out around us, the ones not on fire now browned and muddied by the Greeks who had cut through them on their way to finally raid us. The only place for me to run was towards the citadel's walls, usually an entire day's walk.

Instead, I'd watched the boar of a man pin my husband

to the ground like a fish. Even his Greek armour did not hide the barrel of his huge torso, and he wore no helmet, so I could see his dark hair and beard. Matching dark cold eyes stared down at my husband, bulging arms holding the spear as Alcander's body convulsed and writhed on the ground with its dying breaths.

I may have cried out, tried to reach for him; I do not know. I do not remember everything that happened in those moments. I remember strange things instead. When my husband's blood seeped into the ground outside our family home, I had thought of the gods and our sacrifices to them. The demands they made of us. The blood offerings over doorways to ward off evil spirits. I remember being on my knees as my eyes went to the heavens.

My offerings had gone unnoticed. I had lost everything. The gods wanted this war regardless, just like the men.

"You owe me a debt that cannot be repaid."

It was a calm statement, said in a moment of utter surrender to facts I could not change, and something in it stilled the air. The winds died, the screams stopped. It was as if Gaia herself cocked her head and watched me. One mother to another.

I watched back.

Perhaps mercifully, my boy was already dead when the soldiers arrived. None of the men or boys of the village had survived; only we remained – the herd of women on our knees in the courtyard, rounded up like cattle. Together we'd watched as the soldiers looted our homes, taking anything of value to them and placing it in a pile beside us. War prizes and property. Some of the women cried, others begged the soldiers to let them go, that they wouldn't say a word to anyone. They had not been told what to expect from the coming war.

I had.

I remember glancing at the body of my dear Alcander lying a few feet away. He had warned me as best he could. He had been a good man, in his own way. Yet, there would be no funeral pyre for him, no coins laid on his eyes for the ferryman's crossing of Styx to the Underworld. These brutes would not do our men that courtesy. Nor our children. Their souls would remain to travel these plains for the rest of their existence.

So, when the flames went up in our homes and the wailing women's cries with them, mine had not joined in. Instead I had watched the boar soldier, the one responsible for the death of my husband and by proxy, my son. He stood there, arms folded as he watched the flames with us.

Some of his brothers in arms laughed. He did not. He just stood and watched, vigilant in his task. Then his eyes turned to me. He didn't smile, didn't leer. He and I both knew there was nothing more he could take from me. Not even with what we both knew would come next. These brutes could not take my agency if I had already resigned myself to the fact. Which left my pride, and that had died last night when I put the hemlock to my son's lips. To spare him from this.

I hoped the soldier saw the promise in my eyes even as I swore an oath to the gods under my breath.

"If I am never to return here, may he never return to his home, either."

WE WALKED in silence along the road that would lead to the beaches. Most of the women were barefoot, having been dragged from their homes before dawn broke along the horizon. The soldiers had not allowed them to retrieve their shoes, and those women struggled as the sharp rocks dug into their heels. But, they didn't complain out loud. I only saw them wince, and the soldiers must have seen it, too.

The crying finally stopped when the women tasted ash in the air. The fires continued to burn at our backs, and once the Greeks were satisfied nothing would remain, we had been ordered up. The one I watched, the boar, had said something in Greek that most of the women didn't understand. I pretended not to, either. In our small village, Thracian or Lydian were more common tongues. The soldiers gestured and prodded enough that it was obvious they expected us to walk.

"Let's go," he'd said.

His voice was surprisingly melodic. I'd expected something gruff, something that matched his facial features, but from his tone and pacing, even in a different tongue, it was clear he'd been trained in the art of speech. This wasn't just one of the soldiers, then. This was a general. That made me hate him even more.

The smell of fire stayed with us for a long time.

I took small satisfaction in the soldiers' frustration with our slow pace. Every now and then, one would shove us forward, but since the entire group moved sluggishly, they had no choice but to let us continue at our own speed.

No one asked why I was wearing shoes.

Not sandals, either; buskins my husband had gifted me, that weaved their way halfway up my calves to protect my legs from dirt and bristles. I had told him if he expected me to work on the farm, then I needed proper attire. I had worn them in the fields all six years of our marriage.

Then, once I'd heard the Greeks had begun raiding villages and towns not far from our own, I had worn them to bed every night.

Our Trojan soldiers had met the Greeks when they'd arrived, of course, but there were no natural defences on a beach. It didn't take a seasoned general, like Hector, to figure that out. You only had to look at the land to realise a force mighty enough could push Troy's army back behind the citadel – exactly as the Greeks had.

I discovered that for myself when I surveyed the land, hours after we had started walking from our village. The sun was beginning its descent, a heavy summer's dusk settling in the sky and signalling a cloyingly warm night, despite the breeze blowing off the ocean. The Greeks had occupied the land around the beach, which was grassy but still plagued by sand. Tents were pitched haphazardly, as if the soldiers had anticipated a swift victory and thus a swift departure.

As we trudged through the camp, the men began to gather in front of their tents. Some followed us, some jeered, some grabbed their cocks and waved them at us, as if we had never seen them before. We were farm girls and women, did they really think we did not know the realities of life? Most of these women had not actually waited to lose their maidenhoods in marriage, but practised in the hay bales and empty fields with boys desperate to know what lay between a woman's legs, what it felt like to hold heavy breasts in their palms.

The jeers continued until we reached what I assumed was the centre of camp. A rug woven with rich reds and golds was spread across the grass and sand. At each corner stood a column and ropes stretched up to support the tent overhead. Fire torches were planted at each point, and in the middle of the rug was a throne on which sat a large, red-faced man. If the soldier who stood to the right of him was a boar, this man was a pig.

"I am King Agamemnon," he declared.

As if that meant anything to us.

The women didn't say anything, didn't bow their heads or curtsy, and I could have sworn this turned the man redder. We heard murmurs from the crowd of Greek soldiers that had now gathered around us, and then the king gestured to one of the soldiers by his side.

"A good haul, men of Greece! I shall take this fair, shapely female at the front as mine, along with the gold pieces you found. Bring them to my tent. For the others who won their loot today, come forward and claim your prizes."

A bronzed blonde soldier stepped forward first. Hard narrowed eyes roamed the collection of us and then lithe, muscular arms gleaming with sweat grabbed the second-prettiest.

"Very well, Achilles."

The women realised what was happening and started to panic, their heads turning this way and that. It must have looked like chickens in a coop because the men started laughing again. I grabbed the hand of the woman closest to me and stroked it in reassurance.

The boar's eyes zeroed in.

The woman whose hand I held did the same to the woman beside her, and that woman beside her, and so on. Eventually, all the women calmed.

Agamemnon chuckled. "You next, Odysseus. You led the raid, after all."

No man stepped forward, so I did not know who the king was talking to until the boar man lifted his chin. He didn't even bother to survey the other women as he looked me dead in the eye.

"I want her."

"Very well," the king said again.

The boar, *Odysseus* as he was called, did not step forward to claim me. Instead, he continued to look me in the eye, as if he knew I could understand him. But, the gods would be damned before I took a step. We eyed each other, both unblinking, until he finally stepped towards me. His calloused fingers on my upper arm gripped tight enough to bruise as he yanked me forward to stand beside him; to watch as the rest of the women were distributed like platters of meat.

Once the business of the day had been decided, the fire torches doused with water and dunked in the sand for good measure, the crowd of men dispersed with their new spear-wives and bed-slaves. Any names or titles we'd held had died with our husbands and fathers. One by one, the women left with their new masters until I was left standing on the dais alone. With him.

"Come," he grunted.

When I refused, his eyes hardened. That was the only warning I got before he seized my wrist and dragged me along beside him.

THE BOAR'S tent was lavish compared to the others in the camp. I hadn't seen inside them, but this was larger than the other tents around it, with a rug and plenty of cushions and blankets on the pallets. Another pallet doubled as a serving table. I had never imagined such wealth could exist in a war camp. More riches were here than had filled my modest home. I doubt they had brought this all over themselves, which confirmed the rumours – in my mind – that they'd already raided other villages, too. There would be other women here.

The tent, however, was empty except for the two of us. The minute we got inside, he released his vice-like grip on my wrist.

"Take a seat," he grunted.

Instead, I surveyed the space and then turned to face him.

He chuckled. "I know perfectly well you can understand Greek."

I shot him a piercing glare, but he turned his back to do something as he continued talking. I took the opportunity to scan the tent some more. The only weapons I saw were the sword still attached to his hip and the spear he had just placed on the wall beside him. There was no way I could get it in time. Even if I could, where would I go? There were a thousand Greeks out there waiting to chase me.

"I suggest you take a seat and break your fast with me." He turned and eyed me again. His hands were now full with two plates, each with bread and cheese and fruits. My stomach chose that moment to betray me with a large growl. We hadn't eaten the entire walk here.

He chuckled again and my hackles rose. The sound felt too easy, too intimate, after what he had done in the early hours of the morning.

He noticed my eyes scanning my husband's blood still splattered on his skin. "Ah."

He put the plates down on the pallet before grabbing a jug of water. He then went to the tent's opening and poured water over each arm, one at a time, and scrubbed with his hands. He returned and placed the jug on the pallet, the remaining water sloshing inside as it hit the surface.

"Better?"

"How kind of you," I remarked in Thracian.

He must have understood it, for his brow darkened. "Sit."

Begrudgingly I agreed, because starving wasn't going to serve me. But, to break my fast in the evening with the man who had killed my husband, to sit opposite him ... My stomach may have physically needed the food, but my appetite was not there. It took conscious effort to take a bite of bread, to chew every mouthful, to swallow. Every movement felt like an act of betrayal.

The deaths of the day clearly did not affect him so much. He ate quickly, efficiently. As if the food was merely fuel for his body and nothing more. Perhaps he didn't savour life, only death.

"So, where did you learn Greek?" he asked.

From the man you killed, I muttered in my head. But how did he know? He must have seen the question in my eyes, because he answered.

"You don't have that glassy-eyed confused look that the other women do. I'm assuming your husband taught you? Your father?"

I didn't bother nodding at either guess.

"Rare for a farmer to know Greek."

It was. But my husband hadn't wanted to be a farmer; he'd wanted to be a scholar. We'd met outside the citadel library ...

. . .

I HAD RUN into him on the library steps. I wasn't supposed to be there, but my mother was busy chatting away to a woman who had called for her by name: Callidora. After she'd commented on how long my hair was getting, just the same shade as my mother's, and 'wasn't I turning into a proper young lady' now that my body was starting to fill out with 'womanly hormones' (though I didn't know what they were), I stopped listening. So, I decided to make a game on the steps. I was only eleven. I hadn't been watching where I was going and bumped into a much taller boy, whose flat brown hair fell into his eyes as he looked up from his book.

"Oh, hello," he said, as he snapped the book shut and smiled at me.

Mortified, I stood there looking at him with eyes wide, afraid to blink. I think, at the time, I hoped he would mistake me for a statue, though I didn't have the porcelain skin to pull that off.

He laughed. "Shy one, are you? Me too. That's why I come here," he whispered conspiratorially as he pointed at the overwhelmingly huge building behind me. I'd never been in it. My mother told me only the smartest of men got to visit. But, this one didn't look much like a man, all long-limbed with no meat on his bones, as she would say. He definitely wasn't as old as my father, but he was older than the boys I knew.

"You're allowed in there?" I folded my arms over my chest and fixed him with my sternest look, the one my mother gave me when she knew I was lying.

He laughed at me again. "When I have time to study, yes."

I hesitated. "What do you study?"

He shrugged. "All sorts. The kings, the politics, the geography of the land."

"Geo-gra-fee?"

"The arrangement of the land."

"Why would you want to learn a thing like that, in there? Why not just look at it?" I gestured at the land around us as if that would prove my point, and caught my mother watching us. She was wearing a peacock-blue tunic, her hair in a braid atop her head to signal she was no longer a maiden and half down her back – to shock the neighbours, my father said. She looked like a goddess surveying the steps, as if she was about to walk up into the temple herself. But, there was a strange expression on her face. I couldn't tell if she was angry at me or not, but I could see her eyes peering intently at us from all the way over here. I turned to look back to the older boy.

"My family are farmers. My brother will inherit the land, but I thought I'd do something useful to help. Study it. See if we can't get a bit more coin for our crops if we're smart about it," he continued.

"Oh." I didn't have anything smarter to say. I don't think he realised I was distracted by my mother.

Luckily, she chose that moment to call my name. "Odette!"

"Bye!" I turned and rushed down the stairs as fast as my legs could carry me, which was quite fast given I was unnaturally tall for my age. According to my mother, I got my height from my father (even though she was taller than most of the ladies around here, too).

"Who was that?" she asked when I arrived beside her, out of breath.

"No one."

"Looks like you had a lot to say to no one."

I turned back to see him still watching me. I shrugged. "He was chatty."

I hadn't known it then, but Alcander had asked around,

figured out who I was and where my family lived. Then, on the eve of my fourteenth birthday, he came to ask my father for my hand in marriage. His proposal was initially rejected, my parents unorthodox enough to let me wait until I was sixteen to give me a chance to mature into a young woman. But their plan for me was always to be a wife, to bear children, to be a good Trojan woman of solid stock and breed. To do my part and to do it well. Given that Alcander was only eight-and-ten himself, the two-year wait had been approved by both families.

His marriage hadn't been as important as his elder brother's, who would inherit the land, which was good because my dowry wasn't very large. But it was good enough for him, and the match suited my parents just fine. It perhaps would not have been fine had his family known that their eldest would come down with a fever he could not break. But by then it was too late; Alcander and I were already married.

I was one of the lucky ones, losing my maidenhead to a good man. A studious man. Not one of those rough-and-tumbles in the barn I later heard about from other women. They'd given me looks of pity when they'd discovered I'd only had dalliances with my husband, even though that was the proper way to do things. I'd simply smiled at them. He found his pleasure and gave us a good life, what more did I need?

I found it far more invigorating when he would share with me the texts he'd been reading in the library. No other farmers' wives got that privilege. Alcander liked nothing more than to tell me what he had learned, in a time before he had to take over the farm, and I liked nothing more than to listen by the fire at night. Geography, as he had loved, the history of our townships, and ... Greek.

Then our son had arrived, and those conversations made way for the ones all new parents have. The Greek was barely practised, until we'd heard the greatest Grecian Army the world had ever seen was coming to our shores. Then, Alcander had dug through his memory to recall everything he could to help us survive what was to come, knowing he likely wouldn't, if – and when – they raided us.

I DIDN'T SAY any of this to the boar across from me, who continued eating. Watching me and eating. Eating and watching. Until he finished and stood, leaving his empty plate on the makeshift table beside my barely-touched one.

"That's your pallet over there," he pointed to the one farthest away from the entrance of the tent, lined with burgundy cushions and a thick blanket. "I suspect you'll eat when I'm gone and then I'd suggest you stay here and sleep. You need it."

At the look of confusion on my face, he nodded towards my feet. "If you were smart enough to be wearing buskins when we arrived, then you knew we were coming, which means you weren't sleeping when we raided your village. You must be tired. Rest. I'll be back later."

But, he'd mistaken my look of confusion for something else. When I looked between one pallet and the other – his and mine it seemed – he realised where my concern lay.

"Ah." He gave me a long, measured look while he stood at the tent opening, his hand on the fabric, ready to leave. "I have no interest in sleeping with you, spear-wife. I didn't pick you for that."

2

ODETTE

I didn't want to sleep, not when any one of those Greek soldiers could walk into this tent at any moment. But after the day's events, the heightened adrenaline, and the long arduous walk on no food or sleep, exhaustion soon sucked me under.

Hypnos was waiting for me. He was not, it appeared, fond of mothers who had killed their sons. And so he sent his son Morpheus to haunt me. I stared at the flapping of the tent and whenever Hypnos dragged my eyelids shut, the flickering sound of the tent became the crackle of the log fire Alcander and I had lit last night.

"THEY'LL COME TONIGHT." Alcander's voice was quiet.

I had only just put our son Lykas to bed. "You sound certain."

He sent me a pained look, and I knew what it meant. He was begging me to take this seriously, but when faced with the certainty of eternal damnation, what better way to beat back the desperation than with glib statements?

"*We could still take Lykas and run,*" *I pleaded, for the millionth time.*

"*Run where, exactly? To the next village on their warpath? Did you hear what they did to the people in Old Theronika, only one village away from our own?*"

I shook my head, not wanting to hear, already having heard the rumours, but Alcander was intent on continuing.

"*They hung the men's bodies from their own homes and left the ground slick with their entrails for their wives and children to walk through, as the Greek soldiers dragged them out of their houses kicking and screaming. Then, they hauled the boys by their hair and crushed their skulls against the rocks, until their small bodies were limp and left for the crows to peck at. Those close enough to report back say you can still hear the flies buzzing over their remains from miles away. And the smell of blood, and piss, and shit – and fear – becomes so overwhelming you can't help but retch. That is what will catch up with us eventually, no matter how far we run. And when it does, we will wish we had stayed to face the sword here, because what waits out there is a death so slow, even the gods look away.*"

I had closed my eyes to avoid watching Alcander's mouth paint such a vivid, crushing picture while also humming a sound-less tune in my head to block out his words, but it had not worked. The scene had sunk in regardless, until it took me several moments to catch my breath, to force the bile that had risen in my throat back down again, so I could speak. "*We could go to the citadel to seek refuge.*"

"*The citadel won't open until the people are banging down the door, and even when they do, the overcrowding is likely to cause disease and death to sweep the streets.*"

"*At least it would give us a fighting chance,*" *I countered, but I already knew it was useless. Alcander would say what he had said every time we had this argument. Still, some parts of me hoped he would change his mind at the eleventh hour. But he was already shaking his head.*

"Odette, stop it. We would be hunted down like animals. These are soldiers, barbarians. They want to see the fall of Troy — not just the citadel, but the fall of the Trojan people. All of us. I will die and they will butcher our boy like he's nothing." His voice hardened. "You know what they do to women. You'd be forced to watch them brutalise us before they dragged you away in chains."

"They might still spare him, raise him as their own, he's so young …" I tried, but even I heard the patheticness in my voice.

Alcander shook his head, his stare boring into me. "I am trying to offer you the only final kindness I can, as your husband. Do not fight me on this. My plan is the only thing keeping us from a fate worse than death." He stepped closer to me. "I won't let them take you or our son. I won't let you put us through that on a thread of foolish hope."

For the first time, I heard it in his voice. Defeat. Said quietly, resignedly, yet there was a crescendo roaring through my ears and a crushing weight on my chest that felt like someone was robbing my lungs of air. This had not been a discussion. There was no room for defiance, no space for hope. The poison I had purchased was not a back-up plan, but our only chance to be spared a brutal life, a brutal death, and die peacefully together as a family.

"Go. Make the tea," he ordered.

Nodding mechanically, I slowly rose from the fireside and walked as quietly as I could into our tiled kitchen. Above the sink, a rack where I usually kept jars of herbs for cooking and preserving. Behind them, the hemlock I had quietly purchased from one of the women in the village over, now gone. She had been quite clear in her instruction: crush the plant in my mortar and pestle, then add hot water, brew it for no more than five minutes, and serve it as a tea.

I boiled the water and steeped the tea.

The gods would never forgive me for this. They did not like poison. We were their little playthings. Anything that gave us some measure of control was abhorrent to them. Hera, in particular, would curse me for what I was about to do. But she didn't understand; how could she? Her children were gods. They would never know pain or suffering, so they did not understand the concept of mercy. That's what separated us and them, the mortals and the gods. True, compassionate mercy.

That's what I told myself as I poured the tea.

Alcander came in behind me and pressed his body warmth against mine. His attempt at comfort. His thumb stroked the curve of my neck, ran along the length of my bare shoulder, which he pressed a kiss to before he left. I heard him head up the stairs and imagined him going in to check on our son, stroking those curls off his forehead and pressing a kiss to his temple, before quietly moving into our bedroom.

I had already been told how this was to go. I did not agree with his approach, but in the end, I was his wife. I was supposed to follow my husband's instruction. And he would not – could not – watch his little boy die. As if I wanted this task. As if I had asked for it. As if I hadn't screamed and pleaded and begged the gods to keep the Greeks from our doorstep.

It had worked, for a time. Until it hadn't.

I held the cup firmly in my palms, as if spilling any of this poison on the floor would erode the stone beneath my buskins. Up each step, one by one. A light push on the door until it creaked open and there was my son, in his bed, bathed by the moonlight from the window above.

"Mummy?" he murmured drowsily.

Gathering myself, I took the four small steps into his room and sat on the floor beside his bed.

"It's alright, darling. I just came to say goodnight. Are you thirsty?"

He nodded as he sat up.

"H—Here." I swallowed hard, willing my voice not to break. This was a kindness, I reminded myself. "Drink this."

His small pudgy hands clasped either side of the cup. So small, so perfect. How could I think of ending something so precious? I went to snatch the cup out of his hand, but it was too late; he had already taken a giant gulp.

"Mummy, it tastes funny," he complained, and then took another gulp as if that would change his mind. Like I had frequently told him to do when trying new vegetables at the dinner table. Oh gods, what had I done?

He handed the empty cup back to me. "I don't think I'd like to drink that again, Mummy."

A tear fell down my cheek and I couldn't help but let out a small sob. "No, I don't think you should."

Climbing into bed beside him, I stroked his soft arms, forehead, hair, and sang to him. When he complained that he couldn't feel his legs and that his tummy felt funny, I shushed him and told him it would be alright. When his body trembled as his breaths got shallower and more rapid, I cradled him in my arms and assured him it would be alright. Not much longer, I promised.

And when he was still and the last of my wretched sobs had been torn from my throat, I went back down to prepare the two remaining cups.

I woke to the knowledge that there was someone in the tent. Someone trying to muffle their footsteps in a failed attempt to keep quiet. Unlike the soldiers who'd made no such attempt when they stormed their way into our homes.

The boar was wrong. I *had* been sleeping when they'd come to raid us. I had gone to make the remaining two cups of hemlock. Alcander and I had sat by the fire together and drunk them. It had an acrid, bitter taste and it wasn't long before I had felt the muscles in my limbs weaken and my breathing become laboured. I remembered my head lolling to the side, as if I was having an out-of-body experience, before my eyes had flickered shut.

I don't know what happened, why I had awoken to the banging on the door. Or why Alcander was staring wild-eyed at me as the banging seemed to get impossibly louder. Perhaps the gods had spared us for a reason. I ran immediately to Lykas' room, in case he too was awake, only to crumble in the doorway at the sight of his still, lifeless body.

The gods hadn't spared us.

They'd ensured there wasn't enough poison to take us all. I was certain I had measured it out as the witch had said. Had she lied? Had one of the gods interfered? It didn't matter though, as rough calloused hands yanked my arms behind my back and dragged me from our home.

Now my little Lykas lay dead, my husband killed before my eyes, and my worst fear had come to pass: life without either of them, with me left behind to carry on. I was no longer a desperate mother pleading with the gods to no avail. I was a murderer. And for trying to take control of my fate, the gods were content to make me suffer. Hera certainly knew how to punish those who went against her.

That's why I had ended up a slave – *to him.*

I opened the slits of my eyes to try and make out who was walking around, but it was just the boar. He stopped and I tried to breathe evenly to maintain my feigned sleep. Grunting, he found whatever he was looking for and left again.

I did not wish to fall back into Hypnos' arms, so I got up, finding the jug by the entrance of the tent to wash my face and under my arms. Outside, the camp didn't sound so busy, so I dared to look.

Turning my head from left to right, I saw two rows of simple but sturdy tents staged like houses along a sandy road. These ones were all emblazoned with the same circular emblem stitched onto the beige canvas. The line that ran across the middle of the symbol was jagged, clearly a clifftop, with a swirling line below it representing a bay. In the centre of the emblem, balanced on the jagged clifftop, was a palace surrounded by olive branches. Above the palace emblem was a rising sun, as if the place was a beacon of enduring hope.

I knew from my studies with Alcander that the island of Ithaca was famed for its rugged mountains and olive groves. I wondered if the boar was from there.

There weren't many soldiers out, but I could hear roaring laughter in the distance and smell a fire; the aroma of roasted meat mingled with the salty tang of sea air. Perhaps that's where Odysseus had gone, to have a real dinner, the paltry plate he offered me earlier merely honouring some weird Greek guesthood rule I didn't know about.

But, why would he feed me at all if I was now nothing more than property to him? I shook my head, my thoughts foggy from weariness, and quite possibly the aftereffects of the hemlock still working its way out of my bloodstream.

My memories, even from earlier in the day, were muddled at best. I was sure on my walk here that there were rows upon rows of these tents, a sprawling tent city, nestled beneath the shadow of mighty warships drawn up to shore. I could imagine that during the day the place pulsed with an energy equal to the citadel of Troy, which I'd visited on the few occasions I ventured beyond the walls.

For now, though, the place was muted and seemingly deserted. Most of the soldiers must have been up by the bonfire. I hesitated, not wanting to get lost in what was undoubtedly a labyrinth, but also desperate to explore. To not be an easy target for the boar to return to.

So, I stepped out onto the path. Each tent along the way was a miniature fortress, its entrance flanked by spears thrust into the ground and shields propped up against the fabric walls. Whetstones to sharpen weapons lay abandoned beside them. Somewhere, horses whinnied and stamped their hooves impatiently. I imagined they were tethered to wooden stakes.

At least I had been spared that.

Rows of tents gave way to more rows of tents, and I could see more than one bonfire scattered up the coast of the shoreline. Of course, if a hundred thousand Greek soldiers were here, then there had to be other areas for the different islands all gathered under one Greek banner.

Just as I'd had the thought, I saw a pennant with a different emblem of another Greek city-state wrapped around a wooden pole and stuck into the ground, clearly marking the boundary between one encampment and the next.

"What are you doing here?"

The harsh voice to my right threw me and I froze, like a deer that's just scented a predator in the glen. I went to swallow, to talk, but my mouth was dry and no words would come to mind.

"I asked you a question," the soldier rounded on me, grabbing my hair and harshly tugging it until my face was cast in moonlight.

"I—I was just ... taking a walk," I managed.

"Without your master? I don't think so," he sneered. His flat sloping nose looked like it had been dented in with a shovel. His dull eyes, slightly too far apart, lingered on my face then dragged their way down the rest of my body, his sneer turning salacious as his tongue swiped out against fat lips. His grip on my hair tightened.

Then, before I could so much as curse myself for my foolishness (of course there would be guards on watch duty), a commanding voice with the weight of a church bell and yet somehow like warm wood and honey cleared through the heavy breaths of the man holding me.

"There you are." Odysseus appeared from the shadows of a tent, along the track between the two encampments that obviously led elsewhere. To one of the bonfires, probably. "Release her, Thersites."

"Odysseus ... *Lord* Odysseus," he corrected himself. Was that fear I heard in his voice? His hand unclenched from my scalp as he shoved me. "I was just showing this slave back to her proper place."

"And where would that be, Thersites?"

I actually sensed the man behind me begin to tremble as Odysseus strode towards him.

"You would be particularly stupid to take what does not belong to you just to increase your own status. Are you dumb as well as ugly, Thersites? To take another man's property when his tent is not five hundred metres from your own? What were you going to do, cut her tongue out so she couldn't talk? Or just hope she wouldn't open her mouth for anything but your stump of a cock?"

"I wasn't—"

"Thinking? No, I don't imagine you do much of that," Odysseus said quietly, ignoring the soldier's blabbering entirely as he stopped beside me, crooked a finger under my chin and turned my head one way and then the other, examining my skin for marks. Satisfied he saw none, though my scalp was still on fire, he took the remaining steps until he was inches from Thersites' face.

The smell of fresh sweat emanated from unwashed pores and coloured the air around us.

"Even without talking, all bodies – slave or soldier – can do an awful lot of explaining. Just as yours is doing right now. Do not let me find you touching my property again. Do you understand me, Thersites?"

Thersites gave an audible swallow, the soldier's fear palpable. I realised in that moment that Odysseus must have been more than just a general, or done *something* on the battlefield, something renowned, in order to inspire that kind of fear in another man, particularly one on his side of the war. Thersites nodded in deference before shuffling off into the shadows of his encampment.

"Come," Odysseus motioned for me to take his hand. My legs were now jelly-like from exhaustion and fear, so to avoid tripping over the fabric of my chiton, I gathered the dusty and sand-spattered hem around me and reached for his hand. His was large and calloused, dwarfing mine as he interlocked our fingers and tugged me back to Ithaca territory.

We had just returned to the tent, Odysseus holding the flap open for me as I nodded my thanks, when a cry pierced the air. My head snapped back towards the outside, but no one came declaring war. Instead, an uproar of laughter followed as Odysseus stepped into the tent. I realised it must have been one of the women from my village. I stepped back, to avoid being crushed into the boar's broad chest and cringed simultaneously, trying to keep my show of displeasure to myself.

He noted it.

"It is the only way kings can convince men to go to war," he said as he moved past me and I remained standing near the doorway, loath to be here but even more loath to leave. "That and glory. Next time, you would be wise to stay where I tell you."

I went to thank him for what he'd done with Thersites. It was a force of habit, of manners that had long been drilled into me as I'd been raised a good woman, a good wife. Then I realised the absurdity of such a thing – to thank my captor for sparing me from degradation. He hadn't done it for me. He had done it because to take and debase another's property was to question a man's social status.

The boar had no more rescued me than he had asserted his position. That was all.

He wasn't a good man. He wasn't a kind man. He was a feared general in the great Grecian Army. And I would do well to remember that.

3

ODYSSEUS

She reminded me a little of my Penelope, with that proud, strong nose and those sharp eyes that said she was noting everything, just waiting for a chance to use that information to her advantage. Just like Penelope. But, her lips were bigger – both plumper and wider on her face. My wife had more of an oval-shaped face, compared to the sweetheart shape of the slave's in front of me. She didn't have hair as dark as Penelope's, nor skin as white and creamy. A splattering of freckles across her cheekbones made it clear the men in her life had put her to work in the fields. Her arms were slim but muscular and tanned. From what I saw when she lifted her chiton, her calves were, too.

I appreciated a woman who could do hard labour. I thought it would make her more useful, but that wasn't the only reason I chose her.

It was entirely possible that she was spying for the Trojans. Why else would she have been wearing buskins on her feet when we raided her village at the fourth hour before dawn? If it were to run, she would have done so. But, no –

she'd been gathered with the rest of the wailing women. We hadn't had to chase any of them down. Had she known we were coming? If so, how?

Then, there had been that neat trick of hers at the dais, calming all the women with that show of solidarity before they were picked off one by one. The fact that she, a farmer's girl from the provinces, could speak Greek fluently enough to understand what was going on was suspicious in itself. Why did she need to know the language of scholars and great men? One thing I was certain of: she was no fool.

Hector could have trained her in the art of speech himself, for her to report back to him, and placed her in plain sight for us to capture and retain. Most of the men in the Grecian camp wouldn't think a woman capable of it – spying – but I'd been married to clever Penelope long enough to know it could be true. It was a smart move, a clever move, one I would have considered myself.

When I returned to the tent earlier, I half expected to find her poking her nose into things, looking for plans or something to use as leverage. Instead, she'd been evenly breathing on the pallet, her back turned to me, sleeping. As I'd suggested she should. But then, she'd gone for that little walkabout in the camp.

It was a good thing I'd waited, followed, and watched as I found her with Thersites, truth be told. Anyone smarter and quicker would have already had her, unaware what a double-edged prize she might be. She would have been ruined; I'd have had to discard her, as keeping her would have raised questions.

Besides, Thersites, with all his moaning about the state of our leadership during the war, had become a bothersome talisman of the grumbling that stirred beneath the surfaces of the men. I'd already beaten him once with a gold staff for voicing his poisonous thoughts about the war and how we were handling it. It was a pleasure to taste his fear on my tongue again, while he shrunk into the shadows like the coward he was. Those who agreed to something and then claimed themselves the victims were the most repugnant in character.

With that, my thoughts turned back to this strange creature in front of me. She'd been watching me, a slight tilt to her head that reminded me of a feline. I could see her breathing return to normal, by the rise and fall of her slim chest. I had felt her heartbeat in her hand when she had taken mine earlier, the adrenaline flooding through her small frame. She'd stopped shaking now. I was impressed by her ability to control it so well.

Another cry pierced the air, and another round of jeers and laughter followed, like thunder chasing lightning. She didn't flinch this time, but I saw the disgust slither behind her eyes as her gaze held mine. She was probably expecting the same treatment from me, judging me by my actions rather than my words, despite what I told her earlier this evening.

Like I said – clever.

But, my heart and whole being rested with a woman back on the isle of Ithaca. How I longed to be in those soft arms of Penelope's and that softer bed, ruminating on the day, asking for her thoughts and opinions on how I led our people.

So, as pretty as my new spear-wife was, I had no desire to bed her. I wouldn't be led by my cock.

There was nothing for it but to turn in and go to bed myself. If I left the tent again, who knew what she would do.

Perhaps she would stay. By the look in her eyes, I suspected she worried that I'd come back with other men, or another woman, and trade her in. Although she couldn't know that thanks to Agamemnon's appetites, spear-wives and bed-slaves were becoming currency.

It was a foolish king who decided to play his war games in the camp we all called home.

The only way she would relax, and which would allow me to relax after this long, arduous day, was to sleep. Our Lady Dawn always had a way of making the terrors of the night seem less fearful come morning.

***

"You look like a Trojan piece of shit."

Diomedes, a king in his own right, made the remark as he slapped me between the shoulders. I turned to survey him as we headed back to camp after another day of killing Trojans on the battlefield. What tedious drudgery.

My body ached from the constant movement; of finding steady footing on sand, soil and mud, stepping over bodies, twisting my torso to aim, lunge, thrust, and avoid blow after blow. My arms were heavy, even though my shield and spear were in the chariot being driven by one of my captains. I could have rode in it, but something about walking at a slower pace with the men back to camp seemed good for morale, and got my mind back into a calm place after being constantly on the lookout for the next threat, the next Trojan.

"If you weren't just beside me killing those bastards, I would have thought your bed-slave had kept you up all night," Diomedes boomed loud enough for all the men around us to hear. Several of our subordinate soldiers, those who hadn't done anything to earn any war prizes of their own yet, sniggered.

I enjoyed fighting beside Diomedes on the field. His courage, strength, and skill had seen several Trojans sent down to the Underworld. We could have passed for brothers, I'd been told. But Diomedes' dark curls were shorn close to his head, while mine kissed my nape. Where my beard dusted a shadow across my jawline every day, his only grew beneath his chin, as if his hair was strapped to him like the helmet he now held under his arm. We were of similar build, both broad-shouldered, but he was a few years younger than me – and it was at times like this, when he said something childish and vulgar to gain traction with the crowd around him, that I remembered it. On the battlefield, he was the perfect general. Off it – well, he was still a young king.

"Unlike you, my friend, I happen to let her sleep."

"Sleep? A strange concept for a spear-wife, surely?" he jabbed again.

I knew what he was angling for. He wanted to meet her. He wanted to see why I had chosen her, when I had either refused slaves in past prize collections in favour of gold or precious goods or handed them off to one of my captains in thanks instead. It would be a dangerous play. I didn't want to tell him what I suspected until I had confirmation, which meant he might let something slip in her presence in the meantime. Then again, it could be a good way to confirm my suspicions if anything did come of Diomedes' yammering.

"Why don't you come and meet her properly tonight? Dine with us in my tent."

"I thought you'd never ask!" Diomedes slapped me on the back again as we finally arrived at camp. The twenty-minute walk always felt harder and longer on the way back. "I'll be 'round within the hour, yes? Give me a chance to wash off this Trojan scum!"

Those were his parting words as he peeled off to the left, towards Argos' camp territory. A bunch of soldiers following him laughed at his retort. I merely nodded in response.

I continued on with my own men who had survived the day, and in the few minutes it took to reach my quarters in the Ithaca encampment, each step got heavier than the last, as if my body knew how eagerly respite waited for me in the privacy of my own tent.

Except, of course, it wasn't waiting for me. As I batted back the tent flap, there she was, lying on her pallet, staring up at the ceiling, making a fidgeting movement with her thumbs. It seemed she was either playing a game with herself, or reciting something to remember, to report back, using a physical mnemonic device of her own creation. My brain snapped back to full alert, and as if that were her siren call, she immediately stopped her hand movements and sat bolt upright, staring at me.

"We have company coming for dinner tonight. Make sure there is enough wine and food for three within the hour." My voice was gruff, gruffer than I intended, but the frustration of needing to stay on guard in my own tent had me grinding my molars.

She nodded, scrambling to her feet and scurrying out of the tent – her chin pulled down, refusing to look at me – as she went to gather supplies. She hadn't hesitated at my request, so she must have met one of the other spear-wives today who would tell her what to do.

With no other nervous, anxious energy buzzing around me, I could allow the weight of the day to collapse on me as my shoulders sagged with the relief that it was almost over.

I was relieved to see the jug by the tent entrance full of water. Stripping off quickly, I poured half of it over my naked frame in the small area of the tent where I'd dug a shallow trench for water to drain beneath the canvas. Nothing would have brought me more joy than submerging myself in the warm salty water of the ocean and washing off the blood and grime caked to my skin. But there would be no time for that, not today, with Diomedes on his way. Taking a handful of coarse sand from a small ceramic pot, I scrubbed at the blood and grime until every inch of my skin felt like it was on fire. A fire I doused with the remaining wash water before I slathered oil across my body.

When she returned, I was dressed in a short-sleeved white linen chiton layered with a dark blue-trimmed himation. Her arms were laden with goods that she settled on a spare crate before she got to work. First, she walked over to the chest by the foot of my bed pallet and pulled out a purple cloth that she then laid on the dining pallet, smoothing out the crinkles. Next came three wine goblets and a beautifully decorated jug depicting one of the many feasts of Dionysus that I had scored in a previous raid. Then she wiped three plates – also pulled from the crate – and placed them on the table.

A scowl settled on my face. Before I could comment that she'd clearly been snooping, she began to unpack the goods she'd brought back with her.

There were brine-cured olives and goat cheese in a wide, shallow ceramic dish, half a dozen slices of barley bread that still looked fresh, honey-glazed carrots and leeks, stuffed vine leaves, walnuts, and almonds. She left the tent again and returned with a leg of roasted lamb, its rich and smoky aroma suddenly making me salivate.

It was exactly what I would have expected of a house-maid. Though, the speed with which she'd picked it up had my suspicions roaring back to life even as my stomach growled. No new slave was this resourceful. These were larger quantities than the ration allowance.

"Is everything to your liking?" she asked, as she poured the wine, and then water, into the jug. I held up a hand to stop her when it was diluted the way I liked best.

Her voice was softer than last night, when she'd spoken to me with such an attitude. Perhaps the ordeal with Thersites had spooked her. But even softly spoken, her Greek pronunciation was clear, measured. As if she considered every word before she spoke it. There was a lilt in her accent that made it obvious she was from the Western provinces of Troy, but that simply added to the poetry of her voice, as if the words had rolled around on her tongue and come out smooth.

"This is good," I replied slowly.

She quirked an eyebrow at me, a small smile on her face. There it was – the fire behind her eyes. The slightest flicker that said she knew exactly what she was doing.

"You've been here less than a day. You've done more than what's expected of you."

It wasn't a compliment and she knew it by the warning tone, for her smile dropped at the same time her hands did.

"What's your name?" I asked her.

She frowned ever so slightly. "What does it matter?"

I paused, considering my answer. "Because I do not wish to call you spear-wife. That is why it matters."

"Odette," she eventually acquiesced. "My name is Odette."

"Odette," I said, rolling her name across my tongue, getting used to the feel of it, before I nodded. "It suits you."

"Better than spear-wife."

A sharp bark of laughter burst from me. "That it does."

She opened her mouth to respond and I instinctively leaned in, frustrated yet intrigued by her complexity, when Diomedes' voice rang out as he entered the tent.

"Odysseus, my friend, how lovely of you to have me over for a meal! Pray, what are we giving the gods this night, and what are we saving for ourselves? And where is your spear-w—"

"Odette," I interrupted, before Diomedes had a chance to corner her and wrangle her for more information I wasn't yet ready to give him. With that sly look on his face, I knew that's exactly what he would do. My friend had always been a brash man, made for the war, and he'd always had a penchant for using women as little more than objects. I took a step forward to prevent him putting his hands on her. Should she slap him or show malice of any kind, it would be seen as weak of me if I let it go unpunished. I was still uncertain of her motivations; unsure how she would act. She was like a spooked horse: calm one minute, ready to bolt the next. Calm, yet feisty. Certainly skittish. She couldn't be trusted, and I wondered if inviting Diomedes hadn't been one of my more stupid ideas.

"My, my, he is protective over you already, isn't he?" Diomedes sent a knowing smirk my way before he offered Odette a dazzling smile and reached out to bring her hand to his lips. "A pleasure," he said, as he tilted and bowed his head.

She smiled at him – actually smiled. Chin lifted, she was looking him squarely in the eye.

"Odette, this is Diomedes. A fellow lord and general." Once again, my tone was harsher than I'd intended. I coughed to pretend it was something other than my annoyance that she would smile at him but revolt at me.

"Welcome Lord Diomedes. Please, won't you come and sit? We have fresh lamb with bread tonight, and plenty of wine, of course."

Diomedes sat. I followed. Odette poured his wine first – as was custom – before she threw him another smile. She was charming him, I realised, and my blood heated in anger at the thought. Inviting Diomedes had definitely been one of my stupider ideas, and she was making the most of this opportunity.

"Well, wine is what we need, woman! This war against the Trojans is becoming more tedious with every passing day. We have your man here to thank, of course." Diomedes gestured wildly with wine in hand, almost spilling it right across the table before throwing it down his throat.

Odette looked at me. I offered a grimace in return as she refilled Diomedes' already empty goblet.

"And why is that, Lord Diomedes?"

"He hasn't told you the story already?" Diomedes threw me a shocked look. "Why is it that you don't brag about your most marvellous of ideas? Is it because, perhaps, you're ashamed of them? Will you finally admit that you don't always get it right?"

I chose to smile as I lifted my cup to my lips. "Not a chance, my friend."

I glanced over at Odette, deliberately drawing out the moment as I sipped my wine. I wanted her to feel the weight of my regard, to understand that I was fully aware of her scheming, and that I would win whatever dangerous game she was trying to play with me.

"Well, Odette, let me tell you how this all came to pass, shall I? How we ended up on your shores."

"Certainly, Lord Diomedes."

There was no falter in her voice. Her shoulders didn't tighten at the horrors she had been through since the war had touched her village. Her voice wasn't tight with pain or guilt. She was either the perfect hostess, or the perfect liar.

Yet, Diomedes was so pleased with her, he poured *her* a wine before he patted the cushion beside him for her to sit on, and Odette complied.

"Our Odysseus was right there when the stunning Helen of Troy was to be married. Now, you know how men can be – fighting tooth and nail over a beautiful woman! Well, Odysseus, ever the strategist, hatched a brilliant plan. He proposed that Helen herself should decide. Can you imagine such a thing? Letting a woman choose her own husband! It was nothing short of genius. By letting Helen choose, he cleverly sidestepped the inevitable brawls and potential wars that would have erupted among the kings vying for her favour."

He paused for effect, his focus lingering on Odette.

"Do you see? By making Helen's choice the deciding factor, each king had to swear a blood oath to respect her decision and protect her from any man who might try to take her from her chosen husband. It was a fail-safe against any disputes. And who did Helen choose? Our very own Menelaus. So, when your bold young prince, Paris, came along and snatched her away, we were all bound by our oaths to uphold our word. Even Odysseus here was bound by that oath."

Diomedes let out a belch before he foraged through the spread of food with his giant hands. Wine and exhaustion created a heady combo that would still not deny hunger. Despite the distraction, my gaze remained fixed on Odette as he ate.

Her eyes, hawklike in both manner and colour, flitted back and forth as if she were trying to piece something together. Eventually, she reached her conclusion.

"You let her choose?" Odette asked me.

"It seemed like a good idea at the time."

"And of course, you had already sneakily arranged to be married to her cousin before the rest of the men had even arrived, so what did you care?" Diomedes added between bites.

"I care very much about being away from my wife now," I managed through gritted teeth.

I waited for Odette to ask about my wife, but instead she kept her attention on Diomedes. "Tell me, Lord Diomedes, how long will the Greek Army remain here?"

"Oh, a while yet, I should imagine."

"So certain?"

She sounded shocked. Diomedes was still scarfing down food, too busy to reply, but Odette wouldn't tear her eyes away from him. The knot in my chest grew larger until I felt myself wanting to growl.

"It was foreseen by the soothsayer Calchas before we arrived," I butted in.

She glanced my way – a mere acknowledgement she'd heard me – before turning to him once again. "But haven't you been on Trojan shores for seven years already?"

Diomedes grunted. "With little to show for it."

She frowned, not fully understanding what was being said between the words.

I got up and collected the bowl of sand usually reserved for bathing scrub. I sprinkled some on my empty plate and sketched out clumsy pictures with my thick fingers. First, a prophet, using the symbol of Urania – the muse of astronomy, known for her fortune-telling – to show Odette that we'd had a seer guide us with Urania's good graces.

I looked at Odette, who nodded that she understood, and continued.

I then drew the symbol for Hydra, a water snake, and nine wide vee's above it – bird wings. I travelled my finger along the snake and up into the air, my finger 'eating' the nine birds one by one, before travelling back into the snake's belly each time with a smudge of my finger.

"Do you see?" I asked her. "Nine years will pass before we will finally take Troy. There are two more years to go."

"The war will be long," she said.

"The war *has* been long," Diomedes interjected.

Odette's brow furrowed. "I don't understand. It will be over soon, though?"

Diomedes and I shared a look.

"Two years on the battlefield feels like twenty. We have already lived a lifetime here," I said quietly.

"Why not just leave if you are all so unhappy?"

"Because of your *upstart* of a prince, Paris. He broke the blood oath. We cannot break from this war until he pays for it," I said.

To my surprise, Odette shook her head. "He is not my prince."

Diomedes laughed boisterously, but I waited, watched,

to hear what she had to say next. She was trying to get us on side for something, of that I was certain, and my friend was falling for it.

"She's already one of us! Well done, Odysseus. You definitely chose well. And her Greek is really rather marvellous, isn't it? Is that what you two have been doing all this time in the tent together, hmm?" Diomedes wiggled a sly look between us and smirked at the crude joke.

Odette's shoulders hunched towards her ears, but then I watched her take a controlled breath and actively work to lower them. "You misunderstand, my Lord," she eventually replied. "Paris is not my prince. I am not one of the citadel members. I am just, *was* just, a farmer's wife. Kings, princes, oaths and wars … these are not my business."

Odette threw me an inscrutable look, which irked me even more. Was she laying blame at my feet for dragging her into this? War would have come regardless. If anyone, Odette should lay the blame with Paris. And she should be grateful she ended up with me and not one of the more animalistic men.

"Quite right. You are much better suited here where you can help," Diomedes quipped between bites.

"Perhaps that is enough talk of the war," I suggested, not in the mood to tolerate more accusations and inscrutable looks. Reaching out, I ripped some bread and dipped it in oil before plunging my knife and cutting away a section of lamb.

Diomedes chuckled. "How can one forget the war, when you gut that lamb like you gut a man on the battlefield?" He turned to Odette once more. "I know you don't belong on the battlefield my dear, but you should see how this one fights! He crouches down behind his shield, then once they throw their spear he *lunges* forward and spits them like a pig." He mimicked the actions with his own knife.

Odette slowly finished chewing her mouthful, before she dabbed at the corner of her mouth with her thumb. I fixated on the action, waiting for whatever words would come next. For her to reveal her hand. When it came, I realised just how dangerous a creature she was.

"I thought it looked more like gutting a fish, myself. But yes, I would say that is exactly how he killed my husband."

4

ODETTE

A thrum of expectation hummed through my bones at the declaration. A beat of silence so long it engulfed everything that followed. I wasn't sure what I expected, exactly, but it wasn't what happened. Was I waiting for Odysseus to deny it, so I had just cause to claw out his eyeballs with my fingernails? For the two oafs charading as civilised men to condescendingly explain the art of war to me, as if I did not know?

No, it was worse than that.

They simply looked at one another and kept on eating. The roaring silence in my head turned into a buzzing. Eventually I could see their mouths moving again, but I could not hear the words. *Would not* hear them. I had just admitted that my life had been ruined over the man who now claimed me as his property and they had ... *ignored* it. I grimaced as the smacks of saliva and chewing beside me broke through the hum in my head.

Alcander had been right – they were savages.

Diomedes, of course, was exactly that. Alcander had told

me of the famous heroes known for their legendary prowess and bravery, but I saw none of this in Diomedes. Here in the tent his words, even in another language, felt delivered by a dull hammer. Subtlety was not this Greek hero's strong suit, further emphasised by the sheer size of him. He could likely snap me in half like a twig and my organs would just bleed out onto the ground.

For some reason, the thought didn't arouse anything but mild curiosity in me now.

Odysseus, on the other hand ... His eyes sent a shudder through my body whenever they landed on me.

After the disaster that had been my wanderings last night, I had convinced myself that perfect compliance in Odysseus' presence would fix the tension he aimed at me like a barbed arrow. I'm not sure why I cared, beyond not wanting to be given to another man like the one who had cornered me last night. Yet, for reasons even I could not comprehend, I had just blurted out something sure to relace the strain between us. And if anything, he seemed less irked now than earlier in the evening. It had to be a trap of some kind.

I believed my dead husband's words that the Greeks tended to employ cunning and deceptive tactics, and that I should expect ambushes and feigned retreats from them. I felt like I was in the middle of one such ambush. Like they were trying to be normal to lull me into a false sense of security.

I still couldn't understand why he'd asked for my name before Diomedes arrived. If it mattered to him, he might have assumed I was from an important family, but then surely he would have reacted differently when I accused him of killing my husband. It was hard to believe he simply wanted to call me something other than 'spear-wife'. After all, he'd made it clear last night that to him, I was nothing more than property.

After I had sniped that the name 'spear-wife' did not suit me, I'd felt a thrill tremble up from my stomach and into my chest at the sound of his laugh. The shame of that burned more than the acid in my throat afterwards.

If I was a good wife to Alcander, a good woman, I would be repulsed by everything about Odysseus. But, repulsion seems difficult to dredge up on command. Instead, it feels as though I am falling backwards into an endless vat of molasses, unable to stop the process. Vulnerable to the all-encompassing darkness, so cloying I'm choking on it; the charade of strong men pretending to be civilised.

Perhaps that was just the stench of Diomedes' belch.

"Well," he said, as he washed down his last mouthful with the last drop of wine, "that was delicious. I thank you for the food and your company." Diomedes nodded at me, the charming suave of earlier gone, before he rose. Odysseus followed suit, as did I, to avoid being the only one sitting.

"I will see you on the battlefield tomorrow, my friend." Odysseus clasped forearms with Diomedes and then the latter left with a dramatic flourish of the tent flap.

I went to clear the table, to busy myself, when Odysseus turned his attention back to me, his eyes narrowing. "Stop."

His look was as sharp as his tone, each word carefully aimed.

"You say I killed your husband?" he began, his eyes not leaving mine.

I could feel my spine getting straighter as he approached. In defiance or fear, I couldn't truly say.

"Do you take me for a fool, woman?" He strode forward,

smoothly and deliberately, the embodiment of controlled strength, closing the gap between us until my back hit the centre pole of the tent, the coarse wood grating against the thin fabric of my chiton and shawl, his palm flat against the wood above my head.

"I do not." The words tumbled out before I could stop them.

Odysseus tsked. "You disobey me, you attempt to humiliate me in front of a fellow king, and now you lie to me."

I grimaced and went to rebut, but he was already shaking his head, shushing me.

"Let's indulge this little fantasy of yours, shall we? You accuse me of the highest grievance, yet I can't help but notice your ... *fascination* with Diomedes. You showed far too much interest in him tonight."

Odysseus leaned in, so close our foreheads were almost touching, as his voice lowered to a menacing whisper. "Is it guilt, I wonder? Perhaps he reminds you of your dead husband? Or is it something more ... strategic?"

I glowered at that, even though he was right about the latter.

"Was it to curry favour with Diomedes by painting me as a villain you can no longer stand to be around? Did you think you could loosen his tongue but not mine? Is that it? Are you seeking a new master?"

I didn't answer, my eyes furiously darting between his, trying to understand his meaning. *Why didn't he believe he had killed my husband? Was he really that arrogant? That obtuse?*

He straightened, his expression becoming one of contemptuous amusement. "Did you think I wouldn't see through your little charade?"

When I didn't answer, he continued, his voice low and dangerous. "You're too calm, woman. Too calm for a widow whose husband was just murdered."

Ironically, it was Alcander's smile that formed in my mind's eye at that moment. That little lopsided grin he would give me when he knew I was angry and about to retaliate. I could almost hear him in my head telling me to calm down, that I didn't have to right all the world's wrongs immediately.

"Perhaps I have accepted my fate," I replied evenly, even as my heart pounded against my chest.

Odysseus scoffed, leaning in closer, his breath hot against my cheek. I tried to move away, to give myself room to breathe, to *think*, when he grabbed me roughly by the arms. His expression hardened, and the room seemed to grow colder as he delivered his next words with a venomous calm. "If I find you trying to get so much as a word out of the other men and generals in this camp, I will feel no compunction at whoring you out to the highest bidder and telling them to gag and blindfold you as they take you. Do you understand me?"

My back stiffened. To be given to someone else ... I would not have a chance to realise my vow, to hold this man accountable for his crimes. I clenched my fists in a desperate attempt to maintain my composure. The muscles in my jaw protested as I kept clenching every fibre of my being, willing myself not to lash out, though my fingers itched to retaliate.

Eventually, I could hold my tongue no longer. "I want nothing from Diomedes," I spat, my voice trembling as I fought to keep my rage suppressed. "I want nothing to do with any of you."

He regarded me for a moment before dismissing my

words as worthless. "Continue being dishonest and manipulative and I'll be keeping a very close eye on you."

Good. Maybe I could poke one of them out.

His hold on my arms tightened. "You will be obedient, Odette," he warned. "Or there will be consequences."

And then it bubbled out of me, a laugh I could not stop, as if it were a fountain sprung to life out of devastation. The sound was hollow and bitter to my ears as it echoed in the tight space between us.

"I have been nothing *but* obedient!" I bit back. "To you today, to my husband before, and to my father before him. And where has it gotten me? Here. You don't get to lecture me on obedience and consequences. Men like you know nothing of either."

His gaze bore into mine, assessing, calculating. But I refused to cower under his scrutiny.

"You do not want to believe me? Fine." I continued, defiance fueling my words. "But there is nothing you can say and nothing you can do to hurt me further. Do you not see? It has all been taken from me. So, go ahead. Believe me. Or do not. Punish me if you must. I. Do. Not. Care."

On the final word, I wrenched myself free from his grasp. He stood there still assessing me, but he didn't make a move to grab me again, or to shake a confession out of me I would not give. Maybe something I'd said had finally convinced him to believe me. I knew I should not have made such an angry outburst – it was not what Trojan women did – but I had never been good at keeping my opinions to myself, even at the best of times.

We regarded each other, predator and prey. When it became evident that this was as close to a truce as we would come, I turned my back on him, retreating to the pathetic sanctuary of my pallet bed. I did not undress. I simply lifted one of the thin, worn blankets, its threadbare fabric offering little protection against the chill that seeped in from the night, tucked it around my body as if it were a cocoon, and crossed my arms, scowling at the edge of the tent that was inches from my nose.

I heard him potter around the tent for a little, gathering the plates when that should have been my job. I wondered why he would do such a thing, but before I could look, he had put out the oil lamp.

And in the dark, I waited for the nightmares to take me.

WHEN MORNING CAME, he was already gone.

My sleep had been fitful at best, Hypnos and Morpheus dragging me down into the depths of my own personal hell, Alcander and Lykas' faces almost close enough to touch, only to disappear into a cold wisp when I reached out. Realising I was in the depths of a nightmare, I would try to drag myself to consciousness. Then my mind would remind me of what awaited me when I woke: a boar of a man who threatened me because he was threatened *by* me, and would undoubtedly find a way to make that my fault, then either sell me off or beat me. So the nightmares called me back – an insanity I would rather swim in forever than wake.

But Eos refused to be denied. Her saffron robes and rosy complexion painted the light against the tent canvas and then over my eyelids, forcing them to flutter open, despite my resistance.

Once I'd roused, it took all of a moment to realise the space surrounding me was vacant. As if Odysseus' presence was larger than his physical form, the space felt like a ghost of itself without him in it. With a heavy sigh, I pushed myself upright, the blankets tangled around me. There was the worn, threadbare one closest to my skin, cocooned around my shoulders as I'd twisted and turned. But another had fallen to my waist as I'd sat up, pooling on my lap, the weight of it surprising me. I stared at the burnt-red blanket in confusion. There was only one explanation as to how it had got there, and the thought made me shudder.

To have the boar that close, while I had been asleep and vulnerable; that I hadn't awoken when he had been mere centimetres from me ... No, I did not want to think about that.

My attention fell upon his armour sitting against the leather chest that held all manner of spoils he had already collected from the war. It was scuffed and stained with Trojan blood. Beside it, a bowl of paste sat on the chest, a clear indication of his expectation that I would polish the armor while he was away, just as any dutiful spear-wife would.

You will be obedient, Odette.

Rising, I walked over to the silent reminder of the duties expected of me. I sniffed the mixture and almost gagged at the pungent fumes of vinegar and lead that assaulted my nose. I'd be smelling that for days now. I regarded the dull metal of the armour. My hand itched to pick up the cloth beside it and get to gwork, the compulsion coming from something long-drilled into me.

What was the point in being shackled by the demands and roles men sought to impose on me now?

That feeling settled over my skin again, the one I'd felt as I knelt in the dirt staring into Alcander's eyes as the light was beaten out of them. No external force could harm me; nothing could penetrate me. That sensation had faltered over the past two days with all that had happened, but in my current solitude, it returned. So, with silent resolve, I slipped from the tent.

My footsteps carried through the camp, on and on and on. Empty tents as far as I could see flapped gently in the morning breeze, while flies buzzed around the morning crusts of stale bread and rinds of fatty meats haphazardly eaten and discarded on plates and cups left scattered around. The grime and filth, the relentless sand, and the lingering stench of the men, even in their absence, left me desperate to find a place to bathe. If only I could escape this labyrinth of a camp.

I stepped carefully around a precariously balanced pile of dishes, wondering when they would finally be cleaned. Just then, a woman emerged from the nearest tent and started to tidy up. She looked older than her years, her green chiton highlighting the rosiness of her plump cheeks and her oiled black hair pulled back into a sleek bun. It wasn't until I noticed the faint, knowing glimmer in her eyes and a small, enigmatic smile that I realised she was watching me.

"Ah, kóρη[1]. New here, are we?"

"Yes," I replied, stepping forward with my chin raised in defiant indignation. That tone, the way she spoke, as if I were a child to be taught the ways of the war classroom.

"What's your name?"

"Odette."

The woman nodded. "Pretty name for a duckling like

---

1. Meaning girl, maiden, lassie, maid, etc.

you, with a swan neck like that. Come, I will show you around."

The woman, whose name I learned was Τάιλορία[2], showed me where slopping buckets of water were gathered, near the tents closest to the ocean. There, the fires were perpetually tended, and the water was boiled and then cooled. We then walked along the sandy banks toward the western forest, where the waters thinned and the reeds grew denser. Here, Τάιλορία explained, the women spun the finest threads. If I encountered anything beyond my skill to mend, I was to seek their help. I pondered what thread could repair a cracked heart and a broken mind, but I did not say such a thing.

Instead, we continued on and Τάιλορία introduced me to those who skinned the best rabbits. That was who to get your rabbit from if you wanted to cook a private meal for your soldier, Τάιλορία told me with a wink. Then she took me back the way we had come, to the best tents for morning fruits and cheeses, closer to Agamemnon's quarters. Finally, she led me to the central storage for the finest wine in the camp. As we came full circle, I noticed even at this early hour, women were already on their knees in the dias, breastplates between their thighs as they polished the plates and armour.

Τάιλορία cocked her head, watching me. "Would you like to go and grab yours and join the circle?"

"No." I wrinkled my nose in disgust.

Τάιλορία laughed. "Yes, the smell does take some getting used to."

I didn't correct her. I was too busy watching the women

---

2. Pronounced Tay-lor-ee-a.

smiling and laughing with each other. They seemed to genuinely be enjoying themselves. The bustle of their industry had me bristling. How could they do this day in and day out?

"What did you used to do?" Τάιλορία probed. "Odette?"

"Huh?"

"Before you were here in the camp, what did you spend your days doing?"

As if it hadn't been just a few days ago that I'd been in my wheat fields. "My husband and I are … were … wheat farmers."

"Ah – you'll be able to help with the grain. Excellent. We don't have many of those girls about. I'm assuming the other girls that came with you are probably good with grain too, yes?"

I nodded, too stunned to speak. This woman simply seemed pleased I'd appeared to help, with little to no concern for how I'd gotten here.

"Your soldier – he keep you up at night?"

The words registered, but it felt as if they were being said through a tunnel far, far away. I had no idea how much time had passed between Τάιλορία saying them and them reaching my ears, but, eventually, I shook my head.

"Then you're one of the lucky ones."

Those words registered.

The scowl on my face was immediate and had Τάιλορία smiling. She patted me on the arm. "I know it's hard. You'll learn to make the best of it. That is the only way."

"Excuse me." I gave her a curt nod and went to turn away.

"Wait. Don't leave without some of the extras we

collected today." Τάιλορία gestured to the bucket of water, the fish, the cured meats, fig leaves, and cheeses.

"Oh, I thought those were all for you."

Τάιλορία laughed. "Diomedes can eat, but he can't eat *this* much."

My jaw dropped open. Τάιλορία was *Diomedes'* servant.

Before I could ask her any questions, she'd begun piling the goods into my arms despite my protests. I could barely see over the stack once she'd finished and pushed me in the direction of Ithaca's camp. By the time I'd returned to Odysseus' tent, to *my* tent, I felt as if I had done a full day's work. The fact that I'd been pulled into the current of the day, unable to swim against it, irked me even more. To finally come back to that armour, sitting there, still waiting for me, making a mockery of what my life had become ...

Dumping the goods on the nearest makeshift surface, practically falling to my knees as I did so, I half stumbled, half crawled to the pallet bed. The ragged blanket I scrambled to pull over my head scratched at my skin, just another reminder of the harsh reality of my existence.

Odysseus returned hours later, the stench of death clinging to him. It saturated the air so thoroughly that I felt as if I could scarcely breathe. I actively held my breath, hoping the smell would dissipate while I waited. In the silence, beyond the blood thrumming in my ears, I heard his footsteps stop. I imagined him observing the untouched armour.

Let him think of that what he would.

I heard him sigh in a manner that sounded like resignation, and then retreat. I hugged the blanket closer to myself, quietly smug in the solace of my small victory.

The next morning he was sitting on the end of his higher

pallet bed, watching me as I turned to survey the tent. We regarded one another, his stare growing darker the longer he watched me. The silence stretched on until, just when I thought he wasn't going to speak, Odysseus cleared his throat. "Penelope used to rise with the sun."

I gave him a questioning look. After our confrontation the night before last, surely he did not expect me to be compliant and willing?

"Our marriage bed was my gift to her," he continued. "I carved it myself. One of the legs is a living olive tree. If it's still there. It used to irritate the shit out of me that she'd rise with Athena's birds, that she didn't want to laze in its magnificence like I wanted her to. She'd always laugh and say it was my fault she slept so soundly. That she lounged around in it before the night swept through while I went to bed with the dawn. Then she'd press a drink into my hand, kiss me sweetly, and head about her day."

I cocked my head as his black eyes continued to drill into me.

"You are more like me. You wake up and drag the turmoil with you. I can see the remnants of your nightmares burning in your eyes. You are as drunk on death as I am. It's like looking in a mirror."

I flinched. "Why are you telling me this?"

"Because I find myself missing the sweet world I once knew. I miss my wife."

With that, he stood, already in his armour for the day, and left the tent.

If his intention had been to make me feel guilty for neglecting the duties expected of me, his blow landed. I stared at the goods Ταιλορία had given me yesterday and wondered if I should get up, unpack and put away the goods that Odysseus hadn't.

He had dealt with the fish, no doubt salting it. There would be a bucket of brine somewhere the fish was immersed in. The meat would need to be cured too, and the cheeses stored in a amphorae[3]. The list of all the things I would have to do today grew in my mind, just as it had when I had been in that modest marriage bed Alcander's parents had gifted us. Long before the sun had risen, before Lykas would wake up crying for his breakfast and my husband still snoring gently beside me. They had never needed to worry that things were done, and they never would again.

Legs heavy, I slid back down under my blankets and rested my head on the pillow.

Back to the madness.

---

3. Ceramic jar.

5

ODETTE

Hypnos
Morpheus
Eos
Lupe[1]

Hypnos
Morpheus
Eos
Achos[2]

Hypnos
Morpheus
Eos
Ania[3]

---

1. Pain and grief.
2. Sorrow and anguish.
3. Distress and suffering.

Hypnos
Morpheus
Eos

Algos.[4]

---

4. The personification of pain.

6

ODYSSEUS

Greek women, slaves or not, didn't defy men. They didn't show anger. They didn't make the circumstances around them about themselves. A good woman was a reflection of a good man.

I had no reason to suspect Trojan women were any different, until that little outburst of hers.

It had forced me to look at the situation with an outsider's eyes, and indeed – though I'd admit it to no man – my suspicion had coloured my judgement. Odette *had* been attentive to Diomedes, but no more than any other slave would have been. Knowing what I know now, that attentiveness born of being bred as a good wife, coupled with her undoubted hatred towards me, would have made it easy for her to be so lavish in her attention with Diomedes.

I was right. She *had* been trying to get one over on me, but not for the reasons I had initially suspected.

Her confession had thrown me. I would have thought a woman who'd watched her husband killed in battle would be fearful, cowering, quiet – secretive, even. Not defiant and loud about such a thing. It was obnoxious during a civilised meal.

It unsettled me, this behaviour, until my suspicions morphed into something deeper. A mere mortal woman wouldn't dare challenge a general like myself; it just didn't happen. So, if she wasn't a spy, she had to be something more – something otherworldly. She must have been a goddess in disguise. Which one, though? If she bore the essence of either Aphrodite or Artemis, she was a formidable adversary for the Greeks, her presence here more dangerous than I had thought. With that swan-like neck of hers, Aphrodite seemed the most likely contender.

Then again, with those eyes like a hawk, perhaps it was Athena disguised in a mortal woman's body. Everyone knew the goddess was grey-eyed, but the gods could morph however they saw fit when they wanted to walk among us. If it *was* Athena, who had sided with us Greeks, then perhaps she had come to guide my men to victory and cement my place in the history of it all.

I had killed a mortal man she'd obviously cared about and she was displeased. Regardless of which goddess inhabited the form, I was not about to anger her further. Instead, I had cleaned up as she had taken her leave. I hated the flies getting in. They reminded me of the battlefield.

Tidiness, order; those things were necessary for me to rest. Penelope had known that and indulged my need to check everything was as it should be, however unorthodox it was.

I had hoped that mentioning my wife to the goddess inhabiting Odette's body would prompt her to reveal her decree – a typically risky endeavor designed to fulfill her purpose while ultimately granting my human desires. I knew how the gods loved to bargain.

But, the goddess hadn't chosen that moment.

The last time I was in the presence of a goddess, I'd been certain. It had been an age since Athena had appeared to me in Ithaca. I wondered if my memory had morphed such an event, coloured it with nostalgia, and called it accurate. As I laid in my pallet bed, one arm stretched out over my head, one leg cocked outside of the rich red blanket – one of the only treasures I'd brought from home – I wracked my memory.

IT HAD BEEN A STILL NIGHT, *the sky a deep purple velvet as it settled over the sky, Orion's star a shining beacon that seemed to blink at me. Perched on the rocks that led down to the Ionian Sea, the water lapping gently at the rocks, I searched the sky for the star cluster of the Pleiades – the seven daughters of the titan Atlas that Orion had pursued obsessively – but they were nowhere to be found on this night.*

I continued searching, breathing in the sea breeze that carried salt and the subtle promise of something to come, when there was a shift in the air. Barely perceptible, it was so subtle that had the night not been so still, I would not have noticed it. I knew a god now stood behind me, and I knew they would not let me see them unless they wanted to be seen, so I continued looking out towards the horizon.

"Odysseus," a female voice began, as clear and commanding as the wind itself. "Son of Laertes. You know the Fates call for you beyond these shores." She paused, allowing the weight of her words to settle in the cool air before continuing. "The assembly of Greeks prepare for an expedition unlike any seen before. One that

shall be etched in the memories of men for generations to come. They seek to reclaim Helen and restore the honour of Menelaus."

I had known this was coming. I'd heard word that Agamemnon was gathering an army to rally and defend the rights of his younger brother. A convenient excuse to go to war over a trade route Agamemnon had long wanted access to. I wondered if Paris making such a move against Menelaus was truly for love, or convenient propaganda.

"Lady Athena, you honour me with your presence." There was no other goddess that would speak to me of such things. I bowed my head, still refusing to face her.

She stepped closer, and from the periphery of my vision I saw an ethereal figure in full battle regalia glowing faintly under the moonlight. "This venture will require not just the brawn my brother Ares seeks, but a leader of intellect." Another pause. "Your cunning is famed far and wide, Odysseus. None can weave strategies and tactics as you can. Troy's walls, mighty as they are, will yield to your schemes."

Another pause, though now I knew she expected an answer. I hesitated, knowing to do so was a dangerous move. "My son ..." I began. Penelope had given birth only months ago.

"Your heart longs for the peace of Ithaca, I see that. It is what makes you such a wise king. But think of the legacy you wish to leave for your son, Telemachus. Will he not grow prouder knowing his father was a key architect in the greatest siege known to all?"

I felt a feminine hand rest on my shoulder as she turned me to face her. The full effect of the goddess punched through me with such power I had to fight my knees not to buckle.

"Your story is not finished, Odysseus. There is a reason you seek out Orion and his quest." Her stare remained intense and unyielding. "I will be with you. With your wisdom and my favour, *there is no fortress so impregnable, no enemy so formidable. Join this cause, Odysseus. Answer the call of the Fates. In the tapestry of time, let your thread shine with unmatched brilliance."*

Above her, Orion shone brighter. Even the seas of Poseidon seemed to fall silent, the lapping waves coming to a halt. I knew Athena would not be denied. My future had been mapped out before me, stretching out to the horizon. A path that would no doubt lead to glory. But would it also lead to death? As I gave my answer to the divine persuader, Athena, her grey eyes burned with the promise of one or the other. I just wasn't certain of which.

I woke with renewed vigor the next morning, certain that Athena had come to me in Odette's form. She had arrived to help me bring this war to its conclusion.

The thought was further enforced when the day's battles unfolded with unexpected ease: the men fought with greater skill, their movements swifter and sharper, winning skirmishes with increasing success. Then each day after that, the Trojans were driven further back, retreating behind their walls as Greek cheers rang out across the camp. By the seventh day, as I made my way back through the bustling camp to the tent and to her, the echoes of victory lingered in my ears.

In the confines of the tent, the air was heavy, filled with a stench that made even me gag. I was aware I was no picture of cleanliness myself, my armour coated with mud, blood, and sweat. I could taste my own scent, sharp and acrid, yet it had nothing on the foul smell in here.

It had been a week, and still Odette's form had not risen from the bed on which she slept, her back always to the canvas tent opening. It irked me. One should never have their back to where enemies could come in. Athena, even in a mortal form, would not be so foolish.

I'd had enough. The irritation that had been stretching from hours into days began to harden into something else – something slower, heavier. I had let it sink in, gnawing at me, until now begrudging acceptance took root. This wasn't, as I'd first believed, a goddess inhabiting a mortal form. It couldn't be. Even Artemis would not have allowed herself to fall into such a grotesque state. No goddess would.

That thought alone made my chest tighten, and the fact that I now had to accept it fanned the flames of my frustration.

And then the deeper sting followed – a bitter acknowledgment that I had allowed a mere slave to speak to me with such audacity, to challenge me. The truth of her actions, of mine, settled uncomfortably in my bones and crawled under my skin like a slow poison.

How had I been so blind?

Storming out of the tent, I grabbed the two largest buckets I could find and filled them with cold water before marching back inside. She had not moved when I returned and, as had become her custom, didn't even shift to acknowledge my presence.

So I placed one bucket down and hurled the other over her.

There was a banshee-like shriek, her body instinctively recoiling from its position and into a protective crouch, huddled into the corner of the tent, facing me. Her skin was smeared with grime, her eyes defiant. Then, her survival instincts kicked in. With a snarl she lunged at me, her hands clawing, driven by a raw desperation like a cornered animal.

I shoved the second bucket of water into her

outstretched arms with enough force to her chest that she physically stopped in her tracks, winded. "You'll clean yourself, or by Hades, I'll drag you to the river and hold you under until the mud dissolves."

She spat a curse at me, something in that pig-language derivative of Greek that farmers used around the provincial parts, but her voice was hoarse, her energy sapped. She'd also decided not to eat these past days.

I crouched down, tossing her the rough cloth and bathing salts. "Scrub yourself clean," I ordered. "Unless you prefer I do it for you?" I eyed her body deliberately.

Her response was a venomous glare, but she took up the cloth and the bathing salts, slowly beginning to rub them into her skin. Each motion was stilted, a silent 'απόλοιο'[1], but at least she was washing.

I continued watching her, my expression deliberately blank. When she reached the parts not for my eyes, she stopped scrubbing. I debated for a moment planting my feet more firmly and insisting she finish the wash in front of me so that at least I knew it was done, but she equally stared me down.

"Do not make me drag you kicking and screaming into the river." I pointed a finger at her. I surveyed Odette a moment longer, something in me stirring her spirit. It was a wisp of a thing, a flame on the precipice of extinguishing itself. But, it was there, fighting the complexities that came with the cruel hand the Fates had dealt.

I wondered if she realised that we both wallowed in the same predicament. That I also wished to not be here, in a war that had made me a dull blade. That if it were up to me,

---

1. "May you be destroyed."

and not the societal expectations burdened upon me, I would rather see her walk free. But that was not the way of things.

The irony of war: it strips us all of our humanity in the end, no matter the role we play.

It was admiration, I realised, that stirred in my gut as Odette stared me down. I longed to have that fire, that spirit instilled in me, so that I might have turned a goddess down on that Ithican shore all those years ago.

WHEN I RETURNED, freshly washed from the ocean, I carried two bowls of goat stew that I had picked up at the feeding fires. Upon entering the tent, I sniffed the air first. Satisfied the smell was beginning to dissipate, I surveyed Odette next. Her hair, which had clung to her face in greasy matted strands, had now been brushed through. Her skin gleamed, like sunlight striking the surface of sand. I nodded in pleasure then held the bowls up.

"You will also eat tonight. This is not a crypt. I will not sleep in the same room as a corpse."

I placed the two bowls down on the same table we had dined at with Diomedes and sat, watching and waiting for her to decide if she was going to join me. The offer of force-feeding her was on the tip of my tongue, when she warily got up from her spot and dragged herself to the table.

As we ate in silence, I noticed the rough cloth I had thrown at her had been rung out and was hanging on one of the tent poles. The scrub jar was empty, which meant at some point Odette had gotten up and used more of the salts to wash herself more thoroughly. *Good.*

It was then that I noticed she was wearing one of my chitons. Too big for her, she had used a torn strip of fabric as a zoster[2] to secure it around her waist. The fabric fell in waves past it, as if that had been a purposeful design. It emphasised her thin waist, her wider hips. I had to force myself to look away.

It had been so long since I had truly looked at a woman. There were other spear-wives and bed-slaves around, but they scurried past, their heads down, trying not to attract attention. Beyond them serving food or providing necessities that kept the camp running, I'd had no cause to acknowledge them, to watch them, as I watched Odette now – with her delicate wrist holding the wooden spoon to her lips, her breath rippling over the stew, the small swell of her breasts as she took another breath ...

Shaking my head clear of those thoughts, I addressed her. "We will need to find you some more clothing. You can wash that ratty one tomorrow, but it looks like it isn't going to last long. You will need to speak to the women, organise an exchange of services to get them to make you something."

She glanced up at me, and I could have sworn her eyes were calling me stupid for pointing out the obvious. I willed her to say something, anything, as she had on those first nights here. But she turned her focus back to her bowl and didn't speak.

When I returned from battle the following day, she was up, dressed, and the tent had been tidied. Standing in the doorway of the tent, I surveyed Odette, assessing. "You're up."

Without a word, she pointed to the jug of water and the

---

2. Also known as a belt or a cord, typically made of fabric or leather.

bowl of coarse sand she had freshly filled. There was also a small amphorae of olive oil, warm to my touch when I reached out for it. I laughed heartily, appreciating her efforts to maintain a semblance of civility in such a barbaric environment. The oil would warm and soothe my muscles after the cold water washed away the grime of the day.

"What is amusing?" she frowned.

"You, Odette, exist in extremes. And this—" I gestured to the collection in front of me, "is really rather excellent."

She crinkled her nose and I could not tell if it was a reaction to the compliment or because now she could distinguish between a clean scent and the one I had returned with. "I am aware I smell like a dead Trojan. Or several."

"I will wait outside." Odette bowed her head, making for the opening.

"No, stay here. I'll be right back." I began stripping off my armour, before grabbing a towel and the bathing items and heading off to wash outside the tent.

Once behind the tent, I dropped the items as usual, draping the towel over a tent rope. I grabbed the water bucket, dousing myself in double quick time, gritting my teeth at its chill. I leaned my head back and tossed the rest of the water across my face.

Next, I reached for the sand mixed with salts, scrubbing it vigorously across my chest and into my chest hair. It scratched as it always did, but I had already moved on to another scrubbing area. Then it stung. I hastily ran my hands across my chest, and a sharp pinching sensation jolted through me, a distinct and unnatural sting that demanded attention. Peering down, I saw one tiny sand crab scuttle across my skin. Another followed. The stinging jolts made me jump back, my reflexes knocking over the rest of the water bucket. The precious water spilled uselessly onto the ground, leaving me with no way to drown the bastards out.

Cursing, I stumbled, trying to shake off the persistent crabs, and inadvertently staggered back into the tent.

"Oh!"

Furiously trying to dislodge the creatures, I blinked to find Odette staring, wide-eyed.

Accusations had been many in my years, but vanity was never among them, yet I found myself oddly pleased by the faint blush glazing her cheekbones as she studied my form. "You like what your eyes have found?"

Her eyes snapped up to mine. "I do not, I—"

I let a slow smile tug at the corner of my mouth, the crabs forgotten as she continued to stammer. "It's just a naked male body. You've seen one before."

I moved past her, deliberately slowing as I reached for a fresh towel from the trunk, using it to shimmy away the rest of the crabs, before I shrugged on my tunic and turned back to her. A little *v* formed in a cute frown between her brows.

"Only my husband's," she admitted.

I see. "Well," I inhaled sharply, then gave a casual shrug. "It's of no matter to me."

Odette went to open her mouth, then snapped it shut, as fishes do.

"Now, more importantly, would you care to explain how those crabs ended up in the bowl of salts you so diligently refilled?"

She blinked rapidly, and for a moment she hesitated, her gaze shifting nervously from side to side. It was a look I knew well – a familiar sign of evasion I'd seen countless times when my men tried to lie to me after I'd asked them a simple question.

"No, I have no idea," she replied, her eyes wide in feigned innocence.

"Clever girl," I muttered as she collected herself.

Such an audacious act of sabotage – placing those tiny, pinching crabs in my washing sand – was a subtle yet striking way to retaliate.

I stepped closer, until I could tip up her chin with the crook of my finger. "I always did appreciate spirit and wit. Perhaps, in another life, you and I might have been allies. For now, though, let us call it even, hmm?" My grip tightened ever so slightly. "No more surprises, spear-wife."

7

ODETTE

"… **B**y Hades, I'll drag you to the river and hold you under until the mud dissolves … I will not sleep in the same room as a corpse."

Those two statements had lingered in my mind, haunting me. The thought of failing to avenge Alcander and Lykas, and being found unworthy by the Judges of the Dead because I had not fulfilled my vow, was a torment I could not escape. The fear of the punishment awaiting me in the Underworld dragged me to the depths of my despair and longing. But those words … They were enough to remind me of the world beyond my tormenting dreams. It seemed that the vow was the only thread of life keeping me tethered to this world.

A sort of madness had taken over me. As if the oppression and subjugation, anger and resentment, had all bundled up inside my body like a rolling thunderstorm, desperate for an outlet. Desperate for someone to acknowledge the suffering being inflicted on me internally, day after day, the longer I continued to live this farce of a life. I had no other way to justify what I did with the sand crabs.

And then Odysseus had stumbled into the tent, naked.

I tried not to think of that moment since, and so, naturally, it was the *only* thing I was able to think about. That moment shattered any illusion that I was no longer part of this world.

He had stood there, unadorned and unabashed, every line of his body outlining his harsh life as a warrior. His chest was broad, covered in thick, dark hair. As my eyes had travelled down, they had caught on the nicks and scars mapped out across his skin, muscles taut from years of wielding sword and shield. And I, traitorously, found my eyes lingering ... *all* the way down, until warmth bloomed deep within me.

The horror of that moment caused something to snap, and immediately I prayed that I had not severed the tie to my husband.

I had deliberately and rationally attempted to empty myself of all selfish emotions, as widows were expected to do, aiming to remain as ghost-like as possible so that I could stay close to *them*. To Alcander and Lykas. Yet here, that emptiness had been filled with warmth for the very man who had torn my world apart. To find any semblance of desire for him was shameful. I deserved to be sentenced to a punishment befitting my crime by the Judges of the Dead.

Was this normal? When you lost all that you loved, to teeter between the two worlds?

I had already tried to kill myself once; would Hera really intervene a second time? I did not care if they would forgive "the coward's way out" as it was known. What did I want with their forgiveness? They weren't capable of it as far as I was concerned. My husband would understand, should we find each other, provided I cleared this stain on my soul, this vow, as I made my way to the Underworld. Little Lykas would be there too, and we would be reunited. All I had to do was reach the river, Styx. If I could get there, then once I passed Charon's crossing, I could ask Hades to allow me to fulfill my vow in death. Surely that would sate their appetite for divine retribution, wouldn't it? Then, I needed only to ask for my family's forgiveness as I completed my sacred obligation in a corporal form. They would understand.

It had been my first clear thought in days. The rest of what had happened was a shrouded haze in my mind, as if I had watched it unfold from outside my own body. But this, *this*, I was certain of.

So I decided, once again, to die.

I waited until the Greeks had set out for the day. Then, I donned the oversized chiton that belonged to Odysseus, leaving my own dirty one along with a bunch of soiled towels, rags, and other garments in a basket, that I could take down to the river under the guise of doing washing. Exiting the tent, I followed the path that Τάιλορία had laid out for me the day she'd shown me around.

At least, I thought it was the path. There were many well-worn trails trodden daily by the women in the camp. They were always slightly narrower than the soldiers' tracks. My feet wandered around the tents and makeshift structures, the ground still damp with dew, as I tried to avoid the more frequented areas where the soldiers gathered. Like that first night.

I kept my eyes downcast, a shield against the stares of

any others. I didn't want them to see me, to stop me. I *needed* to get to the river. It was a lifeline to the besieged city of Troy and the great Grecian Army alike. It would be to me, too. Once I reached there, I could find a deep enough area in the weeds for the river gods to take me down to Hades' world.

Reaching the edge of the camp, I descended a gentle slope that led to the water. I slipped off my buskins and left them discarded on the hard earth, before the spurts of mud and grass gave way to sinking sands, as I found my bare feet wading into the golden-green reeds. The river flowed quietly here, the occasional soft ripple gently distorting the reflections in the water.

I couldn't bear to look at myself in the mirror of the river. I didn't want to be alive; I wanted this to be the afterlife it felt like. As if I truly had died that night after drinking hemlock and this was what happened when you didn't have the coins to cross Styx – that you wandered the earth as if you were still alive. Playing out what would have happened if you lived. That was the only way my brain could make sense of how I was still functioning without my little Lykas in the world. Perhaps it was a small mercy that still kept me numb.

I could see other slaves, mostly women, at other points along the riverbank. They all had spaces carved out for themselves to set about their work. Some were talking to one another, some were minding their own business.

None of them were paying attention to me.

I placed the basket on the bank behind me and knelt in the shallow water, making a show of beating the clothes against the stones. It was a practised movement I'd done so many times back in my village, the thwacking sound mixing with the gentle lap of the water. I would dunk each swathe of fabric in the water, dragging it and myself deeper into the river. Leaning down to grapple with the material that got heavier with every passing second, my fingers skimmed the edge of the riverbed, searching for rocks large enough to hold the folds of this chiton down.

In the rhythm of washing, as I scrubbed each stain and wrung out the fabric, the water rippling with and against the turns of my body, I forgot where I was. It was quiet here. There were no sounds of soldiers or battle. The quiet hum of women chatting felt like a sound I'd heard a thousand times before and would a thousand times again.

For a moment I forgot my purpose, and then it was torn from me forever as Τάιλορία's eyes locked onto mine.

"There you are, little duckling. What are you doing so deep in the reeds?"

The look on her face said she knew exactly what I was trying to do, and that she wasn't going to let me do it. No, Τάιλορία struck me as a woman who would wade in after me and drag me out kicking and spluttering.

"Why do you care?" I asked quietly.

She didn't pretend not to understand. "You wouldn't be the first, and it never does any good."

"I don't understand how you can all stand it."

Τάιλορία shrugged one shoulder, her other arm holding a washing basket of her own, balanced on her hip. "Like I said, it is not so bad once you get used to it."

The look on my face must have conveyed what I thought of that sentiment.

Τάιλορία just smiled sadly. "It is war, little duck. The men pick the battles and the women pick up the rest."

I scoffed. It had not been like that between Alcander and myself.

At that moment, another spear-wife approached Τάιλορία. In the basket on her hip were three dead rabbits lying on a bed of herbs and other plants she had picked, I assumed, from the forest on the other edge of the river.

"Shamera." Τάιλορία greeted her, then gave a nod towards her belly. "You're looking well."

Shamera turned, and then I saw the bump her basket had been hiding. She stroked the rounded mound of her stomach and smiled at Τάιλορία. Given the size of her belly, I guessed she was perhaps two months away from giving birth. She looked ... happy.

I stared at her, mouth agape.

"This is Odette," Τάιλορία said, with a nod towards me, still thick in the reeds.

"Ah," Shamera murmured, her eyes cutting toward me, as if she were fully aware of exactly what I was up to.

"You're pregnant." It was all I could think to say.

Shamera smiled, her hand once again stroking her belly. "Yes."

"And you're happy about it?"

Shamera's smile spread, her eyes crinkling with knowing kindness. "Yes."

She turned back towards Τάιλορία. "One of these rabbits is for Diomedes, if you could manage to get me one of the better jugs of sweet wine for tonight. Not that bitter stuff they keep passing around." She pulled a face.

Τάιλορία grabbed one of the rabbits by the arms and held it up. "Ah, this should do nicely. Diomedes will happily part with one of his bottles for this."

I continued to gape at them, at the *business* of it all. As if this was simply an exchange at the marketplace. As if sensing my bewilderment, both of them turned towards me.

"You'll catch a cold if you stay in there much longer, duckling," Τάιλορία warned.

"Who's her pairing?" Shamera asked, as she continued to peer at me.

"Odysseus."

"Really ..."

I narrowed my eyes in suspicion at the sound she had made that was more a statement than a question.

Shamera shrugged one of her shoulders in turn, swapping the basket to her other hip as she did so. "To be paired with one of the generals is no easy thing. They are often demanding, in more ..." She seemed to be searching for the word, though we all spoke in Thracian. "*Strenuous* ways than the other soldiers."

"How so?"

"The other soldiers want sex. They want taking care of. Then, you'll find they want mothering, loving, someone to make this place more tolerable. If you're paired with one who loses his male companion, like I was, you quickly find your circumstances change for the better." Shamera rubbed her belly again, and the action was not lost on me with her words. "But generals have other demands. Harsher. Their reputations are more closely watched, their authority more likely to be questioned. To be a spear-wife to a general is to be able to hold your own."

I shook my head. "We are all just slaves to them, nothing more."

"We might be slaves to them, but we are women to ourselves and each other."

I cocked my head at Shamera, desperate to know more but loathe to ask.

She seemed to sense it, but it was Τάιλορία that answered this time.

"If you wish to remain a victim, little duck, then by all means, carry on as you are. We have all been where you are; some have even drowned in that very spot you have chosen. But those of us who chose to live? We keep ourselves busy so we do not get sucked into that endless despair. Stay there, and you'll die, while the world continues turning. The war will continue, you will be forgotten, and nothing good will come of it. But if you stay, perhaps Tyche might find you yet, weaving her thread into the Fates' cruel design. Some good could still come of you."

I shook my head. "You have no idea what I have done."

"As you have no idea what I have," Τάιλορία countered.

There was a pause, where only the wind nymphs seemed to rustle through the reeds and grass.

Then Shamera gazed into the distance as though recalling something long buried in memory. She started speaking, her voice breathy but loud enough to drift on the air. "Men are the masters of death, because they can never bring forth life. They can never hold and know the power we can, so they had to create their own. Their own pain, their own suffering. Theirs exists outside their body, while ours all happens within. Such is the nature of the world and has been long before we were here, and will be long after we are gone. If you choose death, if you choose to die, you let them win. Or, you can choose to *live*. Take the hand the Fates have dealt you and show them *who you are*."

She blinked, then turned her focus back on me until I felt

uncomfortable under the weight of it and found my feet, of their own volition, wading out of the water.

"Smarter than you look," Τάιλορία muttered.

I cast her a withering glare that was patently ignored.

"Here," Τάιλορία said, taking the second rabbit from Shamera's basket along with a bunch of the herbs, wrapping it in a fresh towel of her own and handing it over to me. "Take this back to Odysseus this evening. Have a good meal. Try to find the good moments, however fleeting. Focus on them. Trust us – those moments matter more than you know. They can be everything, if you remember to notice them."

Despite the words of the fellow Trojan women still ringing in my ear, I could not bring myself to play the obedient servant once again to the man who held me captive. Instead, the hours stretched on and I remained rooted to my spot in the corner pallet again, the food untouched, my mind desperately searching for a tether to pull me back to life.

My solitude felt short-lived, even though hours must have passed, when the boar entered the tent again. He glanced at the unprepared food on the pallet between us.

"I thought we agreed we weren't going to play these rebellion games of yours anymore," he murmured. "Are you really back to being silent and stubborn? Does your fire diminish so quickly?"

His words hung heavily between us, a challenge that demanded a response.

"No, you said no more surprises." My voice was dull, even to my own ears.

Odysseus frowned as he pulled his armour off. "I said I liked spirit and wit, but you must know, Odette, that even I cannot suffer insubordination forever. If you complete your duties willingly, life here could be amenable at the very least."

I don't care.

He sighed as if he'd heard my thought. I watched him wash swiftly, as if he hadn't much time, before he threw a tunic and cloak on. "Come with me." He took two strides towards me, yanking me up from under my armpits and dragging me towards the tent opening.

"Where are we going?" I asked him the moment we were outside.

Soldiers bustled past us, hurrying quickly towards the centre of the camps, in good humour, laughing and jostling with one another. Some spear-wives and bed-slaves followed behind more demurely, their heads bowed. I looked around for Τάιλορία or the new acquaintance I met today, Shamera. One of them would have told me what was going on, but I didn't see either of them.

"Keep walking," Odysseus muttered in my ear, pushing me forward with his palm on my lower back.

Eventually, we arrived at the very dais Odysseus and I had first touched.

Again, the rug, woven with rich reds and golds, lay across the grass and sand. At each corner of the square rug stood a column where the tent was strung with rope, fire torches adorning each point. The throne was still there, King Agamemnon still seated on it, his red-face more beetroot this time.

The only difference was that this time, a new group of girls huddled on the dais. The soldiers, just as they had when

I'd been standing in the same place, laughed and jeered, hollered and pointed. I could hear the ones on either side of me debate who was prettier, who looked like they would spread their legs the soonest, who would take the longest to break in. I wanted to throw them an evil glare, but Odysseus chose that moment to curve his hand around my hip and flush my back against his chest.

The body heat was alarming.

"Do I need to choose another, Odette?" he murmured, his words a cruel taunt as he used his other hand to keep my chin in place so that I could not look away from the scene in front of me. "Someone less ... useless?"

I flinched at his words, the sting of his contempt roaring against every instinct in me to just do as he said, to be a good girl, to go along with his wants and needs. The dark voice in my head whispered that it could be worse, that it *would* be worse if he traded me in for another woman and I was handed off to someone else. The voice equally deflated me back into that pit of despair, the thread of my vow thinning in my mind as I fought internally to find my footing.

A part of me *was* grateful for Odysseus' patience with me, that he had spared me a fate that awaited so many others in my position. I had seen the spear-wives and bed-slaves who sported black and blue skin daily. I still heard the screams that woke me from my slumbers. But that knowledge offered little solace when I knew that his patience could wear thin at any moment. That the only way to maintain my position was to go back to a way of being I had sworn I would no longer participate in. It was a bitter reminder of my own worthlessness, as a woman and a slave.

"I do not want to have to make this unpleasant between us. You must shake this persistent despair you seem to be cloaking yourself in or I will be forced to intervene," he continued murmuring against the shell of my ear.

"Is that a promise or a threat?"

I felt the length of him begin to harden against me after the words had fallen from my lips. It was clearly something neither of us wanted to acknowledge because he moved to create an inch of space between us.

Instead of speaking, we both continued to watch the new arrivals on the dais, clustered together in a group, their faces drawn and pale. Some clung to each other for support, as our group had done, and the realisation hit me that I had not searched for the familiar faces of my village ever since I arrived. Too caught up in my own despair.

The thought eradicated what little good was left in my soul.

I could remember being one of those on the dais, fingers intertwined in a desperate bid for comfort amidst unfamiliar surroundings. Their attire bore the unmistakable signs of their newfound status as slaves, the once vibrant colours of their garments already faded with dust from their journey. Tattered shawls draped over weary shoulders, their edges frayed and worn from a day or more spent on the road, and I wondered which village they'd come from.

Each of their faces held a tale of loss and displacement. Others wore expressions of resignation, their eyes dulled. I wondered what mine looked like. But my thoughts were interrupted by what appeared to be a skirmish happening at the centre of the dais. The tension rippled out across the crowd until I felt even Odysseus' muscles tense. He pushed us closer to the dais, soldiers turning to berate us until they saw who stood behind me. Then, they shifted like wind through tall grass, until we were standing at one side of the rug, watching what had caused the ruckus.

In the centre of it all stood Achilles and Agamemnon. The two could not be more different. The king was a pig of a man, his skin weathered and worn from sun and wine, his face framed by the weight that bore countless burdens and yet more indulgences, and draped in robes of richly embroidered fabric. He seemed to have an air of authority about him that demanded attention but not reverence, though I suspected he thought they were the same thing. Achilles, tall and lean, stood toe-to-toe against him. But where Agamemnon was stout, Achilles was broad-shouldered, sculpted with sinewy muscle and sun-kissed skin that stretched taut over chiselled features. His jawline was sharp, his hair a thick mane of gold that cascaded to his shoulders and kissed the golden armour, which was weaved with intricate designs of mythic beasts and still spattered with the blood of the men he had killed today.

"You have no right to claim her as your prize!" he thundered at Agamemnon. "She is not yours to take."

But Agamemnon, his face contorted with rage, refused to back down. "She is mine by right of conquest," he spat, his voice dripping with contempt. "I will not be swayed by your petty protests."

On the dais, a beautiful woman stood between them. Her form was slender and elegant, her chestnut hair flowing in soft waves around her shoulders, accentuating the delicate lines of her face and the flawless porcelain of her skin. High cheekbones and a sculpted nose gave her a regal air, but I suspected it was her fuller figure that had the two men fighting. I noticed her eyes flickered between the two, while her hands trembled at her sides.

"Why her?" I asked, my voice barely above a whisper against the backdrop of their argument, but Odysseus heard it.

"Briseis is a princess of Lyrnessus. Achilles believes she belongs to him, given that he is the one that captured her, but Agamemnon refuses to relinquish his claim."

"Why?"

Odysseus hesitated. "She is more than just a prize of war," he explained, his voice heavy with the weight of uncertainty. "She is a symbol of power and prestige. That is why they both believe she belongs to them."

I looked beyond, to the girl who was standing beside the throne with her wrists tied. Agamemnon's current prize, no doubt. Her skin sported angry welts that stood out in stark relief against the pallor of her flesh, itself an unsightly sickly colour. Deep bruises marred the delicate curve of her jawline, her hair hung limp and lifeless around her shoulders, and dark circles ringed her eyes. *That* was what becoming Agamemnon's 'prize' did to you.

"No," I said, quietly.

"No?" Odysseus whispered back, and I thought I caught a slight bemusement in his tone.

"No, you do not need to choose another."

I could see all too well the human cost of war and the consequences of male ambition and pride. Though I might now be a mere slave to the Greeks, I understood the fragile balance of power that governed their world.

Τάιλορία and Shamera had been right – it was up to me to decide how I played the hand I had been dealt. Not the men nor the whims of the Fates that had brought me to this point. Dying would not absolve me of this helpless feeling. The vow I had made was nothing more than a bargain designed by my mind to keep me tethered to this world. The petulant demands of my behaviour had not changed my circumstance, nor would my longing for death. None of it made any difference.

Alcander and Lykas were not coming back.

I was not joining them.

Odette, the woman who had always tried to do right, was gone.

And now I stood in her place.

8

ODETTE

When I had first arrived, it felt as if every camp had been all but deserted when the men went off to fight, each one willing to earn his glory. That's what all men fought for: honour and glory. The Greeks weren't so different to the Trojan men after all. They just didn't know it.

But now, four months later, more and more men lingered around camp, claiming illness. Each day, it seemed their numbers grew, abandoning their swords and choosing to remain behind. Not that I nor any of the other women knew what these supposed ailments were. We were not allowed to work in the medical tent, for we could not hope to understand the medicine of men, or so we were told. No matter that we'd made tinctures like the medics every day when we had been home with our families.

It was common now to hear the usual morning grumbles and murmurs persist like a dull ache while I went about my business, collecting water and food for the day, doing the washing, each step purposeful but heavy, made heavier by the knowledge of the endless days that stretched before us.

But on this particular day as I passed by the watering tents, I caught a snippet of bitter conversation, the voice familiar but one I could not place.

"Nine years wasted!" he exclaimed. "And for what? Nothing but bloodshed and suffering!"

I scoffed under my breath. The ones who stayed behind always complained the loudest. But I held my tongue and kept moving.

When the men returned from fighting on the plains, weary and worn, covered in blood and sand and dirt, their faces etched with exhaustion and longing for respite, the camp seemed poised on the edge of unrest. The usual routine of washing and gathering around the fires was disrupted by murmurs of discontent that simmered just beneath the surface.

A fire could feed no more than a hundred men at a time before we needed replenishments, and there were tens of thousands of them. At least a thousand in each army. Fires littered stretches of sand all the way up the beach. Each camp, for each king and his men, had gathered its own sort of mini community. Unless one of the other kings or generals was visiting, we tended to see the same faces day in and day out.

By nightfall, the whispers of the discontented had turned the camp alive with the sounds of anger and unrest. The fires seemed to burn higher and brighter, the embers spitting into the air, as men shuffled about in the sand and began to fight one another. King Agamemnon eventually dispatched his men to stop the dissent, to carry away those fighting; but those men were just followed with more cries of outrage.

It was more and more common nowadays that certain women did not turn up at the fires, and we learnt in the following days to look for bruises on their arms, necks, and chins in the mornings. The men did not think the women needed aid, so we would save some goat's milk and honey, hide it, and use it as a balm. Or steal some of the herbs meant for the medical tent. More often than not, those women had been initially presented to that pig of a king, Agamemnon, and he'd later discarded them to his other soldiers.

So the king's soldiers were no better.

The rest of us were left to gather around the fires of our camps lit along the beach. Water was boiling to cook whatever we had harvested that day, game cooked in a broth and then carved for everyone to come and help themselves. Men first, always.

I had just poured some more water in the broth that had begun to reduce down into a stickier sauce when I felt a large, calloused hand between my shoulder blades. Looking up, I saw Odysseus, his weathered features illuminated by the flickering flames. Despite the chaos that surrounded us, there was a warmth in his gaze that softened the harsh lines of his face.

"There you are."

I smiled at him before busying myself gathering him a plate, filling it with the foods I knew he liked best. "Thank you," he said when I handed it to him.

"So polite, Odysseus," one of the nearby generals I didn't know said before chuckling. "You would think your beautiful wife, Penelope, didn't prepare meals for you in all the time you've been married."

I watched Odysseus grin in response, his eyes crinkling at the corners with genuine amusement. "My darling wife is good at many things," he said. "But cooking is not one of them. She'll tell you so herself, next time you see her."

"When do you think that'll be?" one of the younger soldiers piped up. A nervous murmur rippled through the crowd.

"Soon enough," Odysseus said, his voice steady, as if another year or more until he saw his wife was not a lifetime. It was the quiet confidence of a seasoned general, one who knew how to keep his men in line.

As he demolished his plate with surprising speed and handed it off to one of the girls responsible for washing dishes, I couldn't help but feel a twinge of bitterness. If I had it my way, it would be a lot longer than that before he saw his wife again.

Odysseus got up and left, and another man approached me. I couldn't quite place him, but after a while they all started to look the same to me, anyway. But his accent – *that* I recognised. He was speaking at me in Greek, too fast for me to keep up. It was clear he had some plight with the food, whether it wasn't enough or if he wanted more I couldn't quite tell. Portions were rationed for a reason, but I wasn't going to be the fool who told him that. I would wait for another to convey that particular message. Instead, I tried to calm the man down, to ask him to repeat himself with what limited Greek I had, but with each attempt he got more and more incredulous.

"Κουτός!"[1] he cried. "Pórni!"[2] Tossing his plate on the ground and spitting, he then pinned his eyes back on me. "Pick it up."

---

1. Stupid.
2. Also spelt πόρνη: prostitute, whore, slut, harlot, hooker, wench.

I understood that well enough. I bent down to reach for the plate when I felt the man's grip on my hair. I still hadn't been able to bring myself to wear my hair down, even though Alcander was now gone. Not quite the woman I once was, not quite the woman I now had to be. So his fingers tangled in the intricate braid I had weaved and tugged me upright, until he forced my chin to tip back. He raised his other hand, staring into my eyes, his own flickering with malice. I stared back at him, unflinching. Then ...

"Unless you would like to be whipped for touching another man's property, Thersites, I suggest you let her go."

Odysseus.

The man's grip did not immediately recede. But when he looked around, as I too looked up towards Odysseus, I felt his grip loosen and then retreat completely.

"A wise move."

Thersites muttered something under his breath as he went to walk past, until Odysseus' hand reached out and made contact with his chest, halting the man where he stood.

"What did you say?" Odysseus asked.

I'd never heard him talk so softly before. For his sheer size, the softer his voice was, the more menacing his demeanour.

"Did someone wound your hearing in battle today, Thersites? I asked you to repeat yourself."

The soldier muttered something I couldn't hear, though I cocked my head and strained to listen. His answer must have appeased Odysseus though, who eventually removed his hand and let the man continue on his way.

Then he stepped up to me. "Are you hurt?" He gripped

my chin lightly, turning my head one way then the next to survey my face.

"No, I'm fine." Then, when he dropped his hand and nodded with a clenched jaw, I added, "Thank you."

That seemed to cause him to release a breath. "We need to talk. Tonight, once you've finished your duties here."

I nodded in compliance. "As you wish."

When I arrived back at the tent hours later, he had several letters strewn across the palette table. "Come, take a seat."

"What are these?" I asked.

"Practice materials. Letters from home, for you to read. Had you been proficient in Greek already, Thersites could not have so easily made you cower to him. Twice."

Somehow, he made that last word sound like an accusation against me.

I scowled. "A man is always able to make a woman cower to him, by the sheer nature of his size." I mimicked what I meant so that my meaning was clear.

"True," he conceded. "But, where Thersites has size, as you say, you have wit and cunning. It does not take much to overpower a fool – even a large one – with smarts."

"You want me to … read these?" I tapped at the letters on the table.

"Yes, and speak them out loud to me. That way, you can practise your Greek and you'll become familiar with how the letters look on the page too."

I could not recognise all the words, but one word, one name, I did. "These are letters from your wife that she wrote before the war. To take with you."

"They are."

"Don't you want to read them … in private?"

"When you and I are alone, Odette, we are in private."

"Oh." He was right, though I was loath to admit it.

Learning more Greek would come in useful. The longer I was here in this camp, the more frustrated I felt by the lack of things I could say. The girls all knew our common tongue, but the soldiers hated hearing us speak it. They assumed we were talking about them, and the crueller ones would slap the women they heard talking in a foreign language. 'Speak Greek!' they'd yell at us, as if it were that easy. As if we weren't having to translate everything they were saying into our own common tongue in our heads, understand it, form a response, convert that into what little Greek we knew, and then try and pronounce it. Most of the time they jeered and laughed and called us 'slow'.

So, Odysseus' offer was tempting, I could not deny that.

"Why?" I eventually asked him.

He looked at me. "Why would I teach you? I have just explained that to you. You have to be smarter. I can't have you getting on the wrong side of these men."

"No, not that. Why do you care?" I asked slowly.

"You're my property, Odette."

I shook my head. "I have seen how other men treat their property. You are not the same. You once told me you picked me for something. I want to know why, what, you picked me for."

He blinked slowly, as if surprised by the question, before looking at me as though he'd never seen me before. Then he leaned back from the crates we sat on and crossed his arms. His forearms, dusted in dark brown hairs, bulged even larger, and I saw the fabric of his chiton ripple and stretch taut over the power of his quads, solid and unyielding, like carved stone. That amount of muscle on display made me uncomfortable. Almost as uncomfortable as the assessing look he roamed over my face.

"Because you're intelligent. That much is clear, and it's a rare commodity in war."

"In-tell-ig-ent?"

"Smart. Clever."

"Ah."

"And clever slaves," (to his credit, he did scowl at that word) "are rarer than pretty, fuckable ones. It is wise to own rare things."

Nothos.[3]

He might have spat the word 'slaves' with distaste, but he still refused to see me as anything more than a tool to be used, playing on my emotions with a clear understanding of how human I was. My first impression of him had been right: while others admired his cleverness, his stirring speeches, and strategic brilliance, I saw through it. He was cunning, manipulative, and used people for his own gain with a callous disregard for anything else. I wondered if he was even aware of his own cruelty – and if his wife saw it, too.

"Let us begin."

Scowling, I took a seat at the pallet and gently snatched the first letter he held out to me.

When Alcander first taught me all the Greek he knew, I saw it as a vast, sprawling language similar to our own. With that similarity, I had picked it up easily enough. But after I became a mother, relearning had proved challenging. Perhaps it was the stress of the situation, having to learn polite phrases: pleases, thank yous, how can I help, what

---

3.   The equivalent of being called a 'bastard'.

would you like. Knowing they were all phrases designed to keep me alive; if you could call slavery a life.

Penelope, instead, wrote and spoke as eloquently as her husband. She mused over old memories of her and Odysseus enjoying a sweet moment together before he'd left for the war. They ate akratos[4] and half a fig each; the juice of a particularly succulent one she had bitten into dripped down her chin and he had wiped it off with his tongue. Then she recounted quite vividly other things he'd done with his tongue, which I read until I'd blushed and refused to read any more, citing I could not possibly understand all the words.

Still, our lessons continued every night after I had finished my duties, and I got to know Odysseus' wife through her letters. She was clever, sharp, and witty, just as he'd described me. Not all of the letters were so immodest as that first one. My favourites were those in which she'd spun tales of how she'd imagined their son getting older in those first few years, so Odysseus could feel closer to him as he grew up. They warmed my heart, for it was like getting to relive all of Lykas' moments of growth; being absorbed in the letter and able to deny the reality of him being gone. As if he was simply off in a faraway land, like Odysseus' son.

Until, one day, the lessons stopped.

Instead, I found Odysseus in our tent as tired and weary as the rest of the men. He barely offered me a glance before going out to wash away the day, again barely a grunt when I pressed a glass of wine into his hands upon his return. I went about preparing something to eat with what we had as he slumped into a seat on the floor, his back against the centre

---

4. Undiluted wine and bread served at akratisma (breakfast).

wooden pole that held up the tent. One leg was long and straight in front of him, the other bent at the knee with his foot on the floor, as he held the bridge of his nose with his forefinger and thumb.

"Headache, my lord?"

"This whole war is giving me a headache." I mulled over what to say, when he beat me to it. "What have the women noticed about the men of late?"

I stilled, then wiped the knife I'd been using against my tunic, placed it down and turned to him. "How did you know the women have been discussing the men?"

"Your shoulder blades sit much tighter together when you have something to tell me, and you don't know how to broach the subject."

I hadn't realised he'd come to know me so well. I thought I'd been all but a closed book, but apparently any amount of time in close quarters proved that even I could not hide my very nature from others. I wondered how long it would be before my other secrets unknowingly slipped out from beneath my skin. I made a mental resolve to push those thoughts down *further, deeper*, and then cocked my head so I looked inquisitive.

He always liked when I was inquisitive.

"We've all noticed the men are angrier, meaner. Not like they were even three months past. It is as if the straw that broke the camel's back has finally landed. It's not like when the men were chasing glory. This is a ..." I searched for the word. "... *Frustrated* kind of anger. And some of them are taking it out on the women."

"I know," he said quietly.

"Are you not going to do something about it?"

"What would you have me do, Odette? They're men. Their very nature is to fight, feed, and fuck."

"It seems to me they are getting plenty of all of that."

"Yes, but they – we – are losing on the battlefield," he growled. "Day after day, we gain ground only to lose it. We cut down Trojan after Trojan, only for more to pour out of the gates of Troy. Every day, the men lose their friends and brothers in arms. Every day is the same mindless monotony, as war is prone to be."

"They knew what they were signing up for."

"I'm not entirely sure all of them realised the full scope of what it would entail." He thrust a hand through his hair. I would be due to give him one of his haircuts soon.

I held my ground, my arms folded now. "And the women should suffer for this because ...?"

"They shouldn't. But if foolish men can't win one fight, they'll pick another they know they can win against a smaller opponent. It's in their nature."

"Men like to blame a lot on the laws of nature, while they pillage the natural world around them."

"Will you continue to nag me all night, or will you provide a solution to your quandary?"

I uncrossed my arms and rubbed my hands together, before leaning back to grip the makeshift table behind me. He had to see me as open, willing, vulnerable. That was the only way he would listen.

We'd had similar discussions in the past, when the letter reading had turned to more heated, philosophical debates. I had learnt that when Odysseus was cornered, when his intelligence was threatened, it was the boar that I would meet. He would snarl and storm off, only to return much later in the night. But, when I was open, vulnerable ...

it was as if his mind placed me in a certain category. His protective instincts rose to the fore, and often whatever I suggested became an idea planted in his mind that would bloom.

Such an exhausting game it was, playing the willing slave.

"The men are frustrated at the lack of results, yes?"

Odysseus nodded. "Essentially."

"Then you must give them something productive. Useless, but productive; something that yields results. That's what we do, what we used to do, when we had the children count the wheat grains before they were grounded."

Odysseus looked at me for a moment, and I saw the calculation behind his eyes.

"Just a suggestion," I shrugged, turning back to the meagre food preparations.

He stayed quiet for a minute or so, as was his custom when he was working through something in his head. Then I heard him stand. It was not surprising to me when he came to place his empty cup beside me.

What *did* surprise me was how close he stood behind me. I could feel his body heat radiating between us as he leaned in and muttered in my ear. "You are cleverer than half the generals I have to work with, you know that?"

His hands brushed my shoulders gently as he held me in place and pressed a quick kiss to my cheek before releasing me and striding out of the tent.

I lifted my fingertips to my cheek, where the skin still tingled from the bristles of his beard.

Alcander had always been clean-shaven, at my insistence. I had always thought the coarseness of a beard would be too itchy, too unpleasant. But I found myself thrilled at the tingle, at how soft his lips were compared to the harshness of his beard.

How quick it had been – I hadn't even realised what he was doing. My focus had been on his hands at my shoulders, at the close proximity of him.

I wondered why he'd done it.

But what I wondered at more – something I immediately found so horrifying I had to push it down below any other thoughts or feelings I'd had since coming to this camp – was how utterly normal it had felt.

THE NEXT DAY, when I woke, the morning sounds were different to what I was used to. Scrambling into my tunic and quickly tying my hair into a loose plait, I hurried outside to see the men all marching towards the dais.

"What is going on?" I asked Τάιλορία as she, too, marched past.

"I'd have thought you'd know. Apparently Odysseus has asked the men to gather at the dais on King Agamemnon's behalf."

We followed behind the soldiers, curious to see what the announcement was. Surely, it was about the dissent amongst the ranks, and I wondered if today was the day Odysseus would announce what the men would be doing if they would not go to war. They couldn't, after all, have them all whipped into compliance. There would be a mutiny.

Sure enough, Odysseus stood on the top of the dais and called out to the men. "Soldiers of all the Greek islands – I speak to you now. I understand your grumbles and groans. It has been a long time away from home. But, you knew this would happen. So said the oracle who, need I remind you, also ensured we would be victorious! Do you really think Achilles, the greatest warrior of all, would be here, fighting a war he could not find glory in?"

Odysseus stepped down and Achilles, that bronzed god-like man with lithe muscles, took his place to deliver a speech to the men. Of course, Achilles was a favourite amongst the men for his fighting skill and the women for his looks. Not that he ever took a woman to his bed. That place was reserved for his cousin, his companion, Patroclus. No one particularly cared. Patroclus was as passive in nature as most women, so it came as no surprise that he shared a bed with Achilles. Still, the women swooned.

I, however, found my eyes darting towards Odysseus. He was so much more heavily muscled than Achilles, and would naturally be slower in speed. They were slow and fast, dark and light in colouring; complete opposites.

I wondered if I was attracted to the darkness of Odysseus because of the darkness that now stained my spirit. What was good in me had died the day I had accepted my fate, and now I was only attracted to the cunning, the dark, the evilness left on Earth.

Stop it. Focus on their speeches.

Even in speech, Achilles was the opposite of Odysseus. While Achilles corralled the men into lifting their hands, swords and spears into the air chanting, his words were laboured. As if every word he landed was like a blow, trying to get through these dense men's skulls. Odysseus, meanwhile, when he went to speak again, his words were suave, whispering through the men's ears and behind their defences so that they could find no fault in his argument.

A moat would be built, he declared, along the perimeter

of the beach. Wide enough that the Trojans could not simply jump across it, and deep enough that they would not see the spikes that would skewer them. Any man who did not wish to participate in the war and follow Achilles into victory, or who was recovering from wounds, would help build this moat.

I smiled.

It was the perfect pointless project. The Greeks had no need for the moat. The Trojans never came out of their citadel, except to fight the day's battles. But, it would ensure the men had something to do other than moan. They'd feel like they were accomplishing something. and the ones who despised the hard labour of digging trenches (which would certainly not earn them glory), would begrudgingly return to the battlefield.

Odysseus' eyes met mine and he returned my smile. It was slight, barely noticeable from where I was on the edges of the mass of Greeks. More of a faint curl at one corner of his lips. But it was there.

Horrified at the joy that threatened to bubble up inside me, I turned to head back to our camp.

I was completely lost in thought, treacherous and heart wrenching, when another of the women fell alongside me.

"Natalia, how are you?" I asked, shaking my head from my reverie. With one glance at her, I caught the bruise dangerously close to her eye, now turning a putrid green. "Shall we make you another pumice for that?" I nodded at the offence.

"No need. Haven't you heard?"

"Heard what?"

"Your Lord Odysseus only went and had Thersites beaten unconscious last night. I was so worried all night I did not sleep a wink, but I found him today in the medics tent. He's lamenting that he needs to stay at least for a few days, until he can see out of one eye again. At last, I shall get a peaceful two or three nights to myself!"

With that, she practically skipped off.

I stewed over the information, busying myself with the usual chores of the day until Odysseus reappeared in the tent.

"Not off fighting today?" I eyed him warily.

"I've been tasked by King Agamemnon to oversee the project while it gets on its feet. Looks like I, too, get a short reprieve from the war for a change."

I continued pottering about, my back turned to him.

"Odette? There is something you're not telling me ..."

I continued about my chores in silence.

"Odette," he warned.

"Why," I ground out, trying to counter my temper as I shook out the blankets and pillows to be washed, "did you have Thersites beaten half to death?"

Odysseus paused a minute, as if sensing a trap, before replying. "For his effect on the men."

"For his effect on the men?" I almost laughed as I turned to look at him, wringing a loose polishing cloth through my fingers.

"You find that such a strange reason?"

"From a man who is known for his clever ideas and charming words, one who he himself admitted does not like to resort to violence if he can help it ... Yes, I find it strange."

"I am a general, Odette. He was causing insubordination, I had no other choice. If anything, you should be grateful, given the way he targeted you."

I snorted. "Grateful?! What should I be grateful for? That

you did one decent thing amongst all the horrible? Why should I be grateful that I'm a slave? Grateful to you, to this life, that I have the honour of serving 'the great Odysseus'? Yes, let us forget that I had a kind man that used to care about my honour, and that you killed him. Instead let me be *grateful* that I have it so *easy* now."

"Perhaps then, we should address the other reason."

I stilled, eyes immediately darting to the sand floor. I hadn't expected that. *Damn my hot temper and my frivolous tongue.*

"Look at me, Odette."

His tone suggested that if I didn't do so willingly, I would have to regardless.

Odysseus moved until he was standing in front of me. When I went to break eye contact, his thumb and forefinger grabbed my chin with a lightning fast reflex.

But the grip on my chin was not tight as he said, "You and I both know why I resorted to violence."

"If you are going to give me some contrived notion of our base natures again, then I have heard this argument before." I stared at him defiantly.

"Is it not a valid one?"

"When every reasoning boils down to our basic animal instinct to survive, it gets a little tedious." I shook my head, trying to get out of his grip, but he tightened his clasp. The only thing I did was shake my plait loose.

Still, he didn't let go.

"War puts us in those conditions – the most extreme, the most basic," he reasoned.

"For some of us. Not all," I countered, glancing around at the spoils gathered around the tent.

"For all. We all must choose to remain human, or to turn

into animals. Every day, we make hard choices. I can choose to let the hatred for my enemies overwhelm me, or I can choose to retain my humanity."

"And?"

He knew what I was asking.

"I have found that since you arrived, I have been enjoying the simple things for the first time since the war began. Food. Wine. Morning. Company to keep. I find myself loath to lose that."

I didn't know how to respond to that raw admission.

"Your hair – I've never seen it down before," he murmured, his hands curling around the ends.

It was all too much. I slapped his hand away.

"You cannot keep making claims on me as your property and then treating me as you might a free woman you care for," I snapped. "If war invites a choice, then you must choose."

There it was; now that I had voiced it, it was clear as day why I felt unnerved. The sands were shifting beneath my feet, the hand the Fates had dealt me changing once again. I wasn't ready for it.

The look of shock on Odysseus' face turned to piercing clarity in those dark eyes that danced between mine, until his hands leaned onto the table behind me, either side of my hips, effectively caging me.

"Do you think I like to be here? That I like killing inno-cent men? Fighting for that oaf of a king who is greedy and arrogant, who has no concern for others? That I *like* this nagging responsibility I feel for you, a gravity I cannot ignore?"

I didn't answer. I just continued to hold my head up

high, staring into the depths of those unfathomable eyes that I swore went on for eternity.

Odysseus' gaze flicked down to my lips, my cleavage, and then met my eyes again. Our breathing was evenly matched, both dragging in what little air we could between us without our chests crashing into one another.

"You think I want to be here, feeling this *need* to protect you? This desire to damn the gods and this war and *touch* you, hold you? That I wouldn't rather be home with my wife?"

His words were bitter with resentment, yet it did nothing to dull the charge in the air.

"Don't you think I'd rather be with my dead husband than you?" I hissed.

And then he did something I never expected. His hands gripped my face and he crushed his lips to mine, until there was no more oxygen between us.

9

ODYSSEUS

I shouldn't have done it. I knew that.

But it had been nine long years since I'd last felt the warmth of a woman's touch, and in that moment of weakness, I succumbed to the allure of Odette's presence. Yet now, as I rubbed my jaw, remembering the sting of the slap she had delivered afterwards in her rightful anger, I couldn't help but feel a strange fascination alongside the sense of regret.

Penelope was a woman of strength and cunning. Unlike Odette, she possessed a quiet resolve, a calculated wisdom that she wielded with precision. In all our years together, she had never lashed out at me in such a manner, never raised a hand in anger. Her silence spoke volumes, her words measured and deliberate. She'd always held me steady.

Odette was different. She was a tempest of emotions that threatened to consume everything in her path. Her desperation created a vacuum in the very air around her. All of her emotions were so obvious in every action she took, painted across her face, and yet somehow it was not a weakness. For the way it drew me in, it made *me* the weak one.

Had she been in another man's tent, I'm sure she would have taken a beating for her insolence. But violence had never appealed to me, certainly never against one of the opposite sex. Punishing her would just make her fearful and myself displeased. So what would be the point? No one else needed to know what went on between us.

I couldn't ignore the pang of guilt that echoed through my bones for betraying Penelope's trust. But I was aware enough to admit I was lonely. It was an ever-present state in this war; comfort was scarce. I longed for Penelope, who had always challenged me; and now here was Odette, offering the same gift *and* solace in the midst of chaos.

She was both a confidant and a rival. Perhaps she was right. Perhaps I was taking advantage of her station, but she stirred something within me, a longing that I had long since buried beneath the weight of duty and responsibility. And though I knew I should resist, I found myself drawn to her in ways I could not fully understand.

With a heavy heart, I sighed and turned to stare at the horizon, where the shadows of war loomed large on another day in battle.

The moat project had only lasted three weeks, and yet somehow in that time I had forgotten the scent of true battle. Now that I was back, all I could smell was shit. I should have been used to it – how often men shat themselves right before they died. Late in the day, when both sides retreated and each collected their bodies, the ground was always soaked with blood, sweat, and other bodily fluids cast across the plain as we cut down man after man.

Looking out on the barren expanse of the field on a fresh day that offered only death in its void, I felt a wave of despair wash over me. I could feel it in the men beside me, too, sneaking between us on the wind, as we listened for Agamemnon's cry to charge towards the wall of Trojan soldiers awaiting us. The same cry he would have made yesterday, and the day before that, and the day before that.

Except, with each passing day, there were fewer men. Not just on the battlefield itself, but back in camp. A dreaded black plague had begun to sweep through the tent rows and firepits, infecting the men. It had arrived on the night of the first full moon after the moat was built. Many men grumbled that Artemis had sent it, but those of us closer to King Agamemnon knew the truth.

The king hadn't been satisfied with just taking Achilles' war-prize, Briseis. No, he'd also claimed a woman named Chryseis, the daughter of a Trojan priest of Apollo. The priest had come to beg for his daughter back, risking slaughter himself, and still Agamemnon had denied him.

This plague was Apollo's punishment for Agamemnon's greed and cruelty. Twelve nights of fever and chills, swollen faces and discoloured skin. Twelve nights of death to welcome us, even when we returned from the battlefield.

Agamemnon willfully remained ignorant to the rumors like the coward he was. Instead, he turned to us, as if he could sense the despair and offered a cajoling – clearly rehearsed – speech. "Men, I have decided it is time for us to give up this charade. Let us return to Greece, knowing that we have slaughtered a good many Trojans, and have made our point loud and clear. You cannot take from us without losing many of your own."

His tone was prideful, as always, but there was an inflection there, a catch I didn't believe the other men heard. Agamemnon sent me a glance with a small smirk, as if to say 'watch how they rally for me now'.

He and I both knew why despair hung heavily off the men, after all. He'd insulted the great warrior, Achilles, who now refused to fight. Without the one who could win this war for us, what hope did the other men hold?

This, I realised, was a test. One which failed almost immediately as a deafening cheer went up around me and carried back through the crowds of men, who upon hearing the news, turned on their heels and started running for the ships. There were splashes of ocean, an ever-gathering crescendo, as the men quickly waded into the water. I turned back to Agamemnon, who looked more like a forlorn boy than a king.

Then, she whispered in my ear. I knew it was Athena who spoke to me, but for the strangest reason I heard her words in Odette's voice. "You must call them back. You are not done here yet."

"Are you really so cowardly?" I bellowed, catching Agamemnon's look of surprise as I turned around to face the men heading for the ships. "Do you not remember what the soothsayer Calchas said to us before this war began? Do you not remember your vow, that you would not abandon this struggle we *all* face, until this city falls? Are you really so weak to put that all on Achilles' shoulders? Do you have no pride? Have you not held your own on this battlefield day after day, for the last nine years?"

The men shifted on their feet, their faces a mix of shame and defiance, but no one moved closer to the ships.

"You have made it this far, and now you would turn and run when victory is millimetres from your grasp? Nine years, men. That is what the soothsayer said. You know it is darkest before dawn. This is it, the end in sight! Are you so very sure you want to return home when you are so close to claiming honour?"

The silence was thick now, charged with possibility.

"Come, what say you? Will you fight just one more day?"

"Buy them time," Odette whispered in my head. "Buy us time."

Jarring words, for she would almost certainly never say them.

Regardless, whatever I'd said had worked as the men began the battlecry wave towards us. I turned to find Agamemnon standing beside me, a grin on his face that suggested the words were his own. His slap on my back confirmed it.

"To war!" he cried.

"TO WAR!" every man cried back.

Despite the resolve I placed in the men, our steadfastness slipped between us like quicksand. Ares fought alongside Hector. Even my bloodthirsty friend Diomedes sent me a look of fear that paled his face when we watched Tlepolemus slaughtered in front of us. I responded in kind, slaughtering an entire line of Trojans in my wake. A second. A third. But I was no match for Hector.

The Trojans pushed us back and back and back, until we were almost at our own moat. We had lost today's battle miserably.

The men looked to us at the front – myself, Diomedes, the other kings, Agamemnon – for signs of what to do. I waited for Athena, or Odette, to appear in my head, to tell me what to say, when Agamemnon began weeping.

"The war truly is a failure. I was right this morning. We should leave for Greece."

Incredible. Even in defeat, he maintained he was right. This man knew no shame.

Frowning, I considered my reply, when Diomedes beat me to it. "I will stay and fight, for I know the words Odysseus spoke this morning were true." He looked each of the men in the eye, studying each of them just long enough to make sure they were listening. A clever trick I had taught him long ago, when he became king of his own lands. "The prophecy stated that Troy was fated to fall. We may have lost today, but this was just one day of many. Eventually, even a rock relentlessly beaten by the ocean turns to sand."

"He is right," Nestor, another of our generals, urged. At the men's skeptical looks, he made another suggestion. "Perhaps, my Lord and King Agamemnon, we should look to reconcile with Achilles."

Agamemnon looked up from his place of weeping, where he'd collapsed on the ground. "Yes," he said, rising. "Perhaps you are right. I will offer Achilles a great stockpile of gifts, so long as he should return to the frontlines of battle. Odysseus, Ajax, Phoenix – go tell him the good news."

I RETURNED to the tent to wash and gather what I needed for the walk across the long expanse of beach to get to where Achilles and his men had camped, high up on the hill.

To my surprise, Odette was in the tent upon my return. Ever since our altercation, she had taken to being out when I returned, volunteering extra hours to help prep the food, tend to the bonfires, wash rags and the like. We had barely spoken, beyond the day-to-day operations we had to discuss. I had tried to engage her in discussions, suggesting that we go back to our Greek lessons. She had replied in almost fluent Greek where I could 'stick' my saviour-like intentions.

I let out a small, throaty sound.

She glanced up from her place where she was folding blankets and pinned me with a stare a lesser man would wither under. She pushed boundaries far too often, yet even that was a thousand times better than the hollow, despondent shell she'd been when I first brought her here.

"I must speak with Achilles tonight," I began, my focus fixed on her, searching for her understanding. "I'll need food and water for the walk over, something to gift him, and a fresh cloak."

I wanted her to ask why, but she merely nodded, stood, and began to gather the things as requested.

"Agamemnon finally wants to fix his insult of Achilles," I told her.

"What a surprise," she muttered sarcastically, yet in Greek, and for some reason pride swelled in my chest.

"I doubt it will do any good," I continued. "Rumour has it that even when Achilles' men have asked him, he says he intends to return to Phthia so that he might live a long, ordinary life rather than the short, glorious one he was fated to have should he stay, according to his mother."

"Strange."

My chin lifted in surprise at her response. "What is?"

"A Grecian man choosing the ordinary over glory."

I was silent for a moment, contemplating if I should

share a little more of myself with this woman. "I do not blame him. I would choose an ordinary life, too."

Odette snorted, and I had to grit my teeth to stop myself closing the space between us again and shaking her. It would only lead us back to what got us here in the first place.

Instead, I said, "Achilles is young and foolish. He cares too much for his pride. I think he has simply been biding his time in this war. But I am a tired old man, and I would like to go home."

I saw her clench at that, no doubt wondering what her fate would be when the war ended. I was still contemplating that myself. I wanted her to ask; I felt myself yearning for her curiosity, but she didn't broach it. I could feel her hoarding thoughts, and I wanted to tug them out of her, one morsel at a time.

"What are you thinking?"

Once again, she surprised me. "I am thinking, if you want to be successful on your quest this night, you will appeal to the one thing Achilles won't say no to."

"His pride?"

"No. Patroclus."

THE MEN and I had found Achilles engrossed in his lyre within his tent, Patroclus listening intently beside him. Within minutes of being there, it became evident that persuading him to rejoin the war would not be a simple task. Achilles rebuffed Agamemnon's offer immediately after we presented it, his resolve unwavering. The chance to voice my own thoughts, so closely aligned with Odette's, was ripped away as Phoenix launched into a fervent plea, invoking the story of Meleager in a desperate effort to bend Achilles' resolve.

It had failed.

With another meeting scheduled for tonight comprising myself, Diomedes, Nestor, Phoenix, Agamemnon, and Meleanus, the weight of decision loomed before us as Ajax, Phoenix, and I trudged back into Agamemnon's territory. It did not help that the camp remained quiet, as it was when we had left. There had not been revelries around the firepits for weeks. There had been nothing to celebrate. Instead, all we could hear was the scuffing of our feet across the sand and the snores of men behind their tents.

"Well?!" Agamemnon demanded, as soon as we entered his tent.

The others gave him grimaces, while I shook my head and cloak off at the same time.

"Then, pray tell, what are we going to do with wretched Achilles? How can we force him to do what we wish, when he did not kneel to me?"

The men all looked at one another. I wondered which of them would be the first to speak. When the silence stretched on, uncomfortably taut, I sighed. "We cannot force him to do anything. Therefore, it seems obvious to me that we need another plan."

"Well, then, what do you suggest, Odysseus?" Agamemnon snapped.

I crossed my arms as I regarded him. The temptation to say something snide was appealing, but I held my tongue. Just.

"Why don't we send a spy to infiltrate the Trojan ranks?" Nestor suggested, breaking the eye contact – and the tension – between Agamemnon and myself. "If we can figure out their movements, pre-empt them, we will have a greater chance of beating them on the battlefield tomorrow. And if we can show the men that we can do it without Achilles, we can win this war and be done with it."

A round of nods and murmurs followed.

"I would go," Diomedes offered. "Though I wouldn't say no to another joining me?"

"I'll join you, friend," I replied.

"It's decided then," Agamemnon declared. "You'll come back and report to me before dawn and we will show Achilles how pathetic his pride is."

With that, we were dismissed. Diomedes threw me a look and I shrugged. We knew who Agamemnon was when we came to these shores. He hadn't changed; he had only become more petulant and child-like the longer he didn't get his own way. War, like greed, simply highlighted and exacerbated a man's character.

"Well, friend, we best arm ourselves if we're going into the enemies' trenches." Diomedes slapped me on the back and we returned to camp to get what little sleep we could. The best time to raid a man, as we had learned from villages like Odette's, was at the third watch when a clock would strike four in the morning. Then, men were prone to drowsiness and sloppiness. Easier to get past. Easier to kill.

At three, we met again at the intersection of our two camps. Diomedes nodded to me, I to him, and we continued quietly on foot across the plain. Nothing needed to be said. We had been on the battlefield together long enough to know each other's styles. He was quicker on his feet, more brash with his execution of movements. He would inevitably catch any man who spotted us, and I would kill them. I was quieter when it came to that part.

We stuck to the outer edges of the field, where the long grass brushed against our calves, and for some reason, I thought of Odette. A heron called to us with its three rolling 'rohs', and once again I found it puzzling that I saw a sign of Athena while I thought of Odette.

"We should pray," Diomedes whispered loudly to me, nodding at the heron.

Exactly what I was thinking.

We each muttered under our breath. "Lady Athena, protect us. Lady Athena, guide us. There is none wiser than you, particularly in the art of warfare. Guide our path and protect us, good lady, if you should see fit."

In the privacy of my mind, I thought of Odette's inquisitive eyes. That I might see them again.

The heron gave us one calling 'roh' before it flew off.

For the next hour, it was unnervingly quiet. I was used to the grunts of men thrusting swords and spears, shouting, screaming, pleading, groaning as weapons were removed with force from lifeless bodies. Not this unending silence.

I was not used to being able to smell the sea breeze on this battlefield, and I was so enamoured with it, it took me a minute to place the second scent.

Sweat.

Not mine, not Diomedes' – I knew his as well as my own – but another.

A Trojan's.

I motioned to Diomedes to crouch below the tall grass and he immediately followed my order, despite the fact we were equals both in our respective home cities and on the battlefield. Together, we scanned the area and there was a poke in my shoulder when Diomedes spotted him first.

The man was moving quickly, quicker than either of us

as he strode through the thick grass. Diomedes motioned to me that he was going to circle around, on his belly like a snake, and capture the man from behind. I nodded my agreement and crawled forward to capture the man from the front in a pincer movement.

The only signal I got that Diomedes had achieved his quest was a sharp, surprisingly high-pitched yelp. The sound was far too high for Diomedes' guttural tones, so I stood, moving quickly to the source.

I found Diomedes with a grin on his face as he held a rather ugly man in a chokehold. The man, who reminded me of a warthog, was kicking and flailing to no avail – he was far too short. Diomedes' strength alone could lift him off the ground. But he was a fighter, that much was clear by the way he bared his teeth at me.

Time for me to break him.

Over the years, I had learned that breaking a man could take many forms. As a king, diplomacy was your blade. You had to instill the fear of the gods in your people, while showing just enough mercy to hold their loyalty. Cross that line, and the gods would make their displeasure known, and their retribution unpleasant.

With fellow kings, fear alone would not suffice. You had to appeal to their pride, their duty, their honour. You had to outmaneuver them, play the game more shrewdly than they ever could.

But soldiers, especially enemy soldiers, required something far more visceral. You had to show them death, strip away their hope, until the presence of Thanatos lingered around them. Your every move became a ritual, a summons for the God of Death to claim what was his.

And I'd become adept at this.

I unsheathed the blade at my side, dangling it in my fingers, as if I were happy to be careless with it. As if I welcomed the cutting of flesh, regardless if it were my own.

That was tactic one.

Then, I smiled. Not a smile that I would offer Penelope, or even Odette. A smile that did not reach my eyes. One that left them feeling as cold as I was when I inevitably plunged a weapon into their body and bled all the warmth, all the colour, all the life out of them.

Tactic two.

Already the man's grimace wavered as I closed the gap between us with small, slow steps.

"Do you know who I am?" I asked him softly.

That was tactic three – softly does it. There was something far more menacing about a man in control of his voice than one wildly screaming. As if he'd take his time carving you up. It was an effective tactic. Usually.

"Grecian scum!" the man spat at me. Literally.

Very well.

"They call me Odysseus. They speak of me as a patient man. A clever man. But, after years of slaughter on the battlefield – endless, mind-numbing years of it – I find myself bored. Quick kills no longer satisfy me. I think it's time I tried something new. Perhaps, with you, I can practise patience again. Take my time. Peel off your skin inch by inch until you're willing to talk. Then cut out your tongue if I know your so-called truth is a lie. Yes. I think I might rather enjoy that."

I stepped closer now, until I could smell the man's rotten breath. He would also be able to hear Diomedes breathing against the shell of his ear. We were all so close. The man tried to hide it, but he couldn't – we knew he was trembling.

"What say you, Diomedes? Shall we have some fun with the Trojan?"

My friend squeezed the Trojan's neck until his eyes bulged slightly.

"Wait!" he choked out.

"Why?"

"I can tell you," he gasped, desperately clawing at Diomedes' forearm. He barely managed to scratch it.

"Tell me what?" I purposefully made my voice sound bored, neutral even.

"I can tell you how we position ourselves, and how our allies do, too."

"What good is that to me? You could lie, only for me to find out tomorrow. I told you how I feel about liars and their tongues." I tapped my blade against his lips to make a point and heard him whimper.

I smiled. *Good.*

"Well? I'm waiting."

"The Thracians. They – they're vulnerable to attack. They just arrived. With their king, Rheus. You could slaughter them now, the two of you, they're that unprepared. I—I could show you where they are and then you could let me go."

"Oh, could I just?"

"Please, I—"

But he had already given it away. I had been watching his eyes, which had darted to the left one too many times. Another tactic I had learned. Men were desperate to have you believe them when you put them under just enough pressure. So desperate, in fact, that they practically begged you to believe them by pointing out the truth of their words. Even if it was with their eyes.

I nodded to Diomedes, who with one quick jarring motion, broke the man's neck and he crumpled to the ground at our feet. Almost methodically, we stripped him of his armour. If we were going into the Thracian camp, it would help to have items of familiar armour to disguise us. Just long enough for us to fool them.

The Trojan scout wasn't lying; we found the camp lying just beyond the next hill. It was a small camp, no more than thirteen men in total. Each of us had slain more Trojans alone. Making our way down the hill on our bellies was slow going, but by the time we hit the base of their camp, Diomedes and I were quick on our feet, whipping out our weapons. He crouched and circled the camp and I waited for five beats before I knew I could move.

The man closest to me had his back to me. A deep slit across his carotid and he was dead. The man opposite him cried out, but Diomedes got to him. The others realised what was going on and tried to rally, but drawing swords or running for weapons when you'd just been lying lazy-limbed by a fire was no match for two already bloodthirsty generals. We cut them down one by one, Diomedes and I both moving in a circular motion that mirrored one another. A death dance these untried and untested soldiers had never seen before. They barely had a chance to fight for their lives.

I didn't feel sorry for them. This was war.

"It's time to go, Odysseus." There it was again, Odette's voice in my head. "You wouldn't want some angry god to wake the other soldiers in the nearby camps."

She was right, of course. She always was. Gesturing to the empty chariot that still had two restless horses bridled, Diomedes nodded and we both made haste. It must have been their king's – Rheus, the scout had called him – chariot.

As Diomedes spurred the horses into action, I looked at the pile of men we were leaving behind and wondered which was their king.

Not that it mattered.

He was dead.

IO

ODETTE

Odysseus had returned under the cover of darkness, his face grim, his armour stained with blood. I did not know whose; I did not want to ask. But though there was no triumph in his steps, only the weariness of a warrior who knew the cost of his actions, it became clear as he wiped himself with a damp rag that the blood was not his own, and I returned to sleep.

My sleep was fitful at best, my dreams haunted as they always were by Alcander and Lykas. Though, more recently, only Lykas had been appearing. I had gotten used to his presence, the lingering melancholy that shrouded me as I woke, how it shook itself off now without my conscious action.

I did not expect to wake to the air heavy and thick with the scent of iron.

The screams followed next.

Alarmed, I bolted upright, my darting eyes searching for Odysseus, only to realise he had already left for the day's battle despite his night activities. I scrambled to dress and see what all the commotion was.

Exiting the tent, my eyes scanned the horizon, trying to make sense of what I was seeing when a single, dark drop splattered onto the ground at my feet. I looked up in confusion, my breath catching. One by one, more drops followed, a macabre drizzle that turned into a steady rain.

Blood. It fell from the sky in dark, crimson streaks.

The other women around me were also looking around, their faces pale, their eyes wide with terror as they observed to the sky. The blood rain soaked into our clothes, painting the earth a gruesome palette of reds and browns. I felt a chill run down my spine. The gods were angry, their displeasure palpable in every drop that fell.

Only one would make such a bold move in war: Zeus. We all knew the rumours that Zeus had sided with the Trojans because his wife Hera had demanded it.

I collapsed to my knees, hands trembling, and began whispering a desperate prayer, my voice drowned out by the relentless patter of blood droplets striking the ground.

"Zeus, hear my plea, for surely most Greek gods will not. Hera, great goddess, undoubtedly shames me as a mother and a wife. I know I have destroyed everything sacred in my life, and she is right to judge me, no matter my good intentions. But I beg you, let this blood rain be a sign of a massacre of the Greeks. Let it be their undoing. If my vow cannot be fulfilled by my own hands, I ask that you ensure Odysseus does not return to his family or homeland on this day. That none of them return. In your wisdom, from my wrath, I ask for this one mercy. End this suffering. Let them fall."

I raised my head to the sky, the blood rain smearing

across my skin as I waited for any sign that the gods had heard my prayer.

The women and I waited together, abandoning the day's duties. None of us could concentrate with blood raining from the sky, anyway. Instead, we watched the ominous dark burgundy clouds as they shifted over the battlefield and moved towards the sea, where the Greek ships waited. Zeus could not be clearer in his demands: *go home.*

It was late afternoon before we got any news. King Agamemnon returned on the arms of two soldiers, carrying him while he moaned about the pain, though I could see no blood or wound to speak of. Limping, they carried him to the medic.

Another two hours passed before we heard anything else. This time, Lord Diomedes returned, carried by his men on a stretcher made of two wooden poles and a strip of dirty linen that was once an off-white. Τάιλορία and I both rushed to his side, but the questions we had died when we saw what had caused Τάιλορία's patron to be carried so.

There was a giant arrow splintered in his thigh. Either an incredibly unlucky shot, or a perfectly calculated one.

"Paris' handiwork," Diomedes barely murmured to Τάιλορία, who ignored the men who attempted to push her aside, and gripped her lord's hand. Her face was a picture of worry, and a sharp pang in my stomach told me that would be my face soon, too.

Why should I have cause to worry? I scolded myself and focused back on Diomedes' words.

"I managed to spook Hector enough to force his retreat, but I left Odysseus with a pack of remaining Trojans. I'm sorry." This last he said to me before he, Τάιλορία, and the men marched into the medical tent.

I fumbled for a seat and fixed my attention on the camp's entrance, watching the men return from the battlefield. And, I waited.

Eventually, the Great Ajax appeared. From a distance, he looked more than formidable, a giant of a man with shoulders the size of boulders. The closer he got, though, the easier it was to see that the boulders on Ajax's shoulders were not muscle, but a body he carried in his arms.

Odysseus.

Struggling to stand on legs as weak as a newborn deer's, I pushed myself up and stumbled towards him. There was blood dripping from Ajax's chest, down the hair on his torso and onto his thick thigh. I searched for the injury, though Ajax was a good foot taller than me, but saw no wound. And if he was walking, with that serious look on his face as he peered down at me, that meant ...

"Where is he hurt?" I demanded.

"Socus wounded him with a sword through the ribs," Ajax replied in that low deep rumble of his. He spoke so seldom that I always forgot how deep his voice was, how it vibrated through your bones. Odysseus groaned in pain. His ribs must have vibrated at Ajax's words, too.

Following the giant into the tent, I heard another groan from Odysseus as he set him down in the third bed, one along from Diomedes and two along from Agamemnon. The generals' line.

There were other men, in other beds, on the other side of the tent. I didn't care to look at them. My gaze was solely on Odysseus and the pale, pale clamminess of his skin. I had never seen his bronzed body so white and sickly.

I watched as the physician worked on Odysseus' wound, my stomach churning at the sight. The wound to his ribs was deep, the flesh torn and raw, and I could see bones exposed at every short breath. The physician, a wiry man with wiry hair and a serious expression, applied a thick paste of crushed herbs and honey to the wound after stitching the flesh together with a needle and thread, a procedure I could not watch. Odysseus winced, his eyes fluttering open briefly before closing again in pain.

"Fetch me the milk of the poppy," the physician ordered, and the young apprentice beside him hurried off to retrieve the potent painkiller. When the milk of the poppy arrived, the physician poured a small amount into a cup and handed it to me.

"Pour this down his throat," he instructed, nodding at Odysseus.

I hesitated, feeling a pang of reluctance. This is what I had prayed for. This is what I wanted. So why had fear suddenly skittered across my skin? Still, I had to be seen playing the part, even now. Gently, I lifted Odysseus' head and carefully poured the milky liquid into his mouth. He swallowed reflexively, and within minutes, a look of relief washed over his face. He relaxed slightly on the makeshift bed, his breathing becoming more even.

As the physician finished his work, binding the wound tightly with clean linen strips, I settled back into my seat, watching over Odysseus as he drifted off into a drugged sleep, the rise and fall of his chest the only sign that he was still alive.

II

ODYSSEUS

I stood with a white-knuckled grip on the prow of my ship as my men rowed in uneasy silence. Their faces were pale in the dim light of the cave we now found ourselves in. I had no recollection of how we had gotten here. All I knew was that my every instinct was screaming at me to turn the ship around, yet no words came.

Our ship continued through murky waters, the mist surrounding us thickening, the air violently cold. I shivered, despite my resolve, and the men continued with their steady, measured strokes, though I knew they did not want to.

We were approaching the edge of the living world, closing in on the gateway to the dead.

I gripped the hilt of my sword tightly, the leather-wrapped handle cool and firm against my palm. I traced each ridge and groove of the intricate design with my forefinger until my breathing evened out as we crossed the threshold. An unsettling silence blanketed the world around us. The scent of decay and freshly turned soil hung heavy. As we reached the pebbled shoreline, I disembarked first, my boots sinking into the cold, damp ground. The landscape was barren, a wasteland of shadow and sorrow. Then came the distant, mournful wail of the spirits.

We had prepared offerings, of course – black sheep for the dead and libations of honey, milk, and wine. The sheep bleated woefully behind me.

I led my men with determined steps to a suitable spot and drew a trench in the earth with the hilt of my sword, a channel through which we would pour the blood of our sacrifices. The ground beneath our feet was unyielding, a reflection of how the dead treated those of us still living. I could tell from the long shadows cast by the eerie glow of the Underworld's twilight that others were watching us. The men could sense it, too; their movements were stilted at best.

Exhaling sharply, I called upon the gods of the Underworld, invoking Hades and Persephone, and began the ritual. The names felt heavy on my tongue, filled with ancient power, and the darkness around us seemed to deepen in response, as if the very air was waiting on us – on me. Tugging the restless animal to me, I slit its throat, letting its rich blood flow into the trench, a river of crimson seeping into the earth, the scent of it overwhelming as it permeated the smell of decay.

More of the dead began to gather.

Next, I poured the honey, milk, and wine into the trench, the libations mixing with the blood. The dead lurched forward, pale and indistinct at first, becoming more corporeal as they drank from the trench. I steeled myself, knowing that among them would be those I had known and lost, that there might be some who blamed me for their early arrival in this place.

The first spirit to approach me was Elpenor, a member of my crew. His presence confused me – how could Elpenor be here among the dead? We had parted ways only days ago on the battlefield, and yet his shade stood before me, skin pale and ethereal, unlike the vibrant man I had last seen.

Had he died in battle and I had not yet been told?

"Elpenor? What brings you here? How is it you've come to be among the dead?"

He did not respond directly. Instead his stare pierced through me with a silent plea. As he spoke, his voice was a hollow echo. "Odysseus, I beg of you, grant me a proper burial. My body lies unburied on Circe's island, left to the mercy of the elements. I cannot find peace in this state."

I shook my head in confusion. "Circe's island? Elpenor, we have never been to such a place. What madness is this?"

A flicker of frustration crossed his spectral face, and his voice grew sharp, tinged with anger. "Do you not see my state? I speak of a future, one where you have failed me! My soul is restless, trapped between worlds, because you did not see to my burial."

My heart pounded in my chest, until I thought I might die from the strength of its hammering beat. I struggled to reconcile Elpenor's words with what I knew to be true. We were still outside the gates of Troy. Yet the anguish in his eyes was undeniable, a testament to a fate I had yet to understand.

"Elpenor, if ever we find ourselves on this Circe's island you speak of, I will seek out your body and ensure you are given a proper burial. You have my word."

His form seemed to flicker, the anger in his eyes dimming slightly as my promise reached him. But the sorrow remained, and I was left with the weight of my oath, and the unsettling knowledge of a future where I had failed a comrade.

The whispers of the dead became more insistent. From the shadows emerged a figure, tall and imposing, a warrior whose mere presence demanded respect. Achilles, the mightiest of the Greeks, strode toward me with the same power and arrogance he had wielded in life.

"Odysseus," he called, his voice carrying a sharp edge. "Have you come to gloat, or to witness the eternal greatness of Achilles, even in death?"

"Achilles, even here, you cling to your glory."

"Glory is all that matters, Odysseus. I am Achilles, the greatest warrior, and even in the Underworld, I deserve to be honoured."

The Achilles I saw before me was not the noble warrior of legends, but a ghost obsessed with his own legacy. As I listened to him continue his tirade, memories of the living world flooded my mind, reminding me that Achilles had not yet returned to the war after I had last seen him. How could he be here, demanding recognition? If our greatest warrior was destined to fall, how could we hope to win this war and find our way home?

My mind raced, connecting pieces of this grim fate. Without Achilles, our mightiest champion, we were exposed. I had to think, had to find another way to outmaneuver our enemies.

Achilles continued to wax lyrical about glory. He spoke of battles not yet fought and victories won, his words dripping with self-absorbed pride. It was as if he were speaking to himself, reliving the moments of triumph that had defined his life. His gaze was distant, fixated on the past glories that now seemed hollow in this shadowed realm. Just as in life, Achilles was consumed by his own legend, deaf to the concerns of others.

His monologue droned on, but I was no longer listening, for another approached me with an air of solemn authority. It was the prophet, Tiresias, his eyes blind but, if the rumours were to be believed, seeing more than any mortal.

"Tiresias, why am I here? I am certain I am not supposed to be here, yet I clearly remember coming to this realm. Help me, old friend."

The prophet nodded, as if expecting my plea. "Odysseus, son of Laertes, many perils await you on your journey. Listen well and heed my words if you wish not to return here before your time. Beware of those that sing you sweet words. Plug your ears with beeswax, bind yourself if you must, but do not succumb to the temptation, for their intentions are treacherous."

I thought over his words. "You speak of sirens."

He continued as if he hadn't heard me, his voice steady and unyielding. "Be careful of being so all-consumed with your goal, shrewd Odysseus, that you are not devoured by the whirlpool that surrounds you, for that grasp is unforgiving. To steer yourself straight down the middle is wise, even if you lose a little along the way, for it is better to lose fewer things than more. Do not fear six-headed monsters when two-faced people are much more dangerous.

"Finally, upon your return to Ithaca, you must make a sacrifice to appease Poseidon, for he will harbour a great anger against you once you wrong him. Only by seeking his forgiveness can you ever hope to find peace in your homeland."

His words lingered, the solemn directives settling heavily upon me. Why would I intentionally wrong a god like Poseidon? Just as I went to ask him, Tiresias raised a hand to silence me.

"Above all, remain vigilant, Odysseus. The greatest danger may come from those you least expect."

I nodded, the finality of his tone telling me I would get no more out of him this night. "I will heed your warnings and follow your counsel. The gods willing, I will see Ithaca once more."

Tiresias nodded, a faint smile across his face. "Then I will leave you in the hands of one who will help you leave this place."

As he retreated into the shadows, I was met by the spirit of my mother, Anticlea. My breath caught as I recognised her form, her face.

"Mother?" I whispered, sorrow bearing down upon me. I had not known she was dead. I had not known the others were dead, was still not yet convinced they were, but for some reason she appeared more substantial, her body more 'material', and I knew. She was truly here. The thought struck me with a pain deeper than any I had felt before. "Mother, how can this be?"

She stepped closer until I could feel her ghost-like hands on my forearms. "Odysseus, my son. Your father is old and in poor health, living in seclusion. He would not see anyone, even me. Between that and a seemingly endless war, I died of grief, my heart broken at the long absence you both left. I could not bear the endlessness of it all."

Tears burned in the back of my eyes as I reached out to embrace her. My arms passed through her, and I was reminded again of the cruel divide between the living and the dead. "Mother, I never meant for this to happen."

She looked at me with a tender smile. "Do not grieve for me, my son. My time has passed, but yours is still unfolding. You must return to the living world. There are dangers that await you on your return home."

I nodded, listening intently as she continued.

"In Ithaca, suitors plague your house, seeking to take your place. They consume your wealth and dishonour your home, believing you are dead. Penelope, your faithful wife, holds them at bay with her cleverness, but she cannot do so forever."

The thought of Penelope, steadfast and enduring, filled me with both hope and dread. "How do I get home, Mother?"

"You have always been resourceful and wise, my boy. The gods

have not finished testing you, but remember that those you love remain ever hopeful of your return. Let that be your fuel."

I nodded at her words even as a gnawing doubt took hold, and my mind flickered back to the last time Penelope saw me, a horrible nightmare come to life ...

She had been standing at the window of our home, a modest estate in Ithaca, watching me plough one of the fields. How strange; I had never considered the event from her perspective before. Perhaps because this was a place of pasts and futures, where I could consider something I should never have done. Something for which the gods would likely never forgive me.

I wondered if Penelope did.

As if thinking of her could conjure her form in this realm, she appeared, speaking the oracle's words at me: if I went to war, I would be away for twenty years and return a beggar. I wasn't sure how this could come to pass if the war was only to last for nine, but my wife seemed certain. Now she watched me as, like a madman, I sowed the field with salt instead of seeds. I knew she wasn't the only one watching me; there were other eyes on me out there. I could feel them. Men who were angry that it was my cunning that originally bound them to this war.

But I did not want to be away from my family for twenty years. My son had just turned one. Please, gods, don't take me away from him.

My mind was now, somehow, in Penelope's body, glued to watching myself out the window. I could tell there were men behind me. I heard them gathering my son into their arms. He was crying out for his mother, but she – I – remained glued to watching myself.

They placed my son in the field. I was driving the plough straight toward him. If I truly were a madman, I would not think. I would run him over without a moment's hesitation. There would be other children between us, I reasoned to myself. I knew what happened in this memory, but I couldn't seem to pull myself away. In case this time it ended differently. In case this time it ended with his cry as the wheel began to crush his skull ...

"You must wake before it is too late," Penelope told me.

"You must wake."

"You must WAKE!"

12

ODETTE

"You must wake!" I said, louder this time, trying to shake Odysseus from his nightmare.

He continued muttering incomprehensible words, caught in the grip of his terror, his hands clenching and unclenching, grappling with unseen adversaries.

Suddenly, his eyes snapped open, wild with confusion and fear as he jerked upright. His movement almost knocked me off the side of the narrow bed, but I grabbed the edge just in time to steady myself. His strong, calloused hand instinctively reached out, grasping my wrist tightly, as if anchoring himself to reality. For a moment, his grip was almost too tight, but then he blinked again, recognition dawning in his eyes as he realised who I was and where we found ourselves.

"You're awake, you're okay." I rested my now released hand on his arm, stroking it gently, hoping to calm him.

His wild panic, near-silent though it was, slowly faded and he nodded, his body falling back on the bed and his breath coming in ragged gasps. When they eventually evened out, I asked the question on my mind, my eyes searching his for the truth.

"Who were you screaming for?"

"I was screaming?" His voice was so hoarse that he answered his own question. He swallowed, as if trying to reconcile reality with whatever had happened in his head. I held a cup of water up to his lips, and waited.

After taking several small sips, he answered me. "My son, Telemachus," he rasped.

I paused, considering my response, the rapid beat of my heart against my ribs. "How did he die?"

Odysseus struggled back up into a sitting position, removing my hand from his arm, which, for some reason, made me feel less than.

"He didn't."

I didn't press, though I wanted to know, and somehow he must have sensed that. Or he needed to get it off his chest, which I could understand. So he continued.

"The men came to fetch me for the war, and I didn't want to go. I pretended to be a madman, but they saw my ruse for what it was. They placed my son in front of my plough, where I'd been sowing salt instead of seed, forcing me to choose between killing my son or going to war."

He paused, watching me closely, as if expecting to see horror or disgust. I worked hard to keep my expression passive, refusing to let him see the turmoil inside me.

"I swerved at the last minute," he continued. "But in the dream, I didn't. I wonder if it is a message that something has happened to my son."

As he said it, the flickering light from the lone lantern in the medical tent cast ghostly shapes on the canvas walls. The scent of medicinal herbs and the faint, metallic tang of blood filled the air. The rest of the injured men slept soundly around us; the only sounds were their soft breaths and occasional sleep murmurs. Otherwise, we were undisturbed.

"You should not say such things." I reached for the cloth beside the bowl on the small table. Dipping it in water, I wrung the cloth and gently applied it to his brow. "Rest."

"How can I rest when I do not know the fate of my boy?"

I could see the tension in Odysseus' muscles, his body still rigid with fear and anguish that the nightmare had conjured. His breaths came in shallow gasps, each exhale a whispered plea. This anguish, this torment, I realised was worse than anything I had planned for him.

"My husband told me that you would come and bash our babes' heads in. That it would be better if we died in our sleep as a family, the night before you raided my village." I hesitated on the next part. "It was I who mixed the hemlock for us that night."

I sat on the edge of Odysseus' bed, watching him. His face was twisted, his brow already damp with sweat again. At first I thought it was disgust that shaped his face, even though he too had just admitted to terrible intentions of his own.

He hadn't acted upon it, I supposed.

"You had a child."

I nodded, reaching for the cloth again, anything to keep my hands busy.

Odysseus frowned. "But I killed your husband."

"I ... I got the doses wrong," I whispered, choking on those last words. I had buried the admission so deep within myself that I did not have to look at it. It had curdled like soured milk and turned to venom in my heart, making it cold, hard, black; and it burnt the back of my throat as it all came back up now.

A horrible silence filled the air afterwards.

Eventually he spoke. "That is a cowardly thing to ask of the mother of your child."

"It is a thing no true mother would ever have considered doing."

"Is that why you looked at me with such ire the day you watched us burn your village to the ground?"

I was momentarily thrown. "You remember me watching you?"

My heart started hammering wildly against my chest.

"I remember every look you've ever given me."

I was waiting for him to confess he had seen my looks of murderous rage, that he knew what I had plotted. Yet, he surprised me once again.

"I thought you were just proud, vengeful for losing your home," he continued. "Now I know that by killing your husband, I stole something from you. Something more than just his life."

That statement stole the air from my lungs.

I had never thought of it in the way Odysseus worded it now, but the words landed true. I felt my soul vibrate in agreement. I had not just lost everything; I had been stripped of my power to *do* anything about it. To hold anyone else to account. Except Odysseus.

But the war had taken him from his family, too.

As he passed back into sleep, my thoughts continued. I had wanted him dead for so long, blaming him for everything I had lost. Yet, seeing him tormented by his own demons ... He was also a victim of this war, in a way. And if he died, I would simply be handed over to another lord, and who knew what fate would await me then?

Whether I liked it or not, my survival – my only hope to reclaim some semblance of control over my life – was now intertwined with Odysseus' life. It was a truth I was still uncertain I wanted to accept.

I awoke to the pitch black of night in the medical tent. It took a moment to register where I was. I hadn't meant to fall asleep beside Odysseus, but here I was, my head resting against his shoulder, his hand gently stroking my arm. I burrowed my head, confused, trying to remember climbing into bed beside him. Perhaps I had sought comfort in my sleep, drawn to the warmth and presence of another.

I shifted slightly, and Odysseus' touch stilled. When I looked up at him, his eyes were open, watching me with a tenderness so at odds with the warrior I had come to know.

"You still have nightmares, too," he murmured. "It kills me that you won't let me touch you, let me hold you, when they come. And when the dawn rises, I know the only thing that dulls the ache of how much I want to, is the violence of the battlefield. It's the only outlet for all this energy."

I glanced at the bandages around his ribs. They were bloodied, but dry. I ran my fingers over them gently, waiting for him to flinch. He didn't. My heart ached for him. Gods curse this wretched war they had thrust us into ... and for what?

"I don't think you're going to be on the battlefield any time soon."

The corner of his mouth twitched. "No, not any time soon."

His hand began stroking my arm again.

"So what are you going to do with all that energy, then?"

I whispered, my voice trembling with something I couldn't quite name.

He lifted my hand from his ribcage and kissed it. He stilled, as if waiting for an attack, waiting for me to slap him away. But for the life of me, I couldn't. Instead, my breath skittered as his hand moved to cup my cheek and pull my face closer to his own.

Our lips cautiously brushed at first, but then the collision crushed us together, his tongue desperately seeking mine, and mine meeting his. Again and again and again. We met each other's fervour with an intensity equal in tenderness and fierceness. The world around us dissolved, leaving only the sensation of his lips on mine, the warmth of his body against mine, and the unspoken understanding that, in this moment, we were each other's refuge. It was a kiss that promised nothing but the present, a brief respite from the pain.

I pulled back when it got too much, too intense, burrowing myself in the space where his shoulder met his collarbone. His hands continued to skim my body until they slid under my chiton and stilled, right over the entrance to my sex.

"I need you," he breathed against my skin.

"I'm here," I whispered back. "I'm here."

I had never heard such a want before. Alcander had never said such things. He had not listened to me or heeded my instruction, instead wanting our final act his way – an act that stole both him and Lykas away from me. Meanwhile, here was a man who listened to me, who had taken action on my advice, who was still listening to what my body was telling him now.

Odysseus' kisses trailed down my neck. His hands moved

more desperately now, over my waist, my breasts, up into my hair and down my back, over my butt. I felt him lengthen against me, and the heat that pooled there made me want to whimper.

The outside world faded once again, and for a moment we were no longer enemies thrust into this pit of death together, no longer slave and master, spear-wife and Odysseus. We were just two people, desperate for some sliver of comfort, of solace, in a world that continued to demand more from us than we wanted or were able to give.

Then, three things pulled us from our stupor. First, Odysseus' fingers slid between my thighs, drawing a sharp gasp from me as a jolt of pleasure surged through my body. Next, a sudden guttural snore erupted from the man beside Odysseus' bed. And lastly, Odysseus' wound started to bleed through the bandage again, the dark spreading stain the reminder we both needed that our actions were bound to reality.

IN THE FOLLOWING DAYS, ODYSSEUS' strength returned. By the eighth day, he sat up straighter, though he still winced as he did so and could only hold the posture for so long before breaking a sweat. Beside him, Agamemnon still lay in his bed, his colour pale, though behind his back the medics said there was nothing wrong with him. Diomedes, too, appeared on the mend.

I could hear him and Τάιλορία having a conversation between the partition divides that gave each man some sliver of privacy, when Nestor, one of the only remaining generals in prime health, broke the quiet atmosphere of recovery as he burst past the tent flap, his expression grave.

"Sire," he said, walking past Odysseus, myself, Diomedes, and Τάιλορία, heading straight for Agamemnon's bed.

"What is it, Nestor? Can't you see I need rest?" Agamemnon snapped.

"The losses for the day have been recorded, my lord."

"And?"

"They are … significant," Nestor said, his voice almost trembling.

"How many?"

Nestor hesitated, and the air grew heavier in his silence.

"HOW MANY?!"

"Thousands, my lord." The words fell like stones into a still pond, sending ripples of shock through the tent.

The silence that followed was potent, suffocating. Since the war began, the daily numbers of losses had been in the hundreds, but never in the thousands. We had now crossed a line that we might not be able to come back from. The Greeks, I reminded myself. Not *us*.

"We should set sail for home, then," King Agamemnon declared, though 'declared' was too strong a word for the strangled, garbled word that tumbled from him.

"No," Odysseus growled, rising once again, his hand pressed against his wound as he pointed at Agamemnon. "This decision no longer lies solely with you. We have all bled, sacrificed, and endured too much to abandon this cause now. We stand on the precipice. Victory is within our grasp if we can find the strength to persevere. We must endure a little longer, for the dawn of our triumph is near."

"My eloquent friend is right," Lord Diomedes added as

he too sat up and looked over at Agamemnon. "This is not just your war anymore. It is all of ours, and I do not wish to be remembered as the king or the general that sacrificed so much for nothing."

"Then what do you suggest I do?" Agamemnon practically whined.

"We ask Poseidon for his assistance," Diomedes suggested.

"No," Odysseus said firmly. Then he looked at me. "We ask Patroclus."

The men turned to look first at Odysseus, then at me. I saw the movements of their heads in my periphery, but my view was focused solely on those dark eyes boring into me, no longer cold, but *trusting*.

"Go, Odette. You know what to say."

He squeezed my hand, but I could not move. To do this now was to forever acknowledge I had aided the Greeks and abandoned my heritage. It was one thing to acknowledge I no longer wanted Odysseus dead. It was quite another to do this bidding.

Odysseus squeezed my hand again, tighter this time, as he noted my hesitation.

I could not be seen to disobey him, not in front of other generals and kings. To do so right now would be to sign my own death warrant, and I could not go to the Underworld. For how could I face my husband and son, and tell them I had not planned on avenging them after all? That I had, in fact, sullied their honour. Even if I was still mad at Alcander. For what I had done at his bequest.

I was trapped. Another decision taken from me. And as I nodded to Odysseus and backed out of the tent, gods damn me, I knew what I must do.

Alcander, Lykas ... forgive me.

If this war had taught me one thing so far, it was that pride loses wars.

Men believed pride was a burning sword, the feeling in their gut that told them to right wrongs, that demanded justice. They believed serving that justice would give them a smug sense of satisfaction from their own achievement. That other men would admire them for acting on it, for holding onto their honour.

There was no honour in such pride.

It was pride that cost me Lykas. Pride that cost me Alcander.

Pride had driven these men to these shores; not indignation at Helen, the blood vow, or a sense of justice.

And it was pride that had Patroclus leading the army of the Myrmidons through the Greek camps in Achilles' armour. Patroclus, who had never been on the battlefield. Some whispered that he was not skilled enough to even lift a spear, and given the little meat on his bones, even less than my own, I could believe that gossip. Though, perhaps he did not go because Achilles preferred to keep him safe.

No matter, because the light that sparked in his eyes when I passed on the generals' message that they needed him was all that was required. That someone, anyone, would think he was worthy enough to be influential in the great Trojan War was the encouragement that stoked the fire of his pride. A chance to put the whispers that plagued him to rest.

As the Myrmidons rallied, running to grab their spears, swords, and shields, quickly attaching their armour and joining the rallying war cry, I headed against the stream of them. Back to the secluded section of the camp where I had sought out Patroclus yesterday. The tents were all but deserted. It was quiet and barren, as if the men had left and would not come back.

Only one man remained: Achilles. His arms were folded, his form stock-still, as he surveyed the men in the distance.

It was pride that kept Achilles from joining Patroclus on the field right then. In that moment, the great warrior turned and looked at me. My blood froze. Achilles was not a dumb man. I was probably one of the last to speak to Patroclus, before this morning when he went off in Achilles' armor. With or without the soldier's blessing, I did not know. But it would not take a genius to put two and two together. I wondered if he would stalk toward me, slap me, hurt me, for taking something precious from him. Looking around, no one would stop him. Most of the camps had gone with Patroclus. Even the women had gone to see what all the fuss was about. We were on our own.

But he simply gave me a nod and turned back to watch the men, now a smudge of colours in the distance.

It was then that I realised why Achilles made no move against me. He too had made an oath, a vow with the gods themselves, just as I had. One he could not break. So he had to continue to pretend to be okay with what Patroclus was doing. Right then, he had to pretend to be something other than he was.

Yes, I understood that well. To know what others must think of you when you stick to your convictions, how it ate you up inside until you weren't sure which parts were you and which were the vow. Which parts were the truth, and which were fabricated from outside sources. You just had to get on with life anyway.

Until you didn't.

Patroclus did not return with the men that evening. The whispers that night around the campfires were that Hector had mistaken him for Achilles and killed the poor boy.

The next morning, I stood on the same spot I had the day before and watched as this time Achilles broke the vow he had made between himself and the gods and went to war once again, his pride forgotten.

Hector died next.

For the nine days that followed, the Trojans prepared Hector's funeral pyre. Achilles had apparently declared a reprieve from battle, much to Agamemnon's displeasure. I saw the declaration for what it was: the chance for him to grieve the loss of Patroclus, and to grieve his own betrayal – his word – of himself.

On the tenth day, we watched from our side of the plain as the pyre was lit and the smoke carried into the air, up towards the gods. Artemis instructed the wind nymphs to blow the ashes towards us and into the sea. But the weight of the ashes fell short across the Greek camp, as if we were all being marked for death.

Ash tasted like burnt sand. That is what I remembered thinking as I stared up into the sun that beat down on us mercilessly, the smoke swirling in the sky, the ashes sprinkling down. The twins Apollo and Artemis had picked their side: they were with the Trojans.

Which is why, when news returned that Achilles had been shot and killed with an arrow – guided by Apollo and executed by Paris – I thought again of pride.

Pride had cost the Greeks the war.

13
ODYSSEUS

The air went out of the soldiers after the death of Achilles. They knew what it was like to fight a war without him. Still, they continued at our insistence. Most of the men didn't understand why we insisted; they hadn't been privy to the conversation we'd had with the seer after Achilles' death.

Calchas had reappeared in his priestly garbs, to the remainder of us lords still in the medical tent, the hem of his robe dusted with sand and blood. Nestor, Ajax, Meleamus, Agamemnon, and myself joined him while the other wounded soldiers were moved out of the tent to give us privacy.

"Calchas," Diomedes started, ever the brash one. Brasher still, it turned out, when he was bedridden. "You promised us victory and yet it has been nine long years, and now victory appears further away than ever before."

"Certain items must be collected if you are to see the end of this war," Calchas replied.

"Didn't fancy telling us that before?" Diomedes

muttered. I, along with a few others, grunted in agreement, but Calchas did not rise to the bait.

Instead, his milky eyes clouded over and he continued. "Achilles has an unknown son. He must be found and brought here. Philoctetes possesses a bow of immense power, and it is vital to our success. Lastly, Athena's Palladium, the sacred statue, lies hidden behind the city walls of Troy. With it, the city cannot fall."

A murmur ran through the gathered lords. I exchanged a glance with Diomedes, seeing my own exhaustion reflected in his eyes. The weight of nine years of warfare pressed down on us all.

Agamemnon was first to break the silence. "And how are we to accomplish these tasks?" he demanded.

"These are not ordinary tasks, but they are the keys to your victory. You must divide your forces wisely. Seek out Achilles' son, persuade Philoctetes to join your cause, and retrieve the Palladium with the cunning that only Odysseus can muster."

All eyes turned to me then, and I felt the familiar weight of expectation settle on my shoulders. The details were discussed, the remaining tasks divided out between the men, and a timeline put in place for when we would be able to act, subject to the medics' discharge.

Nine long weeks I had lain in this infernal medical tent, confined to the pallet as my body slowly knitted itself back together. It would be another three before I would be discharged, I was told. That was not necessarily a bad thing, considering the wound in my side still throbbed relentlessly, a constant reminder of how close I had been, in truth, to travelling down to the Underworld.

That nightmare still haunted me.

Odette came every day, her touch as gentle as the breeze, applying salve to my wound and following the medics' instructions with meticulous care. Yet she remained distant, her interactions with me minimal and perfunctory, as if she didn't trust herself around me after our last encounter. It drove me wild, until all I could do was dream of her.

She came to dress my wound with salve as she always did. But this time, when I captured her wrist, she let me. And when my arms tightened around her chest and pulled her to me, she finally relaxed into me, allowing my hands to stroke her hair.

"Why?"

She knew what I was asking.

"You'll be going home to your precious Penelope soon. Perhaps you should focus on that."

I continued stroking her hair. "You sound jealous."

"No, I am realistic."

"I thought we agreed not to lie to one another."

"We agreed to no more games. Besides, it is not a lie. You will leave this war, and I will remain a slave. This is my homeland. This," – she pushed away from me and gestured to the space between us – "will cease to be anything more. And that will be that. The war will end soon. Nine years by your own declaration. It is almost over."

I crushed her back into me. "You sound disappointed at the thought of my going home."

"I am disappointed in myself."

"For?"

She sucked in a breath and I could feel the raggedness of her heart beating against my stomach, throbbing at the same pace as my wound – two wounded creatures, making one another whole.

Eventually, she answered. "For believing that I mean more to you than I do. For all your precious words about not treating me like a spear-wife, your actions do not match, Odysseus. You use me, just in a different way than the others."

She spun a colourful string of curses then, spitting each one out at me, calling me every heinous name she could think of, until suddenly I was barrelling towards her in our tent until her back hit the centre mast pole and I could crowd her with my body.

"You are right. There is nothing I wouldn't do to get home to my wife."

My eyes roamed over her face before landing on her lips, as the words I had been so desperate to hear fell from my own mouth first.

"But that is not to say I do not care for you, too. I cannot think, Odette, I cannot breathe around you. Not without smelling the scent of you, those herbs you crush into the oil. No matter how hard I try to wrack my brain, I cannot remember what my wife smells like. All I can think of is YOU. It infuriates me. Morning, noon, and night – you hound me. You were right, I probably wouldn't have had Thersites beaten if I could think straight. If this blood roaring in my ears would stop. If I could think calmly, if I could come back to this tent and ignore you, ignore that gods damn scent—"

"You could send me away," she offered.

"And have another man know you?" I chuckled, the sound dark, even to my own ears.

"You don't know me."

A pause, heavy with expectation – as if this moment would be the one to change the very course of our fates.

"I would like to, Odette."

I looked at her expectantly and when she nodded, my hands cupped the backs of her thighs. As I lifted her, her legs hooked around me. I snaked one arm around her waist and carried her back towards my pallet, our eyes never leaving the other's. Her eyes were dark, pupils dilated, her breath coming in ragged gasps, as was my own. Her body trembled against mine, and then we were meeting in a desperate kiss, once again.

She tasted of salt and fire.

I stumbled towards the pallet, my movements frantic and uncoordinated, but even as I lifted her onto the bed, her legs did not fall from my waist. My hands moved with a mind of their own, pushing up her chiton to reveal the smooth skin beneath. The friction of the fabric was coarse, matching the roughness of my movements. It caused tiny goosebumps to break out all over her skin. Her back arched and she bucked against me, pressing the length of her body against mine, demanding more friction, again and again. Over and over.

I complied until she made a needy little sound and I could take it no longer. I pulled away, to strip myself of my tunic, so my bare chest could press against her. I bunched her chiton around her thighs, and watched as my cock pressed against her entrance before sliding all the way home.

Home.

I kept one hand on the curve of her hip, the other landing in the palm of hers above her head in a holy palmers' kiss as I moved over her, in her, through her. She met each thrust with a roll of her hips until I, too, moaned at the pleasure that uncoiled with her every movement, her walls clasped around me. There was no greater pleasure on this earth than where we were right now, even if it was just frantic desperation coupled with such heat in my body that I was certain she would burn me from the inside out.

We were no longer Odysseus and Odette, but just two bodies, moving against each other in a rhythm that needed no words. Words were useless to describe this feeling, this overwhelming sense that everything I was about to become was on the brink of falling apart.

Odette clawed at my back, desperate for some sort of release. Instead, I sat back, looking down at her, spreading her legs wider. My mouth watered at the sight, as if she were some feast gifted by the gods, so I slowed my movements – savouring.

She stilled, and I could practically feel her thinking, so I gave her a short, sharp thrust in warning. I did not want to go back to the roles we had to play in this war. Not yet.

Let the dream last a little longer … please.

Then I thrusted, again and again, until we were both panting and I couldn't tell if it was in pleasure or pain, until the groan ripped through me and I was spilling my seed over her belly.

I woke with a start, my body slick with sweat, cum across my own torso, my breath shallow and unsteady. The tent was dark, the only sound the distant murmurs of the camp.

It was a dream. I knew it was a dream, but it felt so real. Every touch, every kiss, every thrust. But, Odette wasn't there in the tent with me – only the lingering ache of the dream as the vivid reminder of everything I now craved.

I BUCKLED the last strap of my armour. I had finally been discharged from the medical tent with its uniquely clinical smell. I feared the combined scent of herbs and salves, leathers and linens, and the infection-burning fire would never truly leave me.

So here I was, back in my tent, with all the luxuries a man could have in war.

Tonight I would seek out the Palladium, as requested by Calchas. The sacred statue of Athena we supposedly needed to secure our victory.

I secured my xiphos[1] to my belt and then wrapped an old hooded cloak over both that and my armour. The only way to get into Troy under the cover of darkness was if I disguised myself as a beggar. A lot rested on tonight. Without Achilles, without these relics, the war would drag on and on, the cost unimaginable. I had to succeed, for the sake of every man who had endured this endless nightmare.

Of course, it wasn't only the men who had been suffering, I reminded myself as I watched Odette angrily storm about the tent, tidying what need not be tidied. Her movements betrayed her silence, but all I could think of was the way her hair brushed her shoulders, the way her hips swayed as she moved, the way she huffed every time she completed a task unsatisfactorily.

"Will you not wish me well before I go?"

She turned to me, a flash of anger in her eyes. "To what end? Hector and Paris may be gone, but the Trojans still have reinforcements coming, and city walls that will never fall. How can you ask your men to keep fighting for a cause that might as well be a dead horse, while you do something based on the words of a soothsayer whose prophecies have yet to come true?!"

I took three large strides towards her. "Is this about what I asked of you when I was injured? Do you really despise me so much that you still hope the Trojans defeat us? Would you see me harmed again, is that it?"

"I spent twelve weeks, day and night, in that horror of a tent with you. And now you would waste that work once again."

---

1. A double-edged, single-handed sword, typically with a blade around 18 to 24 inches long.

"Ah, so now you're angry at me for jeopardising myself?"

"What does it matter *why* I am angry?"

"Because I cannot assuage your anger before I go if I do not know the root of it, Odette." I said the last part quietly, conscious of how close our fingers were, mere inches from one another though they remained by our sides.

She did not speak for the longest time, her jaw tight. "I am angry at you for all of that, and yet even *I* do not understand the depths of my anger."

Her words stung, but I understood them. I had forced her hands in such ways, just as her husband had. "This is bigger than what is between you and I. It's about the end of this war. Do you not want to see the end of it?"

She sent me a seething look. "Stop manipulating my words. I am not one of your Greek men to be swayed by a crafty tongue and a smart message."

"I must do this. But when I return, Odette, we will unravel that anger of yours."

With that, I left the tent and went to meet Diomedes, who was once again waiting for me at the edge of camp. Given that we had already staked out the places closest to Troy, it made sense for us to partner once again for this mission. We knew the routes to take through the long grass, along the river, until we would come to the western walls of Troy and begin the hike up to the temple of Athena, which overshadowed even Troy's tall walls from where it sat on the mountainside.

We met with no more than a nod to each other before Diomedes and I moved through the shadows, our steps muffled by the soft leather of our sandals. We passed by the remains of what had once been a bustling marketplace, one of the first we'd ransacked on arrival all those years ago. The empty stalls were not much more than scattered debris now and the scent of spices and baked bread had long been replaced by the reminders of war. I could almost imagine the echoes of traders haggling and children laughing, now replaced by the mournful silence of a city under siege.

The high walls of Troy loomed over us as we got closer, until with practised stealth we slipped into the shadows, pressing ourselves against the cool stone surfaces as we regained control of our breathing and listened for the footfalls of patrolling guards.

Together we edged closer towards the temple, until eventually it rose before us, its columns stark and white against the night sky. The entrance was guarded by two Trojan sentries, their armour glinting under the light of the moon. The scent of oil from the burning lamps either side of the entrance mixed with the fragrant scent of laurels and what I thought might be violets.

It reminded me of Odette. Everything did now, her presence woven into the fabric of my thoughts.

The faint rustle of leaves in a nearby tree immediately had me tensing, and Diomedes went deathly still beside me. The night bird gave two craws and then flew off, each flap of its wings amplified in the stillness.

A sign from Athena.

I looked at Diomedes' silhouette, nodded, and received one in return. In a swift, silent motion, he incapacitated the first guard, his blade catching the man's throat before the guard could utter a cry. I dispatched of the second, feeling the warmth of his blood splutter over my hands as my blade sliced his jugular. Together, we dragged their bodies into the shadows and wiped our blades clean on their tunics.

After that, there was no one to stop us. No one thought

we would steal from one of Troy's sacred temples after all this time.

The burning scent of laurels and violets was stronger inside, though the air was cooler. The inside walls were carved with an elaborate olive tree, its branches curling around the circular architecture of the room. The creatures most often associated with our Lady Athena – the owl, the snake, the birds – seemed to watch us as Diomedes and I walked to the centre, where a marble altar sat.

The Palladium stood on a pedestal on the central altar. A pure circle opening overhead showed just a sliver of moonlight that perfectly bounced off the statue, as if Artemis herself was saying, 'Go on, take it.'

So I reached out to grasp the statue of Athena in all her glory. She held a spear in her right hand and a shield in her left, her helmet pulling back her hair, her body clad in a tunic that seemed to flow along her sculpted limbs, all the while protected by the Aegis. Each detail was intricate, right down to the stern expression on her face as her eyes watched me.

This, the Palladium, was heavier than it looked. At only three feet tall and made of pure white stone, its weight was solid and reassuring in my hands.

But, when I looked into its eyes …

The stone turned to liquid silver, running over my hands and onto the floor. My eyes followed the pool of liquid until I turned and saw Diomedes standing in the doorway, not keeping watch as I'd thought, but watching me.

"Diomedes, why aren't you keeping watch?"

He stepped closer. "You should hand me the Palladium," he said.

"Why?" My hands instinctively clenched around it, but it wasn't there – it was liquid silver running through my fingers. Then, I saw that the liquid was pooled around Diomedes' feet, too. He stood *in* Athena's presence. It enraged me.

"Because the glory should be mine." The words were quiet, so quiet, but they bounced off the floor, now stained silver, with crystalline clarity. I stepped closer, too, my hand sliding to the hilt of my concealed dagger. "Yours? When has Athena ever come to you with her plans of war?"

"The war has taken much from me. I deserve this victory." He circled me, our movements reflected in one another and the mirror now beneath our feet.

"So, you would claim glory in her name as you plunge a knife into my chest? Me, the one she has spoken to and guided throughout this war? Do you think Athena will really side with you?"

"There's only one way to know."

Then, there was no more talk other than the clashing of our blades. The fight was fast, fierce, intense, silent other than the ringing of steel meeting steel. But we knew each other too well, and had fought side by side for too long. For every lunge I offered, Diomedes gave a swift and clever side-step. Every time he went to slash across my torso and have my intestines spill from my abdomen, I deftly avoided the blow. When the fatal blow did come, it was not through strength, but an opportunity. The moon shone through the temple roof and reflected off the silver floor, momentarily blinding Diomedes. I struck low, my dagger finding its mark in his side.

He fell with a gasp, clutching at the wound. I stood over him, my breath ragged as the reality of my betrayal sunk in.

"Forgive me, Diomedes."

"Whatever for?"

Diomedes was standing upright, no blood pouring from him, staring straight at me.

The unnaturalness of it was jarring. I looked down at my hand, expecting to see fresh blood mixed with liquid silver. Instead, I saw the stone statue of Athena in my hand. I shook my head clear until I realised *this* was reality.

"For taking a moment to say a prayer to Lady Athena." I gave my voice a moment to steady itself. "We should focus on getting out of here."

He let out a low chuckle in response. "Yes, there's plenty of time for prayers. For now, we must return."

I nodded in agreement, yet when Diomedes held out his hand for the statue, I refused. A look of surprise flashed across his face, but then the moment passed and he shrugged, and we both left the cool air of the temple for the warmth of the night. As we made our way back to camp, the weight of the statue seemed to get heavier, the knowledge it had given me – what it had *told* me I was capable of – weighing on my conscience.

"We did it! Troy's fate is sealed," Diomedes finally declared as we crossed back into Grecian territory.

I offered him a tight smile. "That it is."

The men might see this as a sign of hope, the promise of an end to this endless war. But I knew the gods would demand retribution, and their wrath would find me soon enough.

14

ODETTE

"Odette, I will not leave you with one of the other men. I will return."

Those were the last words he had said to me when he left the tent last night, wearing a threadbare wool cloak he had probably travelled to these shores with all those years ago. It looked like a beggar's cloak, grey and moth-eaten. It had likely been sitting in the trunk since he got here. I couldn't shake the idea that it was a metaphor for him – worn, frayed, still carrying the weight of his past.

I spent the whole night tossing and turning, warring between the woman who craved his return, who wanted to feel his warmth beside me again, and the one who could not forget the hurt he'd caused.

I woke to find him slumped against the tent's centre pole, his focus fixed on something far beyond me, lost in a realm not of this world.

"Odysseus?"

"It holds such power. You can feel it, when you hold it.

You can feel it take your life force and turn it into something ... other," he muttered.

"Odysseus?" I tried again.

"It's like you are touched by the gods when you hold it. Like you can see as they see. No wonder we could not beat the Trojans while they still housed it. Their soothsayers could hold it and see. Do you see?"

This time, his eyes found me.

I crouched down beside him. "Yes, I see."

No, I did not. I hadn't any clue what he was rambling on about. Instead, I tentatively reached out and touched his arm, trying to form some kind of physical tie that would tether him back to this world.

"What happened? Did you find the Palladium? Where is it?"

Odysseus' eyes turned glassy. "When you look into the statue's eyes, if you are chosen, Athena looks back at you. The eyes, they turn silver like hers, like liquid metal, and she shows you what to do. She showed me how to kill Diomedes."

I reeled at the confession. "You didn't ...?"

"I was slow, foolish. I disappointed her. I was so enraptured with being in her true presence that I—I let her down." His eyes turned to me, pleading. "What do I do?"

I did not recognise this Odysseus. I knew two. There was the general everyone was afraid of, the suave shrewd man who made calculating decisions. The one who could make a moment last for eternity just by grounding you in his presence. Then, there was the one I was sure only I had seen these past few years. The one who could be brash, unthinking, wild. No one would ever believe me. But, I had never seen this one – pleading, scared, uncertain. And I'd be lying to myself if I said it didn't unnerve me.

"Show it to me." I put every ounce of command I could muster into my voice, trying desperately not to acknowledge that it reminded me of scolding a toddler, of telling off Lykas when he had displeased me.

"What makes you think you can handle its power?" Odysseus murmured at me, his gaze swimming in and out of focus.

"Perhaps, it only drives men mad."

I made the remark flippantly, but when Odysseus pointed in the direction of the trunk, I saw that the cloak I thought he had let crumple to the floor was actually strategically swaddled around the small statue of Athena, as if the Palladium were a treasured child. Something tingled at the back of my neck at the thought.

Walking over, I bent to scoop it up.

"Don't touch it," I heard Odysseus growl in the background.

But it was too late. Suddenly, the eyes that had been pale orbs snapped open to reveal liquid silver, and I was falling into a pool of thought ...

THE ROOM WAS COLD, even though I could hear a fire crackling. Three high-back chairs faced the warm glow, where I assumed the fire was.

"You come to see us again, Athena."

I tried to speak, to tell them I was not Athena but Odette, when the goddess herself, far taller than I, walked straight through me.

"You knew I was coming, Lachesis."

"You speak to one of us, you speak to all," three voices bellowed in unison. It was harmony and symphony, screams and agony, death and life all rolled into one voice. It made me want to cover my ears to stop them bleeding, yet I was desperate to hear it again.

"My apologies, Moirai, but I do not wish to play games today."

"Your hero is in a spot of bother, isn't he?"

"My brother, Ares, seeks to kill Diomedes for striking him with his spear in the latest skirmish on the Troy borders, but you already knew this."

"Seeks to kill. Not yet killed," one of them reminded her.

"Yes, Atropos, but Moirai, to have it done through my image, with one of my other heroes, was an insult."

"We do not control how it happens, only that it happens. It is not like you, Goddess of Wisdom, to lay such a burden at our feet. Take your quarrel to Ares."

"Taking my quarrel to Ares would result in tempers flaring and brute force exerted. It would gain no actual ground."

"Yes," they all cackled. "That is the problem with men, no? This is why we told you to find the girl."

Athena turned, and suddenly she was looking directly at me. "You found me, mortal."

"L-Lady A-Athena," I stuttered.

She looked behind me, though when I turned, there was nothing there but stone.

"You found me through the Palladium," she muttered, more to herself than to me. "I see I drove Odysseus quite mad."

Her owl-like stare focused back on me, and I realised she was waiting for an answer.

"Oh, yes, my lady."

She sighed. "The Moirai are right – that is the problem with men. War demands rationality, but at the cost of humanity. And men are always so brash with their decisions, are they not?"

"I—I ..."

"I did not take you for a blithering idiot."

I took a deep breath and steadied myself. "No, I suppose you are right, Lady Athena. Apologies, I am not used to being in the presence of a goddess."

She smiled at that. "You're doing much better than others, I confess."

"Can I ask a question of you?"

"You may ask."

The tone was clear. I might not get an answer in return.

"Why, if men are always so brash, do you choose them to be your heroes?"

"Well, they did not question me."

I clamped my mouth shut at that.

"But, every mortal has their uses. Their strengths and weaknesses. Do you know where my Palladium used to reside, mortal?"

"Pallas Athena?"

"Correct," she nodded. "And do you know who used to guard Pallas Athena before the war?"

I thought for a moment. "Your priestesses?"

"Correct again. Why do you think I put them in charge of protecting such an important artifact? One that ties the sculptor's work directly to me? Why not men? Why not heroes?"

I looked back behind me, as if searching for Odysseus in our tent, but he was not there. I turned back to Lady Athena. "Because it drove the men mad?"

Athena smiled. "Indeed. The heroes took the action I instructed them to, and that was recorded in the history books.

But, they did not hear their instructions from me directly. Do you know who they heard them from?"

I shook my head.

"From women like you."

"Women like me?"

"The men who go down in history books are those who know when to take wise counsel from the women at their sides. It is why Achilles listened to his mother, why Diomedes does not sleep with Τάιλορία, why Odysseus listens to you."

"What about his wife, Penelope?"

"She is not in this war. She battles her own and must provide wise counsel to another."

I hesitated to ask my next question, but Athena missed nothing. "Speak, mortal."

"What happens to women like me? After the war? When we are no longer needed?"

"You will always be needed, child." Her tone was almost scolding, yet sad, as if I knew nothing. "But if you wish to become indispensable to the man you currently aid, then you will need more than words."

Another piercing look, and I realised this goddess knew. She knew the vow I had made, and yet she did not seek to strike me down. Why, when my words would have one of her heroes dead?

"Would you?" Athena cocked a tawny eyebrow at me.

"No," I whispered, knowing what she asked of me. "But I made a vow. I cannot … to reconcile …" Words failed me.

"Would be an act of impiety. You are wise not to perform such a reckless act; your rational thoughts serve you well. If you were lucky, you would find yourself at the River of Lethe if the Judges of the Dead could be persuaded."

Despair, never-ending despair, free-fell through my stomach. There was no getting out of this nightmare. Either I was to suffer

*at the hands of Athena's wrath for her hero now, or I was to suffer
divine retribution at the hands of Hera, who had heard my vow.*

*"But you did not wish my hero dead, child. You willed that he
shall never return home, as you might never. I should say that
leaves what you mortals might call a loophole."*

"ODETTE. ODETTE!"

Someone was shaking my shoulders, but it took me what
felt like a lifetime to gather my bearings. Eventually, my
senses returned. My knees were steadfast in the dirt, my
body limp with shaking, and whoever was holding me had
rough calluses on their skin. Then Odysseus' voice, gravelly,
like those mountains on Ithaca he had told me about, echoed
through my ears.

"What in the gods' names were you thinking?"

Blinking my eyes open, I saw Odysseus leaning over me,
a worried look painted across his face.

"I'm fine, I'm fine," I grumbled, shaking his hands off,
while his touch lingered on my skin like a brand. I went to
stand, missed my footing slightly, and felt his strong hand
encircle my waist. His eyes narrowed as he held me, and my
pulse quickened at the proximity of our bodies.

"You were unconscious for many minutes. You are not
fine," he frowned at me.

I glared at him, pushing away as I steadied myself. "I …
am fine."

Odysseus allowed me to step away, but the space
between us remained charged. I stared at him, taking in the
way the light caught the rugged contours of his face, the
intensity in his look that seemed to search for something

within me. As if sensing the direction of my thoughts, his eyes dragged down my body, assessing me. For injuries, I told myself, though that did not stop my thighs from clenching. To break the tension, I softly cleared my voice.

"Last night, before you left, you told me that you needed the Palladium. That it was the last thing you needed in order to win this war once and for all. Why?"

Odyssus scratched his jaw, and I could practically hear the rough bristles of his beard against his palm, though we still stood apart. "Well, seeing as you gave me the idea, I suppose I can share with you."

"Gave you the idea for what?"

"We are going to build them a horse."

"A horse?"

"A dead horse."

It took my mind a minute to remember the words I said to him weeks ago. "I don't understand ..."

"It will be the largest wooden statue ever built. We will fill it with men and then hide our boats further along the coastline with the rest of our soldiers. The Trojans will think it is a peace offering to the gods, and when they take it into the city of Troy for themselves, we will be behind the citadel walls. We can take Troy for our own – all thanks to a dead horse. Do you see?"

He'd moved towards me during his impassioned speech until his palms brushed my elbows. Even the lightest touch sent a wave of warmth through me.

I did see. It was ingenious, as Odysseus' plans tended to be. I just didn't understand what it had to do with the Palladium, and there was just one small wrinkle in his plan. "How do you know the Trojans will take it in? How do you know they won't just burn it where it stands?"

"The Palladium will hang around its neck to convince them it is a gift from Athena."

"Athena's Palladium? The Trojans will know it is missing by now. You really think they are going to be grateful to get back what you stole?"

"Mmm," he replied, his cheek now resting against the top of my head as he pulled me in for a hug. His embrace was warm, solid, and for a moment, I allowed myself to sink into it, feeling the steady rise and fall of his chest against mine. I succumbed to his touch, while Athena's words echoed relentlessly in my mind.

I did not want this man dead, and I was tied to my vow.

For as long as I couldn't return home, he could not either.

The words of wisdom Lady Athena had offered were spoken through the mouths of women; women her heroes trusted with their every confidence.

"Every minute you waste over the Palladium is just that – a wasted minute," I told Odysseus. "You have six days before the Trojans will expect war to resume, following Achilles' funeral games. I suggest you start building that horse."

15

ODYSSEUS

I recruited Epeius, a master carpenter, to build the wooden horse. With him as the men's instructor, we managed to complete the statue within five days. When we were done, we watched as the remaining men and those we had gathered during our time at war boarded the ships. Our tents had been taken down; we'd left the burnt pyres of our dead standing. A few dead men remained on the shore. All to convince the Trojans that we had retreated. And left the dead horse in our place.

To the Trojans, it would look like a solid structure, an offering to one of the gods for our safe passage and return to Greece. On the inside, it was hollow.

As I watched Odette board my ship, the waves lapping at and rocking the boat, a shawl pulled tightly around her shoulders and the moonlight shining down on her, I felt my own ribcage hollow.

Whatever was to happen now was at the mercy of the gods.

Odette and my men would sail around the bay, just

beyond the peak of the mountain, and wait. I, and forty-nine others, would remain inside the horse. We had left one, Sinon, who waited outside.

It took the Trojans a day to find us. No doubt they had wondered why their scouts hadn't reported us marching forward on the battlefield as we had always done, come the dawn. Instead, we had rested inside the belly of the wooden beast for the long night under the light of a full moon, a positive omen from Artemis that our plan – my plan – would come to fruition. Now, we were wide awake and alert, listening for the slightest hint that the Trojans knew we were inside.

"What is it?" one of them asked Sinon.

"Isn't it obvious? It is an offering to Poseidon, to give them safe passage," another Trojan accent answered his friend.

Another man snorted. "We should burn it then."

I could hear my own ragged breathing and clamped my hand over my mouth, an active reminder to myself and the men around me to make as little noise as possible.

We had accepted the risk that they might choose to burn the horse.

"No, it is a gift to Athena," Sinon told them. "The Greeks admit that Troy is impenetrable. So they have given a gift to the Goddess of War, for her wisdom in helping to create such a city. A citadel that cannot be beaten. It is the ultimate place for her warriors to reside. You should take it as a reminder. Troy will always remain impenetrable."

"Why should we believe you?"

I felt my heart hammer in my chest. This had been the other calculated risk – to leave Sinon outside the horse. It slightly negated the chance that the Trojans would outright burn the horse, but it would be Sinon's silver tongue that would determine what they would do next. It was exactly why I had chosen him.

"My commander, Odysseus, left me here to rot, knowing that you would most likely kill me. All because I called him out in front of everyone, that the Palladium he stole showed him that we would never win, no matter what any of the soothsayers said. He had told us we were coming here for honour and glory, but all we got was death and disease. What loyalty should I have to him now?"

"Why did you stay with the horse?"

This time, a female voice asked the question. That was unusual – highly unusual.

"I didn't know where else to go," Sinon mumbled. I could hear his feet scuffing against the sand, and I could imagine his head bowed as he said it. A young man, no more than ten and nine, no doubt attempting to look like the petulant child that needed taking in, especially if there was a woman present. He should be able to play on her weakness, her need to save and nurture.

"We should take the offering into the citadel. Offer it to Athena ourselves as thanks for driving the Greeks from our shores," one of the Trojan males said.

"No, you shouldn't. If you do, Troy will burn," the female voice warned them, turning sharp. A reprimand.

"Luckily, I don't take my orders from you, Cassandra." I could hear the smirk in the unknown man's tone. "Why don't you go back to the temple and make your ominous declarations to someone who will listen? Apollo, perhaps?"

Another man outside the horse sniggered.

I grinned at the soldiers around me. Despite the darkness, slivers of light snuck through some of the gaps in the wooden panelling. Not enough that the outsiders could see in, but just enough to keep fresh air circulating. I was grinning because Cassandra was known for her declarations. No one ever believed her prophecies, which was just as good as cementing our cause.

"I agree with Cassandra. We should set fire to this monstrosity."

Suddenly, we all felt the ground shake. Risking a peek out of one of the slits in the horse, I watched as the earth around one of the men cracked open. It was as if a seam in the soil opened up directly to the Underworld itself. The jagged rocks around the chasm looked like teeth as the man began to fall into it. There was a crunch as he fell face first against the rocks, his scream strangling the air. "I can't see! I can't see! Oh gods, I've gone blind – help me!"

No man made a move to help him. Neither did Cassandra. They all watched on, for this was no freak act of nature – this was a clear act of a god. Or goddess, I considered, given that Sinon had mentioned Athena. And to insult Athena's intelligence was a fool's move.

Eventually the earth stopped shaking and one of the men dared to help the fool to his feet.

"I suggest we all take Laocoön's lesson here to heart. He has clearly been punished for doubting this young man's words, for suggesting we mutilate a gift that has now been claimed in Athena's name. She clearly cares for this offering. Let us wheel it into the citadel and present it to King Priam."

"Agreed," one of the other generals seconded.

Cassandra said nothing.

Laocoön continued moaning.

And that was that.

There was uncomfortable jostling as they rigged the

horse up onto the wheel pulley system. The men and I bumped against each other, trying not to grunt as we swayed between flesh and wood, one way and then the other. We might've been bruised, but this was it – our chance to get behind those Trojan walls. Victory was so close, we could almost taste it.

We waited in silence throughout the long journey across the battlefield where our brothers' blood had been spilled.

We waited in silence as the soldiers called for the gates to the city to be unlocked. As those gates we had never been able to penetrate slowly swung open.

We waited in silence as our horse was pulled through the streets of Troy. As cries of joy and false victory rose around us.

Let them celebrate. Let them have this one last moment.

Celebrate through the night they did. Drums beat throughout the city. Music played, ale flowed. We could hear giddy young Trojan women laugh joyously as soldiers cheered and danced with them. Every time one of them would get too close, the men and I would close our eyes and hold our breaths. Until, eventually, the flutes and other instruments drowned out our breathing.

The night went on. The celebrations only quietened when King Priam made his speech thanking his people for standing steadfast, telling them to enjoy this era of peace that the Trojan Horse – as they called it – brought with it. A hurrah went up into the air, and they spent the evening dancing and weaving ribbons on the horse in celebration. Throwing garlands of flowers on it.

Until they were all exhausted with joy, drowsy from the exertion, and dawn – as she always did – came to claim them. They slept.

The trapdoor in the horse was in the right leg flank. We had considered putting it under the belly of the horse, but we figured that would be the first place the Trojans would look for a trap, if they'd been smart enough to look. Instead, we'd built little ledges into the right leg flank. I went first, climbing up the leg, unlatching the hinge, climbing out and then shimmying down the leg as one would a tree trunk.

One by one, the Greeks slipped into the shadows behind me until fifty of us stood deep in the heart of Troy's citadel. After years of bloodshed, it had come to this.

We moved silently towards the gates, sticking to the dark, for surely Priam hadn't been foolish enough to let every guard go. I was right. There were still sentries at their posts. We dispatched them expeditiously, steel slicing through flesh, our hands muffling their dying gasps. No alarms raised. Then, we lit the fires. They flared bright, a signal to our comrades from the ships, now cutting across the plains, the Greek Army ready to storm in.

Troy's fall came quickly after that.

I left a handful of men at the gate as the rest of us spread out, igniting fires around the outer perimeter. The flames funneled the panicked citadel folk inward, forcing them towards the palace of Priam and his sons, where my third group waited, poised to slaughter every man who entered. Women and girls would be spared, but no Trojan man would live. We would end this war.

The smoke thickened, the horns blared, and the city stirred. Footsteps thundered, shouts clashed with screams, and the first of their soldiers ran straight into our blades, impaling themselves as they tried to defend what little they had left. Panic reigned. The women shrieked as we advanced, their pleas falling on ears dulled by a thousand sieges before.

These Trojans were no match for us, soft and unprepared for the fury we brought. We moved through them like a wave, drowning any resistance in blood. They buckled quickly, crumbling under the pressure. With every smoky breath they became more docile, helpless beneath our boots.

Menelaus, Pyrrhus – Achilles' son – and I fought our way through the mass of Trojans, now swarmed by Greeks as our brothers poured through the gates. We pushed up the main road, the path our great horse had been dragged up only hours before, now slick with blood and littered with cut-down bodies. Ahead, the palace doors were open, a flood of desperate citizens surging inside, seeking sanctuary. They would find none.

Foolish Priam.

The fight was brutal, but not in its physicality. Most of Troy's soldiers were still drunk, sleepy, or hungover. Only a few fought like they had on the battlefield. No, it was brutal in its decimation. At one point, I passed a woman who lay weeping over the dead body of a man I assumed was her husband. Two of our men were hitting her across her back with their spear butts.

"Pick her up, gods damn it, and take her to where the rest are," I barked at them. If these had all been my men, they would have known that I didn't accept the beating of women. As I reminded my men, war trophies and prizes were to be treasured, polished, and protected if you wanted them to maintain any worth, which the men always did. But these were not all my men; they were from each army that had gathered for the Greeks.

There was no need for this animalistic ritual, this slaying. If only the Trojans would come quietly. If only our men weren't so desperate to get home that they would do anything to achieve it.

If only I hadn't played a hand in forcing this war with my blood vow over Helen. *Stupid.*

Each thrust of my spear after that felt like the heaviest blows I'd had to deliver in these last ten years. Each new death was more difficult than the last, harder to execute, harder still to pull each man from my spear again and watch him fall. I used to be able to watch the eyes of the man I was killing, to honour his final breath, but now all I felt with each stab, each twist, each thrust and grunt, was shame.

I thought there was no more shame in my bones left to give, until I finally made it the naos[1] of the palace. At the end of the long marble room, with its large columns, each one with an intricate carving and dedication to each of the Olympians, where Priam had undoubtedly hosted his war counsel, his sons, his daughters, his family, his royal meetings, was the altar. There, lying across it, was King Priam himself, and Pyrrhus stabbing him up under his ribcage with a smile on his face.

It was the grimmest part of the war, for me. The victory.

The screams quietened by daybreak. The smoke was beginning to clear as I and the other generals examined the royal women who remained at the gates of Troy. They'd been dragged here, to the holding pen the men had formed, by force.

Polyxena. Andromache. Hecuba. Cassandra. Helen.

----

1. The inner sanctuary of a temple, a most sacred area, often inaccessible to the general public and reserved for religious activities, such as prayer and offerings to the gods.

Most of the women in Troy had come kicking and screaming, dragged by their limbs – and in some cases, their hair – by our soldiers. These five royals had not. They held their heads high and now stood before the Greek generals in a semicircle, guards holding them in place.

Myself, Agamemnon, Menelaus, and the rest of the generals stood opposite them. Most of us had our arms crossed as we regarded them, but when I glanced at the others, I saw Pyrrhus puffing out his chest while casually swinging his sword like a child. Agamemnon was leering at Cassandra. Meanwhile, Menelaus appeared like a bull, his breathing heavy and laboured, practically rubbing his heel into the dirt, ready to run towards Helen and drag her back off to where they'd come from.

I shifted my posture, preparing to speak.

One of our men, Talthybius, spoke. "Women of Troy, may I present to you Lord Odysseus, King of Ithaca."

"We recognise no such king." The woman in the middle spoke for them all.

Her voice was like Odette's was when I had first met her: rich and thick in a way that broadened the e's, stressing the last syllable of each word and the only noun in her statement – 'king'. I recognised that it made her declaration sound more ominous than she perhaps intended.

"Queen of Fallen Troy, Hecuba. The generals have gone to a great deal of effort and trouble to decide where each of you shall be placed now that your husbands, brothers, uncles, and cousins are dead," Talthybius continued.

The unspoken words sat heavy between us all; they had to be placed with a male. They couldn't hope to run a city without one. The thought was laughable, though not, it appeared, to the women standing in front of us, who scoffed.

Talthybius hesitated, so I stepped forward a foot, every-one's attention turning to me. "Polyxena, daughter of Priam and Hecuba, seeing as you were requested by the great Achilles and he is now dead, you will be given to the gods at his tomb."

The girl, no more than four and ten years of age, would have buckled on long legs to her knees had the two women either side of her not caught her by the elbows and kept her on small, shaky feet.

Her death would be a waste, for her skin was pure ivory, her hair a shade of raven braided across the crown of her head. She had large eyes, a good nose, pleasant lips. She was, by all standards, the truest definition of beauty to most men, and undoubtedly a virgin as she was not yet married. But, honour for honour's sake had to be taken into account, at least at Pyrrhus' insistence for his father, and so she would die. I had not been able to convince the men otherwise.

"Andromache," I continued, for I could do nothing but. "As Hector's wife, you will be given to Pyrrhus as a token of your husband's rivalry with Achilles."

"Was his death not enough?"

Andromache's voice was as cold as Hecuba's. She would have made a wonderful Queen of Troy. But where the Queen was dark and slim, with round honey-coloured eyes, a long nose, and a calm demeanour, Andromache was shorter with blondish hair and fuller features.

"No," Pyrrhus interrupted. "It was – is – not. We should have every Trojan man killed, even the boy carried in a mother's womb."

A collective gasp fell from the group.

"It's not as if we need to throw children from the battle-ments of the city," I said quietly.

"What an excellent idea!" King Agamemnon boomed.

"You wouldn't" Andromache breathed.

"No, we wouldn't," I confirmed, staring down Agamemnon.

"Well, there is one that must die," Pyrrhus said, his beady eyes lighting up in delight.

"Who?" Agamemnon demanded.

My heart sunk into the pit of my stomach as I realised who exactly Pyrrhus was speaking of.

"Who?" Andromache echoed the king's question.

When no one offered an answer, I took on the task. "A Trojan prince, even a babe, cannot be allowed to live."

"No." Her voice trembled but did not break. Impressive.

"Odysseus is quite right," Agamemnon bleated. "It is the way of such things in war time. If you do not agree to hand the boy over, we will not allow him his burial rites. Now, where is he?"

"You are monsters," Hecuba spat as she held Andromache in her arms.

"We are Greeks, taking what is rightfully ours. So say the gods by granting us this victory. You'd do well to obey them. Take the mother of the prince. Have her bring him back from whatever hole they've hidden him in," Agamemnon barked at the guard behind Andromache, who grappled with the woman trying to shrug him off before forcefully grabbing her hair and pushing her back towards the smouldering city.

"As for the rest of you – what are we doing with them again, Odysseus?"

"Hecuba, Queen of Troy, will come with me back to Ithaca."

"Of course it is my lot to be a slave to a vile and treacherous man," she muttered, just loudly enough for it to carry across our strange group.

I clenched my jaw at the insult. In truth, the reason I'd requested her was because I saw a lot of Penelope in her. My wife would find a great friendship with Hecuba. Who better for a queen than the one who had ruled by her husband's side for more than fifty years?

"Cassandra," I continued, "has been requested by King Agamemnon."

I looked at the woman, the one who it was said spoke false prophecies, yet had that clear-cut warning in her voice when I was in the belly of the wooden horse. She was the shortest and bulkiest of all of them, round-faced too, but with a noble nose and shrewd dark eyes that did not match her straw-coloured hair.

She didn't say anything, which would have surprised me the most had it not been for the small quirk of her dark brow. That was the only indication she gave me that she had even heard the directive.

"And Helen," – the woman we had pinned this war on – "will return to Menelaus."

THE WOMEN WERE LED from their falling city and herded across the desert plains, where they had once watched their men battle from the safety of their keep. Myself and the generals stayed with the royal group, our subordinates taking care of the rest of the Trojan slaves that would now travel like cattle in our ships back to Greece.

The royal entourage was mostly silent, except for Andro-mache's muffled sobs and Hecuba's insistent hushes. It reminded me of Odette's group, when we'd rounded them up from that pathetic village that was really no more than a dirt square with a drinking fountain, bordered by houses and some fields of crops.

The women's steps were small, unsurprisingly, given their stature and fate. None we had collected over the years had been eager to stride into slavery. Still, it irked the men. Even seasoned generals could behave like children, and more than once I caught Menelaus nipping at Helen's calves with the flat face of his sword. They were desperate to get home, anyone could smell it on them. And though no one actually let out a breath, there was a collective sigh from the Greeks when our group could eventually see the ocean.

For the women, the ocean watered down their resolve. It was a brutal slap in the face from their reality, for whichever way they looked spelt a new future. Poseidon had never been a kind master to females. On the horizon, lands they didn't know of or didn't want to return to, unsure of what to expect. Behind them, remnants of a life they'd never have again.

The realities of war.

Andromache was openly weeping now. Hecuba had stopped her hushing. Polyxena began crying in earnest as Pyrrhus grabbed her roughly around the arm and led her away. The others in the group didn't so much as get a chance to say goodbye before she would be sacrificed at Achilles' tomb. Some would say that was cruel of him, but honestly, the extended farewells were worse. Letting them linger in their heartbreak only amplified a woman's feelings.

Better to get it over with.

One of Pyrrhus' soldiers tried to grab Andromache and follow after the young general, but Hecuba clung to her forearms. We all watched him attempt to pull them apart for a moment before I stepped in behind the former Queen of Troy and forced her to relent, crushing her delicate wrists with bruising force.

"Bastard," she hissed at me.

I ignored her.

Instead, I led her away from the pack of royals and towards the ships where my men were setting up our tents once again. We would stay now until the rest of the Trojan spoils were divided up between our counsels, which meant replanting ourselves in the sand.

Just like we had all those years ago.

We were on the easternmost border, which meant we would be some of the last to leave through the Mare Aegeum when the time came. But, for now, it gave us the long-grass hills, the less damp sand, and I was grateful we were away from the rabble of the beaches as we climbed, Hecuba's wrist still in my grasp.

At the top of the hill I spied Odette, her figure outlined against the fading light as she busied herself instructing the men to set up a campfire in that practical way of hers I had come to love. No doubt the men had grumbled of hunger and rather than listen to them gripe, she had set them to work. Things had changed; the men had come to occasionally listen to the women that took care of them. I hoped Hecuba would be able to see that.

I glanced sideways at her. She pressed her lips into a thin line, her gaze sharpening as she took it all in.

"Odette was once a slave," I remarked.

"And what is she now, Lord?" Hecuba replied, disdain dripping from her thick accent.

I snapped my mouth shut when I realised I didn't have

an answer. Not one I could say out loud. Eventually we reached where the men were gathered around the campfire, and I thrust Hecuba towards Odette.

"Get the former queen cleaned and settled into a guest tent," I grunted.

Odette's eyes widened, a small but telling gesture. It was her only giveaway that she still thought me a brute, though she said nothing. Instead she nodded her head, curtsied to Hecuba, and held out her hand. To my surprise, Hecuba took it graciously.

"You don't have to curtsy to her. She is no longer queen," I grumbled.

"Because my city is destroyed?" Hecuba turned and faced me.

Odette watched me too, her head cocked.

"And who, King of Ithaca, is making sure your kingdom still exists? Do you even know? Are you even king any longer?" Hecuba continued. She gave a wry smile at my lack of reply. "Or does your wife keep your seat warm? Surely not, for a woman can't rule a city on her own. You and your comrades laughed at that notion only this morning."

"Just take her to get clean and settled," I muttered. "Feed her, too. She must be hungry."

"Certainly," Odette said with a smile. "Come, my lady, let us freshen you up."

"Thank you, my child."

16

ODYSSEUS

Ten days later, many others arrived on Trojan shores from countries beyond the borders of Greece. They had heard of our victory and were coming to visit the fallen city for themselves, to see if the rumours were true. Well, that was what they said. The reality was they came to see if they could collect any Trojan treasure for themselves.

On the third day of visitors, King Polymestor of Thrace arrived with two of his sons in tow.

"Odysseus." the king came towards me, his hand outstretched. His sons remained behind him, the family resemblance between the three uncanny, as they took resting soldier stances behind their father.

I shook his hand, and turned him towards the camp, the boys following behind us. "I hope your trip was pleasant, King of Thrace?"

"I cannot complain, but please, call me Polymestor. If I may call you Odysseus?"

"Of course," I nodded. "What do you come for?"

"Well, I came to see if it was true. And then, if there was

any treasure you could not take back on your own ships." Polymestor gave me a politician's smile.

I smiled back. "It is true. I can have a soldier take you to the ruined city, if you wish."

Together we began walking towards said city, his sons falling into step behind us. We had not walked five hundred yards when Hecuba exited my tent and caught Polymestor's eye. I felt him stop beside me and then change course.

"Why, Queen Hecuba. I had no idea you were here." Polymestor bowed.

"I'm sure you didn't," she offered him a small smile. "Tell me, my lord, how fares my son?"

Resolve squirmed on Polymestor's face until it settled into a grave expression. "I am afraid, great lady, that your young son did not live to see his twelfth year. Though, perhaps that is a blessing from the gods, that he did not see his family in ruin."

There was a flash of anger in Hecuba's eyes, so quick anyone not looking would have missed it, before her face contorted into utter grief and a sob broke free.

Myself, the king, and his sons, stood there gormless. There could be no comfort from us – had he been here, we would have killed her boy anyway. Agamemnon had been right: it was the way of things.

Hecuba took a few sips of air to steady her breath, her trembling fading with each one, until she regained her composure, again becoming the unyielding queen as she addressed Polymestor once more. "I have had many sons and daughters in my lifetime. Death in one so young is, unfortunately, more common than a mother would like. But I thank you for bringing the news to me in person, King Polymestor."

"Of course."

"My lord?" She bowed her head towards me.

I raised an eyebrow in surprise.

"May I have a moment alone with the King of Thrace, so that I might hear more of my son's final months on this earth?"

I could have denied her the kindness, said no, but I saw no reason to. In the past, I would have probably listened in, taking what information I could glean to save as ammunition. That was before I had met a Trojan farmer's housewife who had poisoned her own son to protect him. I could see her anguish on Hecuba's face, remembering those early days of her grief all too well. I wouldn't get anything out of Hecuba, and I already knew what I needed to know about Polymestor. To try and claim jewels from an old ally won in a war you did not fight ... Well, the man had more greed than honour.

I nodded my consent and walked away, while Hecuba ushered Polymestor and his sons into the tent my men had been keeping her in.

The screams came a half hour later.

Sprinting towards the strangled sounds, I warned the other men to stay back until I knew what we were dealing with, only to stop in my tracks at the carnage.

There, in front of me inside the tent, stood Odette covered in blood, a jewelled dagger falling from her palm onto the ground where the two boys lay in pools of their own blood. Only later would I learn that Odette had gutted them like fish, slicing them from ankle to knee to have them fall, then the lengths of their femurs to ensure they bled out.

For now, all I could see was the chiton soaked in blood pooling around her ankles, the sight freezing me in place. My heart lurched thinking it was hers. The world around me slowed, desperate to buy me time to search for the solution that would stop Odette slipping away from me. But before I could find it, the sharp sound of screaming pierced the air. My eyes shifted, searching for the source.

There, rolling around on the floor, clutching at his brow, was King Polymestor.

It wasn't Odette's blood.

Relief flooded my system, and it took effort to strengthen my knees as my attention turned to the other person on the floor, Hecuba, who reached for the dagger Odette had just dropped. In a sweeping arch, the dagger now in hand, she delivered the steel directly into Polymestor's crotch.

His scream buried sorrow in the hearts of all who heard it.

All, it appeared, except Hecuba, who gathered her blood-soaked skirts to straddle him. When I realised that she now intended to finish the castration, I finally moved. Striding over to her and wrapping my arms underneath her armpits, I pulled her off him as she kicked and screamed.

"Stop this madness!"

"He is a vile, greedy traitor who killed my son, to keep our treasures for himself! He deserves no less," Hecuba hissed. "Let me GO!"

Gone was the gracious former Queen of Troy. In her place was a creature akin to a rabid dog, wriggling and straining against me with all her might.

"Then he shall be tried in a court of man. Not here, not like this."

"She took my eyes! My eyyyesss!" Polymestor moaned. "It's she who should be tried! She is nothing more than a slave. Both of them! Who are they to do this to a king?!" he continued to lament.

"I suggest you shut your mouth before one of them attempts to take your tongue, for I cannot restrain them both."

It wasn't a minute later before one of the messengers barged into the tent, undoubtedly to see the scene for himself. He looked to me, still restraining the former queen, his eyes bulging out of his rat-like face.

"Go and get King Agamemnon! And a doctor while you're at it!" I barked at him.

He nodded, scurrying away.

"Odette – we don't have much time. Who did this? Tell me it was Hecuba only, and let us be done with this."

I felt the woman in question wriggle in my grasp. Then Odette's eyes, bigger than I'd ever seen them, met mine.

"They killed her son. She thought she was entrusting him to them, that she was keeping him safe, and they *killed* him. Then they *laughed* about it, in this tent."

I didn't take my eyes off her face, but in my periphery I saw her fists clench.

She had done this.

The general in me would have had her seized, killed. There was no other way to deal with such a crime. But the man in me … The man in me knew her history, knew her temperament. She wasn't just another woman in this war. She was Odette, and that changed everything.

When I heard the other kings' forces arrive in my camp, I hauled Hecuba to her feet and dragged her outside with me, clasping Odette's hand with my other, tugging her along with us. We left Polymestor in the tent, where a young doctor struggled to staunch the bleeding, struggling against the maimed king's restless thrashing. I could still hear the doctor protesting, telling Polymestor to stay calm, when King Agamemnon approached. I dropped Odette's hand.

"What is the meaning of this, Odysseus? I was getting my ships ready to leave when I got word there was a right royal skirmish in your area. What – can't keep a woman under control?" He eyed Hecuba in front of me with a sneer. "You should do what I've done with mine," he continued, giving a nod to the soldiers behind him. Between them stood Cassandra, who now had a necklace of heavy chains around her throat. On the end of one loop, another chain of metal followed down into a soldier's hand.

A leash.

I felt Hecuba vibrate with anger against me.

"Come and see for yourself. But I suggest we leave the others out here, to spare the dignity of those inside."

Agamemnon nodded, following as I escorted Hecuba back into the tent. This time, Odette followed of her own volition.

Good.

Now, Polymestor sat against the central pole of the tent, holding a damp towel to his crotch, his eye bandages bloody. The doctor had covered the sons' bodies with sheets. The scene was a touch more civilised than it had first been.

"King Polymestor, I have King Agamemnon with me."

"And *her*, I take it. I can still smell her sickly perfume. That siren," he spat. "I want her punished, you hear me? I want her and that other slave that was with her given to me. I'll take them back to Thrace, where they can be whored out to the men for taking their princes from them. Then, once their children are ripped from their wombs, they will be strangled as punishment for their crimes against me!"

"What other slave?" Agamemnon asked.

"Mine," I answered. "And she is mine to do with as I see fit."

"I did you Greeks a favour," Polymestor snivelled. "I made sure her boy couldn't come back and avenge his brothers and his father. And you let THIS happen to me!"

"If I may speak, my lord?" Hecuba's voice was once again that cold, gracious tone I had heard before. Gone was the raging, vengeful monster. In her place, a former royal who even now sought to bend King Agamemnon to her will, as she had with Polymestor an hour ago.

The permission to speak was a nice touch.

"Speak." I wanted to know how she could think to get away with such actions.

"This man did not seek to aid you. He sought to take from you what is rightfully yours. He wanted treasure that you had fought and died for, while he had stayed away from the war, as cowards do. He has taken from the Trojan hand and now looks to take from yours, too. He has already confessed to killing my son, and I do not doubt that was so he could keep the treasure we gave him for safe harbour. He would do it to you, I am sure of it. For he said to his sons when he was in this tent that they could both take the other slave at once, while he had his way with me. And if a king does not respect another king's slaves as property, then what of your gold or other worldly goods?"

Something dark and sinister curled in my gut at the mention of Odette being defiled by his two brutish sons at the same time.

"She lies!"

"What good does it do me to lie now? I am already a slave. Whether I am bound to one master or another, it does not matter."

King Agamemnon looked to me. "Well, they are your slaves, Odysseus. What say you?"

"Murder," I replied quietly.

I felt Hecuba still in my arms.

"I say King Polymestor committed murder, and the former Queen of Troy's retribution was just."

Agamemnon took a moment to pretend like his pea-sized brain was weighing up the merits of the case, but I knew who he would side with. I had won him the war.

"Murder it is. Guards – come and seize this man! We will take his ship for our own, and the goods he would have taken from us on it."

"No, no, no, you can't! You CAN'T!" Polymestor screamed. "If you do, if you do, I'll—"

"Silence!" Agamemnon commanded, booting him in the stomach for good measure.

There was an 'oof' and a crack, as Agamemnon's foot made contact with a lower rib.

"You can't do this, you can't believe her over me, she's just a slave now, she's just—"

I didn't hear the rest as Agamemnon's guards dragged him out.

"What do you want to do with his sons' bodies?" the young doctor asked us.

"I'll get some of the young men to perform their burial rites," I told him and Agamemnon.

They both nodded in agreement, and that was that.

Exiting the tent together, we watched Agamemnon summon the rest of his guard to follow him back to Polymestor's ship. The men had barely begun walking when, to everyone's surprise, Cassandra – coiled to that leash though she was – pulled away, not towards her mother Hecuba, but to Odette. She began talking in low, feverish tones as she gripped Odette's arms and spoke in the old Trojan language to her. Her eyes were wide, desperate, as if she were telling Odette something of vital importance. She stopped only once in her monologue, until Odette nodded, and began again.

Agamemnon, realising his men hadn't followed after he'd taken a dozen or so strides, turned back. He marched towards Cassandra.

"What is with the women today?" he grumbled, tugging at her.

But, Cassandra was as immovable as a marble statue. She held firm, as if Agamemnon was not a fully grown man tugging at her but a mere bug on her shoulder. She continued saying something to Odette that I could not understand. Even if I'd had the language, the speed at which she talked was so rapid, I wondered if Odette was keeping up.

Eventually, Cassandra stopped to take a breath, and the trance was broken. Seeming to slump into herself, Cassandra finally gave in to Agamemnon's tug. With a sharp comical yank, they both nearly fell over at the sheer force. All the men chose to wisely bite their tongues at Agamemnon's huffing, and the entourage left.

"What did she say to you?" I asked Odette, but she refused to answer. "It wasn't a question, spear-wife." I used the title with deliberate weight, meant for the ears of those around us.

At that, her head snapped up at me before she shook it. "Nothing I could understand."

I swung Hecuba around to face me. "Did you understand your daughter's words?"

For the first time, I saw kindness in Hecuba's eyes. "It is Cassandra's plight to be deliberately misunderstood. Even if I could translate it, her words would make no sense – to you, to me, or to anyone else."

"But why would she deliberately seek out Odette to speak to? Why not to you, her own mother?"

Hecuba shrugged and looked forlornly towards the retreating backs of Agamemnon and his marching entourage.

When I went to ask Odette another question, I caught her with a strange look of appraisal on her face, aimed at Hecuba. For some reason, only in that moment did I realise that these two small, slight women had murdered men far larger and stronger than them, and I had let them get away with it.

17
ODETTE

Swinging shadows and death's decree.
Bound together are love and hate
eternally.

Beware the head that turns
when ghosts appear.
Joy is a bird.

For all coins are circles,
and circles, a loop
presented to you.

You have no choice.
One is bound to the other.

The head turns.
The circle loops.
The bind tightens.
The neck snaps.

The spirit drowns.
Swinging shadows.
Eternally bound.

Coup. Coup. Coup.

– Cassandra

18

ODETTE

I had not realised that accidental killing would feel so different from murder. The former was a wound that bled daily, no matter what I had tried to do to stop it, its poison leaking pus at every opportunity. The latter, however, that split-second moment when I had decided to *do* something about the men whose actions harmed the innocent. That was more effective than any bandage I had found so far.

It was power. This was what it felt like.

I had never known it before, never understood the allure of making a split-second decision, seeing it through, having no one stop you, and being fine with where the consequences led you. I understood now why men coveted it.

I would forever be grateful to my queen for gifting me the opportunity to experience it.

Of course, Hecuba was technically no longer a queen, already becoming a shell of the woman she once was. I noticed it as her shoulders curled in on themselves as Cassandra walked away. I recognised myself in her, how I was when we had been led away from my home.

That was what slavery took from you – your sense of self. I think I had expected it to be an immediate thing. That once you were a slave, your lack of control would be a slap in the face every day. But it was more sinister than that; sneakier. There were no physical shackles. Odysseus had still given me the illusion of control in my life, and so each action I had taken had still felt like my own. Until the guilt that I had unwittingly chosen this life for myself churned in my gut.

But now, there was no guilt. Now there were just actions and consequences. A bargain to be struck with every decision.

I suddenly understood Odysseus a lot better.

When he had stumbled into the tent, after the killings, I waited for the guilt to come. I waited for that feeling, buried in my heart and clawing at my stomach since Lykas had died, to desperately rise to the surface once again.

But there was no pain, only calm.

So, I waited for Odysseus' beration instead. That didn't come either.

Then he'd decided in Hecuba's favour, and something in my brain clicked. It wasn't about what was right, or fair. It was about justification. You just had to be right, and to be right you just had to be on the winning side. That was how wars were won, histories were written. By those who were *right*. Individual actions were no different.

I kept that thought in mind as we finally packed up and walked to the ships a day later, leaving Troy behind, this time once and for all.

I had never been on a boat before the Trojan Horse.

This time, as we boarded the twelve black ships with Odysseus' remaining six hundred men, I wasn't so nervous. Ahead of me, the men leered at Hecuba. I did not envy being the newest thing to keep their attention, though I certainly hadn't attracted it, as sullen as I'd been. Hecuba, in contrast, made waves simply with her presence. Of course, word had spread around camp faster than we had boarded the ships of what she had done, what we had done, though no one paid me any mind.

Instead, they watched Hecuba sway through the shallow waters in her azure robes with a beaded belt. It was probably the last fine thing she had left. It draped across her svelte frame in a way that was tasteful but alluring, as all expensive garments were.

It wasn't the right thing to wear.

The men reached out occasionally to stroke the fabric – and more – as they passed her, crude laughter following. Their touches were not enough to be considered brazen contact with Odysseus' property, but enough to make her feel uncomfortable. I could tell by the way she tried to dodge their hands, even as her body swayed. Still, she kept her head down. She didn't snap at them or swat them away like flies, as I expected her to. She just kept walking forward, her head bowed. Walking, walking, walking, all the way into the ocean.

I watched as the waves lapped at her hips, the turquoise of her dress turning a darker and darker blue, until she looked like she was rising from the ocean itself. When it came time to turn, to board the main black ship that Odysseus and myself would be on, to climb the ladder that would take her aboard, she kept walking.

Deeper and deeper into the ocean.

The men didn't notice. She was a bit of fun, nothing to be concerned about. Their focus quickly shifted to the crates of spoils and valuables Odysseus was allowing them to take home to families they hadn't seen in a decade. They jostled and barked orders at one another, struggling to load the heavy goods onto the ships without tipping into the surf.

Just before my queen waded further into the sea than was safe, the clouds above her parted with a crack, and sunlight poured through like a spear from the heavens. I watched as the light hit the surface of the water and danced across it, blinding the men boarding and on the ship, as they squinted and shielded their eyes from the sudden brilliance. A few cried out, stumbling back as a heavy chest of plunder slipped from their grasp and crashed into the shallows, splintering wood and sending coins tumbling into the frothy waves.

"Get it! Before it's lost!" came the frantic shouts, and men dove into the water, scrambling to collect what they could.

I didn't know where Odysseus was, somewhere behind me I suspected, busy making sure all his men got aboard. For surely, if he saw what I saw, he would sprint into the crashing waves to stop her.

But he didn't.

For amidst the chaos, it seemed no one but myself noticed Hecuba walking deeper, until she seemed a part of the sea itself. I did not say a word. I did not cry out, for I had known that feeling that now engulfed my queen. That absolute abyss where happiness could never exist again. She had done what she needed to do, her vengeance complete. Now, she needed peace. I would not be the one to rob her of it.

Instead, I continued to watch her walk. She must have carried something in between the folds of her dress, something to weigh her down, I considered. Rocks that she had probably found around the camp as the men were busy packing away. Because she continued sinking beneath the waves that hit her belly, then her breasts. Until, eventually, her shoulders and head were submerged beneath a wave ... and I never saw her again.

It wasn't until much later, when everyone was aboard and settled on the well-benched ships, that I watched as Odysseus looked around us.

Turning to me, he frowned. "Odette, where is Hecuba?"

"Dead."

A hush fell amongst the men.

"Dead? What do you mean, dead?"

"She wandered into the ocean before we boarded the ships. Did you not see it?" I tried to keep my tone neutral, but some of my sarcasm seeped through and a few of the men sniggered.

Odysseus merely had to send them all a look and that quickly stopped.

He took two steps towards me, until his toes were aligned with mine. "Rise."

I complied. No point disobeying an order unless that disobedience had purpose.

"If you saw this act against the gods, why did you not stop it?"

"I tried, my lord," I lied. He knew it. I could tell by his face he knew it. But if he and none of the other men had seen it, they could not prove my lie, could they? "But you know us women," I continued. "Emotional creatures that we are, we don't listen to reason when it is presented to us."

"Ain't that the truth," one of the men piped up.

"Quiet!" Odysseus barked.

That was surprising. I'd never known him to snap at his men like that.

He turned back to face me, frowning. "You have been given too long a leash if you feel it's okay to answer me with such disdain in that tone, after the freedoms and luxuries you have enjoyed."

"I answered truthfully! I haven't done anything wrong!" I protested.

Odysseus leaned in closer, whispering against the shell of my ear so that the other men could not hear, igniting a fire I despised myself for feeling. Every fibre of my being wanted to recoil, to lash out, yet the heat of his presence stirred something primal, something I wished I could crush.

"Have you not?" His words were a taunt that dripped with the power he wielded over me – power I hated, but could not deny.

"No."

"No, what?"

"No, my lord," I said between gritted teeth.

He grabbed at my chin roughly with a finger and thumb. "I won't have insubordination on my ship. Do you hear me, Odette? I can't have a mutiny while we travel across oceans and time to get back home to Ithaca."

"Yes, my lord."

He was so close now, every deep breath I took pushed my breasts into his chest. Still, he didn't move. It was a power play in front of everyone. And for the first time in a long time, I had to fight the temptation to spit in his face.

"What has gotten into you, hmm? Where has the woman I've come to know gone?"

You have never known me.

I did not say it. I did not have to; he read it in my eyes.

"You are not free just because you are no longer on

Trojan soil, do you understand me?" His tone remained quiet, for my ears only.

When I didn't answer immediately, he squeezed my jaw tightly.

"Yes, my lord." I held my head up and looked him in the eye as I said it. That was one of the lessons I had learnt from observing Queen Hecuba. They could make you a slave, but they could not strip you of your grace. Only the gods could do that.

He noted the slight uptick in my chin, the resolve in my eyes, the clenching of my jaw beneath the pad of his thumb.

"For your insolence, your privileges have been revoked until I say otherwise." The words were so softly spoken I could see the men in my periphery trying to lean in to hear what their king was saying.

I almost laughed when they bounced back as Odysseus shouted his next words for all to hear.

"Get the ship ready to go by the time I get back from escorting Odette back to her proper place."

I wondered where that might be.

"How long will you be, sir?"

"Long enough for you to get it done," he snapped.

He really was out of sorts.

Removing his hand from my face, he used his other hand to capture my wrists before I could catch on to what he was doing. He hauled me towards the stern, where private quarters were reserved for him. The rest of the men, I guessed, would sleep on whichever patch of the deck they could make comfortable enough, or underneath the bow where there were a few makeshift beds amongst the storage.

Odysseus led me into the small, dark chamber that appeared to house nothing more than a wooden bed with a thin sliver of blankets for bedding, that large wooden chest that had once been in the tent we shared, and a small writing desk. Looking around, he grabbed one of the sheets from the bed, tore it with his teeth and one hand, and began to bind my wrists to the bedpost embedded in the floor. There would be no moving from here.

"Is this really necessary?"

Odysseus cast me a dark look, but said nothing. Instead, he tightened the restraints and then tugged on them. He left just enough breathing room that my hands could still get blood flow ... just. Otherwise, there was no moving. The fact he'd tied them above my head while I sat on the ground meant I could not even manoeuvre my way up onto the bed for some comfort.

I was stuck on this dank wooden floor. He'd never tied me up before, not even when I had first come into the camp.

As if sensing my thoughts, Odysseus answered. "You think I want to do this? Do you think I've not had enough of war and death? Now is not the time to start defying me, Odette. You have to be seen as punished. That," he said with one final harsh tug, "is why I do this."

"Isn't being your slave punishment enough?"

He rose then, towering over me, but even in the dark I could make out his forlorn expression. "Not as much as being your master."

Then he turned and left, slamming the door and leaving me enveloped in complete darkness.

———

THE DOOR DID NOT OPEN for a long time. When it did, I pulled my head up from where it had been resting on the bedpost, surprised to see it wasn't Odysseus, but one of the men.

Despite being constantly around them, I didn't know all of their names. They had usually only spoken to each other after a day of fighting. I only ever came to know the ones who were injured and needed my help, and most of them hadn't made it.

This one startled me a little.

"I didn't expect you to be in here."

I stared at him.

"I'm looking for Odysseus' ... Nevermind."

I turned my head away from him.

Huffing, the man searched around the room, looking through the desk drawers and in the chest before he must have found whatever he was looking for and left.

I closed my eyes again.

The next time the door opened, it still wasn't Odysseus. This time it was a man I recognised; I had served dinner to him at those war campfires. Matthias, they called him. A greedy man, who would always demand more than his portion by using his large body to tower over me until I would cave and place another helping onto his plate.

He leered at me. "So, that's where he's put you. On the floor, like a good little pup. We've all been wondering where you were."

Again, I chose not to answer. Instead, I went to close my eyes and rest my head against the bedpost, ignoring him. If you didn't give them attention, they got bored. He would go away soon enough. I heard his boots walk across the creaking floorboards as the ship rocked. We must have been almost finished with the first day of sailing. I was contemplating where we might be, when I felt a sharp sting on my scalp.

My eyes snapped open to see Matthias leering again, this time standing over me, his hand continuing to pull my head up sharply by my hair until I was looking him in his ugly face.

Some may have called him ruggedly handsome. Personally, I thought he looked like he'd had the mumps as a child and never fully recovered. His face was lumpy, his eyes too small for it, his nose large.

"Such a shame he won't let you come out and play with us on deck," he cooed.

I tried not to react, but I couldn't help it. The thought made my lips pucker together in displeasure.

He laughed. Then he leaned in and licked my cheek from chin to temple. I squirmed, but he had that hold on my hair, making sure I wasn't going anywhere.

"Mmm, not nearly as bitter as you look. Sweet, even. Oh, yes, I think the boys and I would most definitely like a taste of that. Keep pissing him off, bed-slave, and he might just let us."

So, I did the only thing I could. I rolled towards him on my left hip, so I could get the momentum I needed. Matthias leaned in thinking I was actually going to cave to his disgusting ways; ugly, stupid fool. Instead, I swung my right leg back and put as much power behind it as I could as I kicked out at him.

I had been meaning to aim for his cock, but given my position, my leg went no higher than his kneecaps. Still, the blow landed and his legs immediately buckled, sending him to the floor with a crash as his brow hit the wooden bed frame and blood poured from that fat nose of his.

I let out a snort of laughter. I couldn't help it.

Dazed, it took Matthias a few moments to come round. He groaned as he got to his feet. Then he looked down at me, still trying to suppress my laughter, before he gathered the blood in his mouth and spat it at me. It landed on the same cheek he'd licked.

Waiting until he left, I wiped the mingled blood and spit from my left cheek by rubbing it against my shoulder.

The third time the door opened, I was sure it would be Odysseus retiring for the night. I had learnt my lesson. My arms were numb and heavy from having them above my head for so long. The discomfort made me wriggle, but I could find no comfortable position on the hard floor. I had tried them all in what must have been, what, eight hours? If not more?

But, it wasn't Odysseus. My heart sank. Because there in the doorway stood Matthias again, this time with two men either side of him.

"There she is, the bitch."

Together, they crowded in. The room really wasn't big enough for all of them. I tried to keep my laboured breathing even, knowing what was coming, but the sheen of sweat coating my skin smelt of fear.

Matthias grinned. "She knows what she's going to get. Hold her down, you'll get your turn," he ordered the other two.

Taking a deep breath into my lungs, I screamed.

"Shut that bitch up, NOW!"

Again, I screamed. Hecuba had held cool decorum, but she'd also had a weapon. The only weapon I had right now was my voice.

The men tried to shove some cotton in my mouth, but I

tossed my head back and forward, until it took the two of them to hold my head still and shove it in. By then, their hands, wrists, and forearms were close enough to my own bound hands that I gouged large scratch marks into them.

"Gods be damned! That little—"

"Matthias."

That voice, the solemn timbre of it. My body sighed in relief. He'd heard me.

"Lord Odysseus. I was just coming to fetch—, and well, then she—," one of the boys started.

"She was trying to escape. So we sought to restrain her for you," Matthias interjected.

"Out," Odysseus pointed at the two sidekicks.

They scuttled away, their heads down, allowing Odysseus to step into the room.

"Thank you, Matthias."

"You're welcome, my lord."

Thank him? *Thank him?* I would have raged against my restraints if I wasn't having so much difficulty breathing with the rag.

"But tell me, if you were so busy trying to restrain her from escaping, why is she gagged?"

Matthias stuttered, stumbling over his words, searching for some excuse that would work.

"Shall we ask her?" Odysseus leaned forward and snatched the fabric out of my mouth.

I took a deep breath and gulped the fresh air into my lungs.

"Did he touch you?"

I took a few more breaths of air, followed by a few swallows to wet my parched throat before I answered. "Not like that," I shook my head. "But he did lick my cheek, and spat on me."

"Did he now?" Odysseus' tone turned dangerous. "Have I done something to offend you, Matthias?"

"No, my lord."

"Have I been a good king? A kind king? A just king?"

"You have."

"Then enlighten me as to why you felt you could disrespect that which is mine."

"She disrespected me first! Besides, she's just a bed-slave—"

THWACK. A slap across Matthias' face, more humiliating than anything, as it brought tears to his eyes.

"Kneel," Odysseus commanded.

I watched as Matthias complied, snivelling.

"Not towards me. Face the desk and rest your chin on it."

Then, I saw the dagger Odysseus pulled from the sheath attached to his hip.

"Let's examine this tongue the bed-slave claims licked her. You see, that way I'll know if she was telling the truth or lying. Bed-slaves are known for their lies, and she'll be punished if I find that to be the case."

Matthias obeyed, whimpering – a strange sound to come out of one so physically large. But Odysseus had played it right, made it sound like he was just humiliating the man further. Matthias had no idea what was about to happen.

The dagger hit his tongue with a dull thud and quickly made its way through to the wood on the other side. Matthias screamed, unable to go anywhere as the blade lodged between his tongue and the desk. Odysseus grasped the hilt of the dagger and yanked it back out, before proceeding to bring it back down and fully sever Matthias' tongue.

Blood immediately took its place, until Matthias had nothing but mouthfuls of blood in the cavity that was his mouth.

Odysseus took the tongue and placed it in Matthias' hands. "Go and throw this overboard and see if one of the men will help you stem the bleeding. If you make it through nightfall, we'll see if we can find you some proper aid at the next port."

Matthias stumbled out of the room.

Shutting the door behind him, Odysseus collapsed into the desk chair and sighed.

"Thank you, for defending my honour," I eventually said into the silence.

Odysseus leaned forward, his elbows balanced on his knees. "This is exactly what I didn't want to happen. What did you think the men were going to do when they learnt you were tied up in here?"

"You didn't have to tie me up."

"After you were insolent with me in front of everyone? And how would that have looked?"

When I didn't answer, he continued. "Tell me, what would you have done if I hadn't come? Truly?"

I bit the inside of my cheek instead of replying. Because I knew what he wanted – a confession that I had been brash and unthinking. That I had experienced a taste of power and was already giddy with it. That, left to my own devices, I would have been attacked and I would not have come out unscathed.

"I know she was your queen, but she had resources to do what she did. You both got lucky, incredibly lucky, to pull off that scene I walked into. And that's likely because Hecuba sat at the right hand of Priam for years and knew how court politics worked. That's how she lured Polymestor to his inevitable death. I understood why you did it, I forgave you your sins. But if I find you playing any more power games, you won't win here. These are volatile men used to war, and I'm the king of an unforgiving mountainside. I don't play games. I win wars."

When I didn't respond, when I couldn't even look him in the eye, feeling like a chastised child, he asked, "Was our time together at Troy really so unpleasant for you?" Then he came closer, tipping up my chin. "Answer me."

But before I could, something happened. We must have hit something, for the ship rolled as clothes might in a washing pail. Then the men were desperately crying out from the deck, trying to get the ship to cooperate with the howling winds that now swept the chamber door open, sea spray spilling into the room and falling fresh on my face.

"Wait here" Odysseus said, as he strode from the room and onto the deck to help the panicked soldiers.

I tugged at my restraints. Despite all the commotion, they still hung tight. "As if I have a choice."

19

ODETTE

After what felt like forever, the winds swept us onto the shore of another island. I overheard some of the men say they thought it was Ismarus, city of the Cicones. If that was true, there would be people here that should be able to help us repair the damage the ships had suffered.

I was still tied up, but the door to the quarters I was in had been ripped off in the savageness of the storm. Beyond me, I could see the damage to the ship caused by hours of relentless battering from Poseidon's waves. Ripped sails, the mast splintered, the men soaked and exhausted.

They were yelling at each other, trying to moor all twelve of the boats along the coastline in a uniform manner, but by the sound of things, it wasn't working. Eventually, I felt our boat settle heavily, the anchor deep in the ocean bed, and then Odysseus' voice rang out across the ship.

"Men, take only what you need. The Cicones are sure to aid us, as they did in the war, but remember this is their land."

The men hollered in agreement and I heard them

clamber over the ship's edge and splash into the shallow waters below. The sound of them was carried away, until I believed myself alone. That was, until I heard a set of footsteps walk towards me and I saw Odysseus in the doorway.

Bending down, he finally loosened the bonds around my wrists. I waited for him to demand answers from me again, to look me in the eye, but his attention stayed on my wrists. Eventually, the coarse material fell to the floor between us.

I was about to ask him if I was free to go when his thumb stroked over the angry, deep red marks on my wrist.

"What are you doing?"

"You told me once I didn't know you," he murmured, his thumb continuing to stroke my sore skin.

"You don't."

"Don't I?"

I hadn't realised quite how close we were. My breath hitched and his eyes shot up to meet mine.

"I know you're grumpy in the mornings," he murmured, his eyes moving down to my lips. "I know you don't like to serve fish, because you don't have the patience for deboning them."

I shuddered at the thought, and he took the opportunity to cup my cheek.

"And I know that you used to hate me; despise me. Despise us all."

I tried to turn away from his touch then, but he didn't let me, instead making sure my eyes were on him.

"But I also know it has not been unpleasant between us. That you were more than just a slave. You were a helpmate to me, and I to you. I know I do not want to lose that between us, Odette."

When I didn't trust myself to answer, Odysseus stood.

"Come. The men would have started a fire by now. You need to get warm, dry those clothes, and eat something hot." He held out his hand.

There was a pause, a moment where the air stilled between us, when we both knew I was making my decision. Power or protection.

Why couldn't I have both?

Then again, I had just spent an entire storm tied to a wooden pole. I took his hand.

Together, we made our way off the ship. Odysseus was right – the men had lit a fire farther up the shore. The landscape looked very different from the barren fighting ground of Troy's plains with the citadel walls in the distance. Instead, here, a mountain of lush greenery towered over us.

Moving up the bank, I saw that the Cicones had indeed come out from within that lush forest and were hosting the men on the beach. The women were pouring wine directly into their mouths from goatskins. A couple of slain goats were already roasting on a spit above the fire. There was laughter and good nature, a camaraderie between everyone that the war was finally over. All was well.

I continued to warm myself by the fire while Odysseus walked off, presumably to talk to the captains of his ships about the plan, what items the Ciconian men had already agreed to give them, when we could set sail again. I spent the time thinking about what he'd said, about how his calloused thumb felt against my delicate skin, about how the shudder hadn't really been about the thought of fish at all.

He was right. I wouldn't survive this new world if I decided to turn against him now. In fact, to do so would be foolish of me. It was likely we would arrive on Ithacan soil long before I could come up with a way to fulfil my vow. In the meantime, I should solidify my place by his side so that come our docking in Ithaca, I might not be tossed aside.

Dark eyes slammed into mine across the fire pit.

My heart thumped wildly against my ribcage, my body reacting, panicked that he could read my thoughts, that he would ask what the vow was.

Suddenly the fire was too hot.

I turned away, desperate to gulp fresh air into my lungs, to get the feel of a cool breeze across my skin. Walking towards the ocean, I chanced a glance behind me, only to find Odysseus striding towards me. I pivoted, walking along the shoreline, away from the campfires, with a plan to turn back towards the forest trees.

I didn't need to check again to know that he still followed. I could feel him behind me, like prey that knew it was being stalked. Until, suddenly, he was grabbing my hand.

"Not here," he muttered in a guttural tone, before dragging me deeper into the tree line.

It took me two strides to keep up with his one. I was out of breath by the time he turned and grabbed my waist, pinning me against a tree, surrounded by enough over-hanging branches to give us a modicum of privacy. Not that there was anyone around us at all. Even the wildlife slept.

"What are y—you doing?"

My back was flush against the tree, Odysseus' hand resting on the smooth bark next to my head. His eyes roamed mine. "Tell me it's all in my head. Tell me there's no desire in your eyes right now. That I'm a mad man who is seeing things."

I should want him driven mad. I should want him on his knees, desperate and sobbing for mercy. I should want that.

I should not want the feel of his hands gripping at the flesh on my hips, or slipping between the folded pleats of my tunic. I should not want to reach out and bite down on that fuller low lip of his, just to see what reaction I would get. I should not be experiencing this heat in my belly, so far from the fire.

But here, away from the men, away from Troy, on land that neither of us belonged to, what if … what if we could just be two people? What if wars and vows, gods and civilizations, didn't matter? What if it was just me and him?

"Say it. Say it one way or the other, Odette."

"I—"

He leant forward and my heart stuttered. I could feel it.

"I want it. I want you."

As soon as I said it, I felt my heart drop down into my stomach and then swoop back up again, as Odysseus' spare hand reached for my bare thigh and hooked it around his hip, thrusting the bulk of him closer to me.

Now, having to tilt my head up to look at him, he cupped my face with his other hand and then tangled it through the base of my hair.

"Thank you," he said, before crushing his lips to mine.

I could feel the desperation pouring from his mouth into mine, and from mine into his, until it all seemed to mingle and my tongue flicked against his. Groaning in agreement, he deepened the kiss between us. He ground his crotch against my sex once, twice, then stopped and pulled back, unhooking my leg from around him.

"What is it?" I asked. "Do you not want this?"

"Oh, I want this very much, Odette."

I knew other men hadn't always treated their spearwives as little more than property, especially in their first couplings. That Odysseus knew exactly who he was doing these things to – these things *with*; the fact he had just said my name, did something funny to my heart.

But, then he did something that had me forgetting all about that, and riding a new flush of heat that travelled down to my belly, then further, lower, as he got on his knees in front of me.

"But you deserve more than a rough, dry hump against a tree for our first time."

The man was on his knees for me. If I was still the woman who had made that vow, I would take the opportunity the Fates had given me, snap a branch, and stab him in the neck with it. Except, these branches were too thick, and he would surely catch me.

Then, his hands were back on my thighs, spreading them apart from inside my tunic, and I forgot all about killing and ways in which to do it.

He gave a slow, long lick with his tongue directly between my thighs, before suckling on my kleitorís. That had me inhaling another sharp breath, trying to process all the sensations.

Another suck, another tug, until I cried out in agreement.

He murmured his approval, the rumble vibrating against my thighs, now slick, before his tongue flicked out a playful lick and then delved back in. His hands grasped at my hips more forcefully, drawing me deeper into him, as if he couldn't get enough.

I relished in the forcefulness, the pain. It made something in me roar to life, and I gripped his hair, pushing him deeper into me.

Again, he murmured in agreement.

When I found myself on the exquisite precipice, where

one more flick of his tongue would allow me to fall into that blissful oblivion where nothing beyond my body would matter ... he stopped.

"What?" I asked breathily, as he observed me.

He rose up to his feet and kissed me. I could smell myself on his beard, taste myself in his kiss. I tasted ... tart. I'd heard about such acts from the other women and had thought it would be revolting. Yet, somehow, with the flavour coating both our tongues, I didn't seem to care. In fact, I savoured the animalistic-ness of it.

Then I felt his cock press against me and my legs widen even farther to accommodate him, as I sheathed him. His powerful thighs thrust into me in one, two, three strokes. I dug my nails into his biceps. He thrust harder. I cried out in the pain of the pleasure. He crushed his lips to mine once again. Then there was only the sound of our laboured breathing.

The sound of two people, each desperately trying to lose themselves in the other.

BETWEEN THE LEAVES of the tree above my head, I could see Artemis had hung a full moon. Somehow we had ended up on the soft moss beneath the tree, on the forest floor. Odysseus' arm was supporting my head as we stared up at a sky so deeply blue it looked black. I was about to comment on it, to break some of the unease I could feel forming in my bones now that conscious thought and clarity had returned, when a rallying war cry echoed up from the beach.

My attention snapped towards Odysseus', our eyes meeting for a fleeting moment as he moved fluidly onto his feet. By the time I had scrambled up, he had already put his fighting leathers back on and was storming towards the beach.

"Stay here!"

I immediately went to object.

"Just until I know the danger has passed. I will return for you."

A silent beat of understanding passed between us, a moment we couldn't afford. I sent him a brief nod.

That was the last moment of peace we had for a long, long time.

I followed him as close to the forest edge as I could get without being seen, where frantic energy filled the air and rushed towards me. On the beach, the men were fighting with the Cicones. Swords clashed, the men desperately grappling and grasping for their weapons and shields that had been abandoned near the fires. The ambush must have happened quickly, given the chaos I saw scattered along the beach – Odysseus' men being cut down, blood raining onto the grains of sand below.

I could feel Zeus' anger, the thunder rolling through the sky from the sea and onto the land. Until I realised it was not Zeus, but footsteps. What sounded like the roar of hordes of men. And horses.

My eyes scanned the scene in front of me desperately, searching for Odysseus amongst the carnage. There he was. Crouching and gutting, his spear a light and deft weapon in his hand as he twirled and stabbed, spun and launched. Always knowing when to press forward. Always knowing when to deflect.

So, this was who he had been on the battlefields of Troy. I could have been mesmerised by the dance of it, had my heart not been beating in the same rhythm as the footsteps that approached, growing ever faster.

Surely he could hear them, I thought. Surely he would force the men to retreat back to the ships soon, knowing what was coming. Feeling them beneath his feet. Then again, in the throes of battle, perhaps he could not hear them. I waited a second too long to cry out. Then I heard it.

"Retreat!" Odysseus' voice boomed over the chaos, a command that carried across the winds, across the beach, all the way to the trees. Every man heard it. Every man turned and ran for the ships as the Cicones followed.

He wasn't coming back for me. He couldn't. And the reinforced ranks of the Cicones were descending down the forest mountainside on all sides of the beach, including mine. There was nothing for it. I would have to run through the battlefield if I was going to have any hope of getting out of here alive.

I stumbled onto the sand, running as fast as I could directly to the shoreline. Men fought all around me, but I was at most of the Cicones' backs for now. I managed to evade most of them. I wasn't the only woman on the shore. The others who had been dancing and feasting amongst the fires were there, too. Some were fighting with their brothers. Others were cowering. Some were being dragged by their hair by Odysseus' men.

One made eye contact with me and flashed her fangs. A fighter. I dug my heels into the sand, forcing myself to run harder, faster, when a hand reached out and grabbed me.

Odysseus.

"Come, we must go. Now. Run, Odette."

At that moment, a spear passed across my chest, a mere millimetre from where I was. Odysseus roared and lunged, gutting the man who had dared, before pushing me towards the boats. I felt every swish of his spear, every countermove at my back as he continued to drive me forward.

It felt like forever before my shins hit cold water. Wading through it to reach the ship felt like it took even longer. But Odysseus' strong forearms bolstered me as I clambered up the rope ladder and onto the ship, even as he continued to fight off the bloodthirsty Cicones that had waded into the water after us.

Most, however, stayed on the shoreline, their message clear. Leave our land. You are not welcome here.

With a triumphant surge, those who had made it cast us off from shore. I stood beside Odysseus at the helm, as we watched the Cicones thrust their weapons in the air with another rallying war cry, this one victorious. Beyond them, dozens of Odysseus' men lay on the beach.

All slaughtered. All unmoving. All dead.

And in the sky beyond, Zeus roared.

20

ODYSSEUS

I counted seventy-two of our men missing.

Meanwhile, Zeus continued to rage. For nine days and nine nights, the north wind swept us along. No matter how many times the men attempted to regain control of the ships, or change course towards Maleia, it seemed Poseidon and Zeus were in agreement, dragging us onwards at their whims. Nine days and nine nights of relentless waves, relentless crashing and swaying. Relentless, endless ocean.

I almost didn't believe it when I saw it, but then there it was. Another island.

Fog hung over the island in a foreboding manner, as if I wasn't supposed to see it. As if we weren't supposed to be there. The nagging feeling tugged in my gut, but the men were desperate for a break. To turn them away from the island would be to cast them to a watery grave. Better to stop, to rest, to take our chances on another island, even if its people could turn on us again.

I prayed that the men had learnt their lesson from last time.

"We're here to replenish food and water only!" I barked at them. "We'll take supper by the ships. There's to be no pillaging of villages, or livestock – none of any kind." I frowned at the men who had dragged unsuspecting Ciconian women with them onto the ships when we had left the island.

"We will light the fires and have supper as close as we can to our ships, to show any folk on this island that we mean them NO HARM. We are to pass through ONLY."

"What if there are men on this island that mean to harm us?" one of the men called out.

"Three of you can go out in search of such men. Who would like to volunteer?"

Nobody volunteered, so I picked out three of my soldiers on the smaller, slighter side. Appearances were important.

"You are to take no weapons. You are to scout and report back what you see. Try to avoid being seen. If you are, do not engage. Do I make myself clear?"

"Yes, sir," they echoed back to me before they wandered off into the lush forest beyond. A gentle breeze swept over the beach and the hairs along my forearms stood on end. There was something not quite right about this place, something that had me thinking we would not see those men again.

They did not return.

THE MEN, their misery still fresh from our losses, started to become antsy. None of them were saying anything directly to one another, but there were shared looks. I could feel the friction the same way I could sense a storm building in the sky.

"Wait here," I told Odette. "I am going to find them."

She threw me an annoyed look.

"What?"

"And what would you have me do in the meantime when the men are spoiling for a fight? Who do you think they are going to take it out on? Each other, or the women?"

The thought of what Matthias and the others had tried before turned my blood molten. I rose to my feet and called out to the men.

"Ready the ships! We leave when I return!"

Grumbles rumbled out from the cloisters of campfires, but I stood steadfast, watching them all until they clambered to their feet and back up. Another night on the ships out at sea wasn't what I wanted for them, but the thought of sleeping here only to be slaughtered was even less appealing.

Satisfied that they were following orders, I looked down at Odette, pressed a kiss to her forehead as I cupped the back of her head – sweet gestures to keep her sweet – and strode into the bushland.

The tracks were fairly obvious to follow. Even though the three men I had sent were of small stature, they were not used to reconnaissance. Their footprints were stomped onto fallen leaves, their legs having dented the natural flow of the luscious plants around me. It was a strange forest. Fruits I'd never seen before, the purest white, yet velvety to the touch, hung from tall thin trees, a host of white flowers blooming around each of them. Eventually, the tracks led me to a clearing.

There, surrounded by natives, sat my three men. Quickly, my eyes scanned the situation, looking for the ropes that bound them in place, the weapons pointed at their bodies. I found none. In fact, the more I watched the scene in front of me, the more it appeared that the natives were friendly folk, though they did not look like us. Their skin was dark, their hair unoiled. They were naked for the most part, draped only in what looked like ceremonial beads. Savages of some kind. But instead of harming my men, they appeared to keep offering them food.

I crept closer.

Cupped in their hands were those white flowers I had seen earlier. Except this time, they were filled with translucent berries of some kind. My men took them gratefully, greedily slurping the contents before consuming the flowers, too. The natives smiled at them, gesturing to eat up, to eat more, while women prepared the next batch of flowers.

There was nothing else for it. I had to make myself known to the men to figure out what in the gods kept them there. I stepped out into the clearing.

Immediately, there were eyes on me. I expected hostility, but instead all I found were smiles.

"Come and join us!" one of my men cheered.

I looked at the natives, who nodded their agreement and gestured for me to take a seat with my men. Only when I got up close to these foreigners did I see that their teeth were black.

Cautiously taking a seat by my men, I watched as the natives turned to grab the next batch of flowers. Lotuses, I realised. That's what they were.

While the Lotus-Eaters' backs were turned, I scolded my men. "Why have you not returned to the ships? Why have you abandoned your task to report back to me?"

The three of them looked at each other, puzzled.

"What ships?" one of them asked me.

Before I had a chance to figure out what he meant, the hosts were back with freshly filled lotuses. The sweet fragrance of the blossoms and whatever they were filled with, what looked more like fish eggs upon closer inspection, was potent. My mouth watered, but I did not take the flower as the others did. Instead, I watched them closely as they ate. I watched their eyes glaze over and a euphoric expression wash over their haggard faces. A worrying suspicion wormed its way into my mind.

Turning to the man closest to me, I asked him, "What is your name?"

He stared at me blankly, smiling, and returned the question. "My name?"

That was it. We had to get out of here. I gently pushed away the flower offered by the native in front of me, who seemed once again to take no offence and continued to smile at me, and stood slowly. Slowly, so as not to spook anyone. So the natives wouldn't turn on us. I kept a smile on my face as I politely bowed to them before scooping my hands under the armpits of each man until they were all standing.

"Come on, men. It's time we leave. Thank these ... people ... for their time. We must leave them in peace and return to the ships."

I may as well not have spoken. The men did not move. Frustrated, I looked around, but I could find nothing that would help me spur the men. I had to find a way to get them to come back to the ship, by force if necessary. If I returned without them, the rest of my men would remain antsy for the rest of the journey home to Ithaca.

I could think of only one thing.

Taking their belts from around their waists, with no

complaints from any of them, I looped each one around their own necks, fastened them through, and then held the ends as if they were leashes.

As if my men were no better than dogs.

Tugging at them, they began to follow, though this time they resisted. Across my shoulder, I held tight to the belt ends and tugged. The men dug their heels in and wept, holding out their arms towards the Lotus-Eaters and their flowers.

The natives simply watched me struggle with them, sad looks adorning their faces. Grunting, I tried a different tactic, shifting the belt ends around until the men were in front of me and I could push them back to camp.

The Lotus-Eaters continued to watch as we left the clearing.

I checked behind me every so often to see if they followed us, but they did not. Not that they needed to track us; the men's wailing was a clear siren to anyone in the near vicinity. Nothing I could do or say could stop them. They only wanted to return to the clearing.

By the time we made it to the beach, I was exhausted. Their friends approached, joyous at the men's return. That joy turned to worry as they realised the men were no longer who they thought they were.

"What is wrong with them?"

"They've eaten something they shouldn't have. A drug of some kind, I suspect. Tie them to the rowing benches. Tie them tightly. If we let them go, they'll escape back into the bush behind us, and we'll never find them."

It took three men to load and tie down each drug-addled soldier in the ships. Meanwhile, I went to each ship to make sure its provisions were restocked with what the men had foraged from nearby the camp, and that we were ready to set sail away from this place immediately. I did not tell them about the native Lotus-Eaters or the fruit – what it could do to them. I was afraid that if I did, some of them might volunteer to stay.

War was a thing most men would rather forget.

Eventually, I made it to my own ship, where Odette was waiting for me with my trusted crew. Something flashed across her eyes, but it was not relief. It was something hard, gone before I knew it, her expression replaced by a smile. I shook it off as paranoia after seeing the effects of the plant and called for my men to set sail.

I watched the treeline as we left, half expecting the Lotus-Eaters to finally make an appearance, to offer up a rallying cry as the previous island's inhabitants did. But, no one appeared. Unease filled me.

Why hadn't they tried to stop us from leaving?

And why had Odette not been happy to see me return?

21

ODETTE

R ain was our constant companion for the next forty nights, a ceaseless torrent. The sky remained an unbroken canvas of lead grey, the sea churned angrily beneath us, and everyone was miserable. Each one of us was soaked through, the cold seeping into our bones – no matter if we were above board or not.

Odysseus had tasked me with drying out the fish, meats, and fruits, so that they might last longer on a journey that seemed never-ending. It was a near impossible task in this weather, and I'm sure all the other slave women would have agreed, should we have been able to see each other through the relentless hammering of rain from the sky.

Guilt and hunger gnawed at my gut, for I suspected it was my vow making this journey so arduous and long. Funny how hindsight could make you rethink things in the moment. I could barely remember the pain of losing Alcander. Even Lykas, though the pang of memory hurt my heart, struggled to contend with the pain of hunger and of my lips, now chapped and blistering from the brine of the olives I was practically living on, to make sure the men were given the majority of bread and cheeses that had not staled.

So, when we finally caught sight of the next island, I was not surprised to hear Odysseus yell to the men to head toward it. The island's outline was dark and foreboding, like a dragon rising from cloud cover or fog, only for us to realise how huge it was. Coupled with the howling wind and the jagged rocks along the shoreline, I was unsure this island *wasn't* a monster disguised in nature – and yet it still presented as a promise of respite from the interminable ocean.

It was twilight by the time we made it to the shore. Ahead of us was a cave, its entrance yawning open before us, further reinforcing my belief that this was some monster. It was too good to be true – an island *and* a cave in which to shelter from the weather?

I was two steps behind every one of Odysseus', even though he was pulling my hand, so I saw him stop and raise his other arm, even as my body lurched forward to catch up to the tug and then swayed as I halted beside him.

His focus was fixed on the cave's entrance, his jaw clenched, and I could practically hear him doing the risk calculations in his head as his eyes darted back and forth and his fingers twitched against mine.

"We go in," he commanded, his voice steady but with an edge that made me nervous. His authority was undeniable to the men, but, for the first time, I wasn't convinced. Perhaps it was because ever since we'd left Troy, trouble had followed us in a way that Odysseus couldn't seem to shake. Or perhaps it was because I had been close to Odysseus when he had been confident in his actions, and this was something ... other. Something I couldn't put my finger on.

Perhaps it was just because I knew, in his position, I would make a different choice. That I *could* make a different choice, and he could not stop me. He could kill me, but he could not stop me.

And let's face it, whatever was in that cave could kill us anyway.

The air grew heavier as we walked towards the entrance, and as we stepped into the cave it felt like the darkness swallowed us whole. The air inside grew colder, almost suffocating. The smell of raw, earthy dampness was mixed with the faint, sickly sweet scent of decay. I heard a crunch and could have sworn I stepped on a bone. Then another crunch followed, and another. The ground was littered with bones. I could only hope they were animal.

But hope, as Odysseus had said once, was a foolish man's method. He wouldn't rely on that.

Would he?

My trepidation immediately subsided upon seeing the cave filled with provisions – there were large wheels of cheese stacked as high as the cavern walls, and clay jars brimming with milk. Sheep bleated from the back recess of the cave, and for some reason I thought that because livestock were here, it was a safe space. Someone who protected the livestock, who respected the laws of nature, would be a decent man.

If only I could ignore the bones.

Suddenly, the ground beneath us trembled and the entrance darkened as some sort of creature lumbered in, his frame so massive it filled the cave. He bent to pick up a log of wood and struck it against the cave wall like it was kindling, throwing it with eerie accuracy into a pit that within minutes became a giant bonfire.

I think we then collectively noticed the single narrow eye, for it seemed as if everyone drew a breath at the same time. He was a grotesque sight, his single eye glaring down at us, completely naked and built like a man – but five times the size.

"Who ... are ... you?" he boomed, his voice reverberating off the stone walls, though his voice was not hostile. Instead he seemed curious, which only made the situation more unnerving.

"We are travellers," Odysseus said smoothly, his eyes never leaving the Cyclops, "blown off course by the whims of the gods."

Even I could not deny it was impressive how he kept his voice steady.

"I am Nobody," he added.

Clever, so clever. Too clever.

"Who are you?" Odysseus asked the Cyclops.

Without warning, he grabbed two of the men, smashing them against the cave walls before devouring them with a sickening crunch. My stomach churned, and I fought to keep my fear at bay.

He did not like us not knowing who he was.

But, he was blocking the entrance, which was also our only exit. I glanced at the provisions around us, wondering how we could use them to our advantage. Then Odysseus pulled out a skin of wine from somewhere.

"Something to wash them down with?"

He held out some of our wine to the monster. I had to stifle a gasp – to offer a gesture of xenia[1] was a sacred duty, watched over by none other than Zeus himself. Admittedly,

---

1. Hospitality.

the beast that stood in the door hadn't exactly greeted us warmly, but to offer food and drink, between one party or the other, took this to the next level. If this ended up being our place of rest, or if he and Odysseus exchanged stories, there is no way we wouldn't be bound by the rules of xenia.

The Cyclops swiped the skin of wine from Odysseus' hand and began gulping it down greedily until he was shaking the dregs of it down his throat. A minute later, a belch echoed around the cave. He eyed all of us, like he was deciding who to eat next, but when his arm swiped forward and the men jumped back, the beast stumbled. His eyelids drooped. Then, with a crash, he collapsed into a drunken stupor, his snores exhaling alcohol.

"You didn't water down the wine," I breathed, turning to Odysseus, who pinned me with a knowing look.

"You think it would have been better to mellow him out?"

I rolled my eyes. "That's not what I meant."

I had meant to compliment his ingenuity in a time of great pressure, but – now that I thought about it – perhaps it had been more opportunity and sheer, dumb luck that Odysseus had undiluted wine on him.

When all he did was smile at me across the fire, I crossed my arms. "Well? What do we do now?" I nodded to the sleeping giant in front of the cave's entrance. "He will wake eventually, and then we will be damned."

Odysseus looked around, as did I and everyone else. But there was nothing other than the original provisions I had already clocked – the cheese, the milk, the sheep, the fire. I watched as Odysseus' eyes focused on the fire.

"You plan on blinding the beast?" I hissed.

Odysseus shrugged. "We could sharpen one of the logs and heat it in the fire first. We have time."

"And when he is blindly scrambling for us? He could wipe us out with a sweep of his arm, whether he could see or not."

Odysseus looked around, scanning the cave. Even in the dim light of the bonfire, I could see his eyes taking in every detail, every possibility, until he moved with purpose towards a long, thick branch. "Here, this will do."

Even as he yanked the branch free from the bonfire, his movements were fluid. He laid the branch on the ground and stripped it of its bark, his hands moving with practiced efficiency.

"We need to sharpen one end," he said to another of the men, not looking up.

One of the younger boys handed him a jagged rock. Odysseus took it without a word. As he worked, I couldn't help but watch him, noting the set of his jaw, the intensity in his eyes, the bulge of his forearms.

I crouched down beside him, while the other men in the cave looked for other ways out, deliberately giving us space. "Odysseus, what happens after this, hmm?"

He didn't pause in his work, but I saw his eyes flicker with something.

"This plan of yours – do you ever think about the lives you gamble with your schemes?"

The muscle in his jaw tightened. "Every day. But right now, we have to survive. We can't afford distractions."

"It's not about distractions, Odysseus. It's the way you treat us all like we're pawns supposed to just go along with your game. I used to think it was just me you did this to, but what you've pulled the men into ...?"

The stake continued to take shape, the point sharpening under his skilled hands as he rebutted. "So what would you have me do? Sit and wait for the gods to decide our fate? I'll let you in on a little secret, Odette. They don't give a damn. I'm trying to save us. And yes, every plan carries risk, Odette. But we don't have the luxury of playing it safe."

I didn't say anything to that. I couldn't; he wasn't wrong. Instead, the silence between us became thick until the stake was ready and Odysseus was turning it in his hands, inspecting it.

"This will do," he told me, his voice resolute.

He met my eyes, and for a moment, the barrier seemed to crumble. Everything that had happened between us since he'd been injured washed over me. The absolute terror that filled me at the prospect of being handed over to another Grecian man. At becoming a new slave; at an unknown territory once again. Then the kiss. The *heat* that had travelled through my body. The war ending, the sadness *and* relief I'd been flooded with. The confusion that had followed at that realisation. The terror of what came next. The thrill of being in Hecuba's presence, the elation of power, the crumbling feeling of losing it as quickly as I'd got it. And the rest ... the rest had just felt like survival.

And through it all, he had been there beside me, my only constant in the horrors of war.

And I couldn't figure out anymore which parts he was responsible for, and which parts he kept me safe from. All I knew was that I didn't want to lose the one constant I had. It left me with no choice but to trust him.

"Trust me, Odette," he said softly, as if he'd heard my thoughts. "We'll get through this."

The Cyclops' snores grew louder, jolting me out of the

moment, and I realised my heart was hammering so hard against my chest that I could hear it in my ears. This was it. But as Odysseus stood, stake in hand, a thought struck me.

I grabbed Odysseus' forearm. "Wait."

"What?"

"Once you stab him, we'll still need a way to get out without being caught. He'll be blinded, but not helpless."

Odysseus frowned. "I know that. We'll use his sheep," he said, as if it wasn't the most obvious solution in the world.

"The sheep?"

"We can cling to the underside of their bellies when he lets them out to graze. He'll feel their backs but not their undersides. It's our best chance."

It was genius, and yet it angered me that he hadn't thought to explain that beforehand.

His eyes searched mine, but when he saw my eyes harden, he moved on with a nod, signalling to others and quietly explaining the plan. The men's expressions shifted in understanding, fear mingling with hope. It was a risky plan, but it was all we had.

While the men moved towards the sheep, Odysseus moved towards the slumbering beast. I stood torn between the two.

When the moment came, Odysseus plunged the stake into the Cyclops' eye. A scream of agony, so painful I felt my eardrums crack, filled the cave. The Cyclops thrashed in pain against the heavy stake firmly lodged in his eye, and I held my breath, every nerve in my body on edge, waiting for him to pull it out. But while his hands clawed at his face, the damage was done, blood and ichor pouring down his body into puddles larger than a man at his feet.

I grabbed Odysseus' arm again and pulled him towards

the sheep. Together, along with the other men, we crawled beneath the animals, clutching their wooly bellies as the monster staggered around, blindly searching for us.

If we could just hold on a little longer, we might have a chance of escaping this nightmare.

The next few moments dissolved into chaos, with the deafening roars of the monster, the frantic bleating of sheep, and all of us scrambling beneath the animals' bellies. Dust and debris filled the air, while the beast's hands blindly groped for any one of us. Finding nothing, he let out a terrifying bellow, one that made me squeeze my sheep tighter until it let out a bleat among the many, and flung open the cave entrance. My sheep immediately bolted for the outside, the giant's hands brushing the back of the sheep as he did so, barely missing me, but I held on tightly. The rough wool scratched at my skin, but I didn't dare let go.

When we passed through the cave entrance, the fresh air that hit my face felt like a blessing. We were outside; we were free. The sheep ran towards the fields at a surprisingly fast speed, until we all tucked and rolled off and each one of us ran for the ships.

Once we were on the vessels safely, I took a chance to look around at the others. The women were cowering in fear, huddled together, crying. The men followed closely, their faces drawn with exhaustion and fear I hadn't been able to see in the darkness of the cave. Even Odysseus was tense, his face haggard in a way I hadn't seen before as he leaned against the mast, his usual confident demeanour sagging in his shoulders. Here was a man weighed down by the burden of leadership, and the impending doom that seemed to follow us.

It made him more human, more real. I reached out, my hand resting lightly on his arm.

"You were scared, we all are, but we made it," I said, my voice barely above a whisper. I stood beside him, close enough to feel the warmth of his body and the tension radiating from him.

He straightened, looking down at me, when the Cyclops' cry pierced the air. "Father, Nobody blinded me!"

Odysseus moved away from me at that moment, and went to stand at the bow. "No, it was Odysseus, King of Ithaca, who blinded you, you dumb monster!" he shouted, glancing back towards the men with a suave smile, once again the confident general they had gone into battle with. The men cheered Odysseus and jeered the creature.

Odysseus glanced at me then, and in that moment, I understood why he had done it. He could not afford to be seen as weak. Better to be arrogant to keep the men on side than be scared and afraid, and have them turn on him. And if I, a mere woman, could see it … Yes, I understood why he believed he had to do it.

I just didn't agree with it.

"Odysseus!" the Cyclops' voice thundered, his words carrying across the island. "I am Polyphemus, son of Poseidon! Father, if it is your will, let this man never return home! Or if he must, let him arrive too late, having lost all his comrades, in a stranger's ship, and find trouble in his house!"

Let this man never return home.

There it was – the god who had taken up my vow. I had always assumed it would be Hera – but this curse was too similar to my own to be a coincidence. I glanced again at

Odysseus, his face hardened at the curse placed upon him. I wondered, knowing this man as I did now, would I rather face the wrath of Athena, or divine retribution at Poseidon's hands?

22

ODYSSEUS

She knew me too intimately. I had been foolish to think that she would not, after our time together. I had picked Odette, after all, for her intelligence. But now her insights left me exposed in a way I could not afford. The bond between us after that night we shared could not be ignored, even amidst the battles and continuous hardships we had faced since. I needed to get her alone, so I could explain; so she could understand her place in the scheme of things.

Odette was too much of an open book, like any woman, unable to hide her emotions as a man could bury them. Her grief when we had first met was all-consuming, then her anger palpable. Her shrewdness now felt ... dangerous, foreboding almost. It set my teeth on edge, and I did not want the men catching on.

So, instead, I gathered the men on deck as I stood at the prow of the ship, watching a new shoreline draw ever closer. When all the men were gathered, the women they kept as their own behind them, I turned to address them.

"We will make a stop at Aeolia," I announced. "Aeolus, Master of Winds, resides here and can aid us on our journey home."

A murmur of approval rippled through the crew, while one of the deckhands raised a forest green banner to signal to the other ships in our fleet that we were to head for shore. Finally, an island I recognised. Finally, a place the men could go without fear of being attacked, or drugged, or killed.

I looked towards the Lotus-Eater men. A crescent moon had hung low on the horizon the night we had left that island, and it had swelled into a gibbous moon before the men had come right, the drug from those plants finally purged from their bodies. Now they, too, were in agreement with the rest.

But, when my eyes met Odette's shrewd gaze, I knew she immediately saw my facade for what it was. Shaking my head slightly, I dismissed her silent enquiry. There would be no further discussion here, not with the men watching. Instead, my eyes directed her to my quarters and she gave a small nod in understanding, following my summons to the small space.

It felt like a lifetime ago that I had tied her up in here for insolence.

Now, the space seemed even smaller with her in it, her presence both a challenge and an allure. I pushed that feeling aside, reminding myself of the stakes.

"Do you even know this Aeolus?" she asked me, as soon as she closed the door of my quarters behind her.

I rounded on her, until I had her pressed up against the door with nowhere to go, and her chin was firmly in my grip.

"You do not get to question my judgement, do you understand?" My voice was low, so the men beyond the door would not hear us, but that charged the air with something electric, and I saw a flash of defiance in her eyes at the same time her nostrils flared.

"You are back to using and discarding people as you see fit, I see."

"You dare ..." My grip slid down to her neck and tightened on her, but Odette didn't so much as wince. "I have treated you with respect, and yes, I have grown to care for you. I place a careful shield around you, to protect you from what others would have me do to you. Yet, at every opportunity, you seek to break it."

Odette tried to let out a laugh, but with my hand on her windpipe, it came out garbled. "Nothing you do is to protect me, Odysseus. It is to protect yourself. You use me as a confidant when it suits you, and when I scratch too close below the surface that it alarms you, you like to remind me that I am a captive."

Rage roared through me and it took everything in my control to only let a drop more strength squeeze her throat before I released her.

She didn't even rub where I had held her when I set her free.

Stubborn woman. Gods, I ...

"Aeolus will help us get home," I said, cutting off that other – that horrifying – thought. "And once we arrive in Ithaca, you will become one of Penelope's maids. You will serve her faithfully, and you will not breathe a word of what has happened between us."

I couldn't lose Odette, not now that I knew what this feeling was. And I was most certainly not going to jeopardise my marriage to Penelope.

Odette's eyes held a mixture of shock and anger. "You

could let me go," she countered, her voice trembling with suppressed fury. "If you cared for me, truly, you would not keep me in bondage."

I shook my head. "You know too much. It would be too dangerous to set you free," I reasoned.

"Liar," she seethed.

And damn me to the Underworld if she wasn't right.

Before she could pull away, my lips crashed into hers, a fierce and desperate kiss that held all the anger that it had to be this way. My hands tangled in her hair, pulling her closer until her warm body was pressed against mine, as if I could erase all the boundaries between us. The heat of her mouth, the taste of salt and longing, it ignited something primal in me.

Only Odette had ever managed to do that.

She responded in kind, matching my intensity. My hands roamed over her back, down her bum, squeezing, pulling her impossibly closer until we could both feel my hard erection against the softness of her. There was only here, only now, only the raw connection between us as our breaths mingled, as her heartbeat became mine. For a brief, blinding instant, nothing else mattered.

Then the reality of our situation clawed its way back into my mind, tearing through the haze of desire. My body shuddered as I broke the kiss, my arms still holding her close, my forehead resting against hers.

She pulled away from me. My arms tensed in resistance, but that only made her more determined. "You are a coward, Odysseus. Afraid of a woman who has nothing left to lose."

I let her go after that, a cold, steely resolve dousing the flame of desire. "Call it what you will, but my decision stands. You will serve in Ithaca, and you will keep your silence."

I turned away from her, signaling the end of our conversation. As I heard her footsteps retreat, I felt a pang of something akin to regret. The weight of my choices pressed heavily on me, but I couldn't afford to show weakness. Not now. Not ever.

I waited in my quarters until I could get myself under control. Rearranging myself – *composing* myself – I made my way to the front of the ship, taking my place at the prow. I watched the shoreline draw closer and the island of Aeolia grow larger, its jagged cliffs adorned in greenery rising majestically amidst the relentless expanse of the Aegean Sea as my men rowed, rowed, *rowed*.

As we drew closer, the scent of salt dissipated and the air became clean, rich, earthy – like the earth after it had just stopped raining. It was a tantalising promise of respite that urged the men to row harder until we hit the shore.

Aeolus was there to greet us as we disembarked. "Odysseus!" he called, his arms open wide, the sleeves of his robes billowing in the winds he conjured. "There was word on the winds of your arrival."

"Aeolus," I replied in greeting, hugging the other king briefly before drawing back. "I'm sure your winds told you why we are here."

"Ah, my friend, there is plenty of time for that. Why don't your men settle here and I'll have my servants come and bring them a fresh kill to cook, replenishments, pots to heat the wash water, and scrubs. You and I can go to my home, and when you too are refreshed, we can talk about what it is you seek."

I looked around at the men, my eyes once again catching

on Odette, always finding her. I couldn't help it. At this point on our journey, it was becoming a bad reflex.

"You can bring the woman," Aeolus noted.

I grunted, gesturing with my head for Odette to follow us, and together, Aeolus and I turned towards the great paved walk up towards his house on the cliffs. Sand gave way to smooth stones and then to a decorative pathway, the borders sculpted by a delicate hand. Almost as delicate as the footsteps behind me that told me Odette had followed.

The house was by no means a palace, but certainly grand with its high ceilings, terracotta columns, and detailed architraves that matched the path that led us here. Aeolus swept us through to a guest suite where one kline bed[1] draped in a gauzy canopy sat in the centre of a room that separated off into two different bathing chambers. His servants were already drawing baths, the fragrant aromas of the dried flowers and oils so potent they made my eyes water.

Once upon a time I was used to such smells, but after so long at sea, the closest thing to them that I remembered was the salt scrub and warmed oil Odette would leave out for me. Then I remembered the sand crabs and had to stop myself from barking with laughter at the woman who now stood at my shoulder.

"We will leave you two to wash and rest. Just follow the hallway to the great home when you are ready for food," Aeolus said, before bowing his head in good will and turning back the way he came.

The servants left not long afterwards, leaving Odette and I still standing in the doorway.

---

1. Similar to a four-post bed.

She turned to her right and headed for one chamber without a word. Turning to the left, I followed suit.

The bathing area was done in the same style as the rest of the house: terracottas, browns, and sand beiges that must have appealed to Aeolus, but felt drab to me. The marble bath, however, was a welcome sight. The steam rising off it beckoned me, and it wasn't long before I was sinking into its depths with a sigh.

Outstretching my arms along the edge of the marble, I leaned my head back, enjoying the water lapping at my chest, watching the candlelight flicker against the damp stone walls. Then I heard it – the water splashing, as if Odette was dipping her dainty toes in and out of the water in a pitter-patter movement, like a child. Her laughter followed. Then the sounds of the water, the movements, became more rhythmic and I had to hold back a groan as the images in my mind took me places.

I gripped my cock as I imagined her touching herself, lathering herself. Imagined her hands becoming mine. I fisted once, twice, the sound of my own movements in the water interrupting hers. I stilled to hear them again, but they'd quietened, as if she knew what I was doing.

Frustrated, I snarled and rose from the water, reaching for the nearest towel and drying myself off with harsh, efficient movements.

"Refreshed?" Aeolus called out as I strode into the great room.

"Thoroughly," I assured him. "I thank you for your hospitality, for myself and my men."

"And your women," Aeolus added, a gleam in his eye.

I turned to see what he was looking at: Odette in a fresh dress, the palest shade of tourmaline blue I had ever seen, the fabric draping across her body in a way that framed her silhouette beautifully, curves and drapes in all the right, flattering places.

I scowled. "I don't need you to *dress* my people too, Aeolus."

The other king was already shaking his head. "A beautiful dress for a beautiful woman, that is all. It was only going to waste away in the closet otherwise."

I doubted that. There were plenty of women, and nymphs, that graced the attention of Master of the Winds.

"It's lovely, thank you," Odette said, her voice softer than I'd ever heard it.

It only made me scowl more deeply. But I had to be careful what I said next. Aeolus was not one to be coerced; he could only be persuaded through diplomacy. The man had an absolute hard-on for "the balance of all things". Though I found that balance often swayed towards respect for his power.

"Not as lovely as you, my dear. Come, sit beside me, and the two of you can tell me what brings you to my island."

Odette did as requested, her eyes briefly meeting mine across the table, before diving back into the feast spread before us. There was an array of choices, reflecting the bounty of both land and sea. There were platters of roasted lamb and pork, seasoned with garlic, thyme, and rosemary and drizzled with olive oil, the smell of which made my mouth water. Bowls of olives, figs, and dates provided sweet and savoury accompaniments. Freshly baked bread, still warm from the oven, sat alongside cheeses made from goat and sheep's milk. The centrepiece was a large swordfish, probably caught that morning, grilled to perfection and garnished with lemon and dill. Pitchers of rich red wine and golden honey mead were placed between the plates, and Aeolus poured us all a generous helping of the two.

"Don't worry, I've ensured your men receive the same bounty. What they don't eat can be taken as replenishments for your ships. There was certainly a lot to go around," Aeolus laughed.

Looking at the feast myself, I wasn't surprised. Most of the men wouldn't be able to stomach this after so long on brined goods and dry bread – though that probably wouldn't stop them from attempting to gorge.

"You are too kind," I told Aeolus. Particularly seeing as we had come here seeking another favour from him – one I had yet to ask.

Aeolus regarded me with knowing eyes, his attention briefly flickering towards Odette before returning to me. "Odysseus," he said, his voice carrying the weight of ages. "You came seeking the Bag of Winds."

I swallowed the tart wine I'd taken a sip of, choosing my next words carefully. "Yes. We are at your mercy. This journey has been long and arduous already, and while I am happy to regale you with tales you will no doubt find entertaining, my friend, I am also anxious to get my men home."

"And no doubt anxious to get home to your wife, Penelope," Aeolus said, his eyes sliding over to Odette before they returned to me.

My eyes met Odette's.

"Yes." I didn't miss the gleam of interest in his eyes when I turned back to him. "I come to ask if you can grant us the winds that will guide us safely home."

The gleam in Aeolus' expression turned ruminative, as if weighing the implications of my request. He glanced between Odette and I once again before leaning back in his chair, his hands braced on the table. "I can conjure the winds you require," he said slowly. "For a price."

He looked to Odette once again, and I had to resist the urge to stab my fork through his eye. As it was, my grip on the utensil bent it when I saw Odette's perfect lips open into an 'O', but otherwise she seemed actually amenable to the suggestion, none of her other features tensing or narrowing at the idea.

Did she really want to stay with this kolaktēs?[2]

"No," I said firmly, surprising even myself. "She is not for sale."

Aeolus sighed, then threw his hands up with a laugh. "Very well, it was worth a try. You cannot have everything you want without a little risk." He chuckled again.

I did not join him.

Aeolus gestured to one of his attendants, who left the room and returned minutes later with a small dark brown pouch, cinched at the top with a leather drawstring. As he got closer, I recognised the accented gold swirl across the top of the pouch. It was a wind symbol, the same one that decorated the pathways and junctures of this house.

Of course.

"The legendary Bag of Winds," I guessed.

Aeolus nodded, taking the bag from his attendant and weighing it in his hands. "Contained within are the winds that will guide you safely back to Ithaca. Except," he paused,

---

2. Flatterer or sycophant, someone who uses charm deceitfully to gain favour.

cocking his head to one side, "for the west wind. Do not use it unless you wish to send another home."

Aeolus looked at Odette as he said that last part, and she paled at his words.

He must have meant Troy, guessing where she'd come from.

I gave a grunt of thanks as I accepted the bag, and abruptly stood. But, keenly aware that I must continue to play the political game until my men were safely on the ship and back out to sea, I gave him one small offering. "Odette – stay, eat, as long as you wish. Aeolus will have plenty of enchanting tales to tell you. I will see you down at the ships before nightfall."

That should appease the wiry fuck.

It took every ounce of me to stride from that hall without her, to not look back. To not see if Aelous had reached his hand across the table to touch her. To show Odette that I trusted her. And all the while, Aeolus' words reverberated in my skull: '*You cannot have everything you want without a little risk', the warning about the west wind, and the implied sugges-tion that Odette's presence was a similar gamble.*

That night, fatigue weighed as heavily upon me as the Bag of Winds, a surprisingly dense pouch, which informed me just how far we had left to travel. Yet, the seas were calm when we set sail under the stars and sleep claimed me.

Visions of home and the challenges ahead flickered like a storybook through my mind. In the hazy realm, I could have sworn Odette took the bag from my chest and replaced it with her hand, a soft whisper in my ear.

"It could take us far from Ithaca," she murmured. "It could give us a chance together."

Her breath on my cheek felt so real, but when I grasped at my chest, the bag was still there.

It was just a dream, a figment of my weary mind, mixing the image of a life I could not have with the reality the gods bestowed upon me.

23

ODETTE

O dysseus was a hypocrite. *Saying I wasn't for sale.* Yet, he would rather tie me to a fate he knew I did not want than care enough to let me go. If he had it his way, we would end up forever bound to the ocean, to Poseidon's whims.

Not that he knew that. Instead, he thought he could keep me by his side indefinitely, another possession to control, another prize of war.

Aeolus may have been pompous, certainly conceited, but life with him would have been bearable. Odysseus could have returned to his wife, and I could have had a chance to start again. But no, he chose to keep me tethered to his desires, regardless of what I wanted. And now my vow would keep us shackled to this cursed voyage. If he continued to have it his way, we would be doomed to wander the waters indefinitely, but how could I tell Odysseus that?

I suppose I should have been grateful that he didn't offer to sell me, that he didn't see me as a commodity to trade anymore, if it hadn't been entirely self-serving. I couldn't deny that there were moments – fleeting, yet undeniable – when I felt something for him, certain he felt something for me, too. A connection, a bond forged in all that time spent in the tent together, the weight of war bearing down on us, the loneliness, the faint bitter taste of longing. But that didn't stop me being trapped in this endless cycle, at the mercy of a man who *could* treat me as property.

I was sick of the sea. Sick of the endless spray of salt and the rocking waves. Sick of the aching solitude and the longing that tugged in my gut.

I needed to find a way out, and the only one I could see was sitting on Odysseus' chest, his hand wrapped loosely around the Bag of Winds. The oil lamp in the corner of the cabin flickered over his sleeping face, softened by sleep. A stark contrast from the man I'd come to know in public. But even in his vulnerability, he still clutched the bag, the key to our fate, as if he knew I might take it.

I could not bargain any longer.

The thought of returning to Ithaca, to a life as one of Penelope's maids ... I shuddered with dread.

Odysseus was no longer a war hero, the war long over. Now he was just a man lost at sea. Perhaps Athena was done with her hero, and if she had abandoned him, why shouldn't I?

I reached out, my fingers trembling as I pried the bag from his grasp. Luckily, he stirred but did not wake.

"It could take us far from Ithaca," I murmured. "It could give us a chance together."

Though what that chance would be, I had no idea. Freedom from the vow I had originally made? Just another form of enslavement under a different guise? Redemption, for both of us? I had no way of knowing.

I remembered Aeolus' warning, his eyes seeming to gleam with mischief at me. What was it he had said? *"Do not use the west wind."* As if he knew my vow, *my wind*, whispered across the ocean and could blow us off course. As if this wind could lend my words its power.

I carefully unthreaded the cord, the wisp of fabric almost deafeningly loud in the quiet of the cabin. I stopped, watching Odysseus and the rise and fall of his chest. Slow, steady, asleep.

I thumbed at the opening of the bag and a plume of air escaped, a faint breeze that carried the scent of distant lands and endless possibilities. It swirled around me before it slipped under the cabin door and out into the wide world beyond.

I glanced back at Odysseus, his rugged face still peaceful in sleep. He would hate me for this if he knew, but it was too late to change course now. Already I could feel the wave patterns beneath us begin to shift. I only hoped it would lead us somewhere – anywhere – other than Ithaca.

Come the morning, our course had shifted with the newfound wind, and I woke from a guilt-ridden poor sleep to the murmurs of the men outside the cabin, their voices filled with confusion and worry. Slipping quietly out the door, I made my way up to the main deck and saw Odysseus standing at the helm, his face set in grim determination as his eyes swept over the men gathered in uneasy clusters.

"Who opened the bag?" he demanded.

That voice – clear as a bell, yet deep and wooden – reminded me of all those moons ago when he'd found me wandering the Grecian camp. I'd been scared then, a powerless farmer's wife who had no idea what to expect. I'd done a lot since then: dined with Greek kings and held my own in conversation, defeated the demons of my mind, stood toe-to-toe against the man in front of me, killed another, tasted power – *true power* – and yet, here I was, terrified again, my heart a wild staccato beat against my ribcage.

If he were to find out it was me …

I watched as Odysseus paced back and forth, his eyes flashing with rage as he assessed the crew. I had never seen him so angry before. Calm, calculated in his fury, yes – but never like this. The men cowered before him.

"It was supposed to be our salvation," he growled. "Now, thanks to one of you, we're back to where we started. Who is responsible for this treachery?"

The men remained silent, their heads bowed in shame. I could see the tension in their shoulders, the way their hands fidgeted at their sides. They were terrified, and rightfully so. Odysseus' rage demanded attention, the force of its nature a battering ram to everyone's defences.

He seized one of the men by the collar, dragging him forward. "Was it you?" he demanded.

The man shook his head frantically, his eyes wide with terror. "It wasn't me, my lord," he stammered. "I swear it."

Odysseus released him with a shove, turning his attention to another man. "And you? Do you have anything to say for yourself?"

The second man shook his head as well, his voice trembling as he spoke. "No, my lord. I had nothing to do with it."

And though the morning sun still reflected off the ocean, the temperature dropped as Odysseus looked out across the deck. "Cowards, the lot of you!" he proclaimed. "All too afraid to admit your mistake, and too weak to take responsibility for your actions."

I shrank back further into the shadows as Odysseus' footsteps clipped against the deck and back towards the cabin, towards me.

Just then, the ship lurched, and we all looked towards the horizon. In the haze of the morning mist, the silhouette of an island loomed. As we drew closer, and the men scrambled to adjust the sails to prepare for landing, I went to stand at the bow of the ship, gripping the wooden railing to get a better look. The haze gave way to what could only be described as a lush paradise, the dense forests cloaking the island in a mantle of green.

"What is this place?"

Odysseus came to stand behind me, his arms wrapping around either side of me, as his hands also gripped the railing.

I turned my chin to look at him, surprised at the closeness, but his eyes were studying the island. "I do not know."

As he said that, for some reason unbeknownst to me a chill ran down my spine.

Eventually the ship came to a stop on the shore, and when we disembarked onto soft, lush grass with the faintest smell of fresh, recently watered earth, I felt a pulse, a beat, as if we had just alerted someone to our presence.

Some of the men, eager to prove their loyalty, or perhaps to lessen Odysseus' anger towards them, decided to go ahead and scout for food and shelter. The place was rich with the scent of pines and wildflowers. We could even see wide meadows that stretched out under the clear, azure sky, and I could hear the insects buzzing – a network of nature at work. There would surely be a freshwater source and at the very least, fresh fruit for us to graze on. After all, there was still plenty of food from Aeolus stored on the ships.

Yet, hours passed and still the men did not return. There would be only hours left again before the world went dark. Anxiousness wrapped itself like an old coat around those of us left behind.

Even Odysseus' concern grew palpable, until he eventually said, "I'll go find them. Sit tight."

He stalked off into the forest, the dense foliage swallowing him whole until there was nothing left to do but wait.

The dimmer the day got, the more time dragged on, the more paranoid I became that someone, or something, was watching us. There were only three guards left, and the women were but a small group of twelve, so easily outnumbered.

That's when I noticed the eyes watching us from the bushes. Several pairs of glowing amber eyes.

As my eyes adjusted to the darkness, I started making out their shapes. There were wolves, lions, even cows. "That's strange ..."

No one answered me. Why would a cow be so close to something that could kill it? Why weren't the predators attacking it? If anything, the creatures all seemed wary of us, and yet seemingly wanted to get closer to us, to the fire. I continued to watch them stalk around the perimeter, edging closer, only to scurry back into the shadows when they thought one of the guards would spot them.

Did they want warmth? Is that what they were seeking?

They moved strangely, with a grace and unnatural intelligence that said they knew exactly who we were and how they would be treated. They treated each other with care, too, which was more unsettling than anything else I had seen.

Suddenly, there came a rustling from the jungle surrounding us, and I was sure the creatures had finally come to some sort of consensus, that they were now ready to act, to attack us, when Odysseus emerged from the trees.

"What happened?" I asked as he strode past me and directly up to one of the guards. They murmured together for a moment before the guard nodded and went off to share whatever necessary information with the other men. The women, as always, were ignored.

I stood, resettling my chiton around my legs and following after Odysseus who was now scrambling through the chest of supplies. He pulled out a small knife, then turned towards me. I saw the wildness in his eyes, the tension drawn across his face.

"Odysseus?"

Within two strides he was in front of me, firmly grabbing one of my bare shoulders and forcing me to kneel on the ground.

"What are you doing? Why are you doing this?" I tried, gods knew I tried, to keep the terror out of my voice.

But when his answer came, it did nothing to assuage the fear in me.

"This is the island of Aeaea, home to the witch Circe. She does not fear men, nor will she tolerate your presence. I have to protect you," he murmured, as he began cutting my hair, the sharp blades slicing through the strands.

I tried to shake my head, but he held me firmly as he continued cutting, until it felt like he wasn't cutting hair but parts of my very being, any last source of the woman I once was dying as the strands fell into my hands.

Only when I saw splashes of water appear beside them did I realise I was crying. "Why?" I whispered.

"She has turned the men to pigs. The creatures you might have spied around here are no creatures, but humans she has tamed to her hand. I can only imagine what she might do to a woman she would see as a threat."

I was quiet for a moment. The only sounds were those of the other women crying around us, as the men did the same to them. "Perhaps she just sought to protect herself from the men. Perhaps this is an unnecessary measure ..."

"You did not see what I saw, Odette. I am doing this to keep you safe." He paused, his eyes locking with mine. "I can't lose you."

His confession hung in the space between us, and I searched his eyes, half expecting him to elaborate, when a voice interrupted, dripping with curiosity and amusement.

"Well, well, well. Who do we have here?"

I turned to see a woman standing at the edge of the forest clearing where we had gathered, her presence an unmistakable otherworldly power.

Circe.

24

ODYSSEUS

A year had passed since we'd arrived on the island of Aeaea.

Circe had seen to it that the rest of my men were also turned into pigs. The women, she turned into birds. "Freed from the slavery they were so clearly in," she claimed. No matter that they were now forced to dig worms from the dirt with beaks that were once their mouths.

All the women, that was, except for Odette.

Odette, Circe had decided in front of all the remaining animals in the clearing that night, was to be her maid, someone to braid her hair and provide companionship, comfort, conversation. While I, under threat of transfiguration, was expected to warm her bed at night. I knew then that she had seen me cutting off Odette's hair, that she knew I cared for her. That she would keep Odette as a woman if only to keep me on a leash, and it grated me that it worked.

For twelve months I had warmed that witch's bed. Whatever she had laced into the wine that first night had worked as she'd intended, and I'd been compliant, if unwilling, while my cock remained hard enough for her to ride. It made me think of Odette, and the other Trojan women in the war. But I clenched my jaw and got through it.

Circe must have also given herself a fertility tonic of some kind that night, for she immediately fell pregnant with my son, Telegonus. He now lay in a crib beside me, slobbering on a wooden horse the size of my palm that I had carved for him one evening in the clearing where we had first landed on Aeaea. I had hoped Odette would meet me that night, in the clearing under the full moon, while Circe was busy with her spells – and whatever else she did at the witch's hour that she felt absolved her of her behaviour – but Odette never showed.

We had only been able to meet half a dozen times at best over the last year, clandestine meetings with whispered words in code, on our guard, alert to the tiniest movement.

I missed her.

I know that before we arrived here, I had wanted to distance myself from her. I had believed in the strength of that, and then I had been brash in my actions to protect her, to the point she probably hated me for what I had taken from her, given she had little. But now, without the men and in the presence of a witch with access to power I could not fathom, I bitterly regretted the trajectory of my actions and my thoughts.

I missed Odette's snarky remarks, the snort she couldn't help but make when she found something I said amusing in an unironic way, and the eyeroll that accompanied it. I missed the way she knew she could predict my moods and movements. How she provided comfort when I thought myself alone; a general who could not turn to anyone, not even fellow generals, for fear of being seen as weak.

Even when Odette had been withdrawn from me, when we had first come to know each other, and whenever something was working around in her little mind that caused her to retreat into herself, it was still better than the shell of the woman who now shuffled around the cottage.

Odette had only withdrawn into herself further after Telegonus had been born. I knew she thought of her own son, Lykas, who would have started school by now. My own firstborn, Telemachus, would be ten and two this year, beginning his journey into manhood.

The thought of not being there for it made me feel like less of a man, less of a father.

I still thought of Penelope often, too. I wondered how she was coping with raising a son, and undoubtedly having to fend off suitors trying to convince her I was lost – or worse – dead at sea.

Although, as I looked at Odette's gaunt face once again as she pottered about keeping the hearth warm while Circe and I sat at the table, I wondered, not for the first time, if this was a fate worse than death. Some cruel trick by the gods, where slavery begot slavery.

"Odette, take Telegonus for his bath, please," Circe interrupted from her seat by the fire, one hand stroking her already swollen belly. No sooner had Telegonus been born than Circe had me drink that vile wine once again, and now she was certain we would have a daughter. How she could tell so soon confounded me, but that was witches for you.

"Yes, mistress," Odette acquiesced, brushing the needles of bark from her hands, wiping them on her apron and then turning to scoop up my son in her arms, paying me no mind whatsoever.

I wish she would, but I understood why she didn't when Circe was around.

I caught the witch smiling slyly at me as she watched the interaction.

"So handsome, our son, isn't he, Odysseus? I'm sure he will make a fine warrior one day, just like his father."

I grunted, lifting my wine cup to my lips for something to do other than respond.

"And our daughter, too. She will be as pretty as me, no?"

"Still so certain it is a girl? Careful, Circe, or you will have everything you need from me and you'll have no reason to deny my request to return to Ithaca," I murmured, my eyes downcast to my drink, trying to hide my smile behind the rim of the cup.

Circe returned a wide smile of her own, her teeth flashing a brilliant white. "Oh, my dear Odysseus, do you not remember what the prophet said to you upon your jaunt to the Underworld? Between the Sirens and the Scylla, you would not survive the journey home."

Sirens and Scylla. They were no monsters of the deep - they were the women in front of me. Odette, the siren I so desperately wished to hear, so much so that I could feel my body falling forward in her presence, just desperate for her to simply *talk* to me again as she once had. That I might hear her thoughts or musings on anything Circe said without having to question in my own mind the choice of her words. There were so many fascinating things about this island, Circe, the creatures - enough to fill a book full of colour, and yet Odette had barely strung more sentences together than digits I had on my hands. I felt as though I was bound to this very chair I sat in. Bees swarmed about my head, cutting me off from ever truly hearing her, ever truly seeing her again, beeswax dripping into my ears.

I wondered if Circe had laced the honey on my bread.

In comparison, the witch before me was Scylla herself, the six-headed monster. For whenever I met one of her demands, another seemed to crop up in its place. First, a maid to keep her company. Then, to become lovers. Then a son. Now a daughter. What would be the other two demands, I wondered? Or perhaps Circe was more like Charybdis, the giant whirlpool, and I was merely the sailor caught up in her schemes.

At least I had been able to bury Elpenor, the first man of my crew who had stumbled across Circe, when I found his body. She had struck him down where he stood, murdered him, for he had found her when she was bathing naked, or so she claimed. He'd obviously gone scouting away from the rest of the men, for the others had found her later in her hut, and because she'd been expecting them, she'd turned them into pigs. Called their behaviour vile and rude, worthy of the creature.

Had I not been to the Underworld, had Elpenor not told me of his plight, I would not have expected murder from Circe. Witchcraft, yes. But, murder ... Well, unlike Odette, I doubted I'd be able to talk the witch out of it.

"Has this truly been so terrible a place to live?" She raised one perfectly arched dark brow at me, her straight black waist-length hair rippling as she adjusted herself to gesture around the room.

Vines and herbs curved around the wooden rafters and decorated the windowsills, the wooden benches either side of the walls well oiled, as was the large wooden table we sat at in the centre of the room. The brick wall, under which the hearth stood, broke up the monotony of the wood in the main room we all shared, the fire a good focal point for when I couldn't stand to look at Circe, or when I needed to will myself not to watch Odette.

Of course, there were other rooms in the cottage, a garden out front, the sty for the pigs - *men* – out the back, a barn for the cows and chickens. In other words, it was the domestic bliss I had craved during war; the simple life I had longed to live. Just not with the one I wanted to live it with. Not like this.

So, I did not even have to consider my answer. "No."

For, in truth, it hadn't been. The cottage had no want for homely comforts, from the solid wooden chairs with supportive lumber for my back, to the steel tub where I could bathe when I wanted hot water to soothe my aching muscles after chopping wood. Even walks in the forests were a balm, to have bare feet on earth that was not soaked with blood, sweat, piss and shit. Birdsong in the morning - charming, if I didn't think too hard about the birds. Warm drinks, good wine (when it wasn't spiked), an iron-framed bed whose comforter was made up of more than a pallet, though that had taken some getting used to, my body not what it once was. Fresh fruit and warm broths, nothing that had to be rationed or fought over.

In truth, the greatest gift was being relieved of the responsibility over the men, but I would never confess that thought aloud.

Circe's smile widened as if she'd heard my thoughts. "Well," she said, slowly rising to her feet, using the back of her own chair as leverage to hoist herself up, the babe in her belly growing bigger by the day. "I shall go and complete my rituals. Will I return to find you in our bed?"

I took another sip of wine and grunted. There was nowhere else I could sleep. The times I had tried, sitting upright in the chair by the fire with my arms crossed and my head rolled forward, thinking I could get away with it under the guise of exhaustion, my feet somehow found their way to the bed, no matter how hard I tried to force them to walk a different way.

"I may take a walk to clear my head of this wine before bed," I told her. That way, she wouldn't come looking for me.

"Very well, I will see you shortly."

When I was certain she was gone, I allowed several more slow minutes to pass, listening only to the sounds of the fire crackling, before downing the rest of my wine and heading out the door and towards the clearing.

SHE WAS HERE.

I could have sworn my soul sighed at the sight of Odette by the ocean. Though it had been a year since we had sailed, the gods knew how I had prayed that we would find permanent land, and there was something about Odette by the shoreline that made me think of freedom.

I crept around the edge of the clearing, placing my feet carefully with each step so as not to startle her. Her shoulders were tense, and her posture seemed unnaturally still, like a statue teetering on the edge of collapse. I paused for a moment, just watching Odette as the ocean breeze tugged at her hair, her knuckles white from clutching her cloak. I wondered what haunted her thoughts.

"Telegonus?" I asked, my voice low.

"Asleep," she replied, not turning to face me. "Being watched over by the birds."

"And yourself?"

She exhaled, but the sound was more like a tremor than a sigh. "Alive in a cage of my own creation."

She always said that, and refused to reply whenever I tried to pry more from her, but there was something darker in her words this time. I could hear the tremble, the tenor of fear in her tone. Usually, when she said that, I would attempt to comfort her, and she would offer me a small smile, as if I were a young boy trying to sweet-talk a grown woman. It was one of those sad, all-knowing smiles that finds your naivety a kind-but-useless balm. Then she would shake her head, tell me it wasn't for me to worry about, tell me whatever other piece of information she thought important for me to know – gathered from listening to Circe – and walk away.

But tonight, she surprised me.

"I cannot keep doing this, Odysseus," she whispered, and I swore I saw her flinch at my name, like speaking it might summon Circe herself from the shadows.

"I will find us a way ..."

"And I will lose my mind while you try." Her voice cracked. "Circe always watches, already *knows*. I know she knows."

"Odette, I—"

"I can't stay here. Not with her watching. Not with this ... this *madness* clawing at my mind." She stepped back, shaking her head, as if trying to shake off the thoughts. "Circe ... The power she has over both of us ... We won't escape it. We'll be stuck here forever."

I reached for her, but she recoiled, her fingers twitching nervously at her sides.

"Just a little bit longer, until—"

"Until what? Until your next child is born? Your son will begin hitting his milestones before the turn of the season, and while I have tried my best while he is but a babe, the change in him …" she trailed off. "Would you really have me stay here until your son surpasses Lykas in age?"

I sighed. "No, I would not."

"And you cannot get us off this island."

She said it with such finality, it knocked all arguments from my lungs.

Before I could gather the breath to implore her, she turned, as she always did, and walked away.

I HAD TRIED everything to convince Circe to free us from this island.

Everything, except the one thing I swore I never would. But with Odette on the brink of breaking, pride was a luxury I could no longer afford. Not if I wanted her to survive.

"Odysseus, what are you doing?"

She was amused. I was on my knees by our bed, and she was amused.

"Circe, I have done all that you have asked of me. I have sacrificed all that I have, given all that I am, gifted you children. What else must I do to be free to return to Ithaca once again? Tell me, please, tell me what I must do."

Her stone-grey eyes, usually so hardened unless they were revelling in my misery, grew wide as I looked up at her. "You do not wish to be here?"

She had to be toying with me. Here I was, my knees pressed into the stone floor of her chamber, the weight of the year spent on Aeaea grounding me down to ... *this*. "No," I gritted out.

Circe's eyes softened with a sadness I hadn't expected. "Odysseus," she murmured, her voice carrying a trace of regret. "I truly thought you would find happiness here. Just as I did, in time." She reached out, her fingers brushing my cheek, and for a moment, I saw the loneliness she tried so hard to mask. "I was miserable when I was first exiled to this island. I thought, in time, you would understand. That you would enjoy making a life here, as I did."

Her words stung, not because they were false, but because they weren't. Part of me had wondered if this was how it would end, if I would be trapped here, losing myself to her and this cursed paradise.

But then, there was Odette. Odette, who had withered in this place, whose spirit had been crushed under the weight of her own despair. I could not, would not, let that be our fate.

"Please, Circe," I whispered. "Let us go."

She withdrew her hand, her gaze hardening as she retreated into the role of the witch once more. But even then, I saw the cracks in her armour – the flicker of hesitation, the pain she concealed so well. "Us?"

"The men, the women, all of us who wish to return to Ithaca."

"You mean Odette," she accused.

I kept my head bowed, begging, praying to the gods that something would be able to sway her.

Circe laughed and a cold dread settled in my chest. "You think her heart is bound as yours is – but it is not. There are whispers that cling to her, promises made that cannot be broken. I cannot speak of it, except to say that saving her will cost you, and despite what you may think of me, I know you, Odysseus. This is a cost you will not want to pay."

"Tell me, Circe. Let me be the decider of that."

She sighed, and when she eventually spoke again, her voice was quiet, almost resigned. "You will not understand until you experience it, I suppose. Such is the way with mortals. Very well. If you wish to leave, Odysseus, you may do so if you make this one vow," she said, her tone now firm. "Swear that when your journey is done, you will return to me."

She gave no date; there would be loopholes to work around this vow.

"Very well, I swear it."

"And ... a final sacrifice," she said, her tone testing, as if she was trying one last time to get me to stay. As if she truly cared. "Six of your men and women must remain here. The rest I will return to you, to help man the ship that will take you back to Ithaca."

My head remained lowered, the enormity of her demand sinking onto my shoulders. Would I really sacrifice six lives for my own freedom? For Odette's?

Gods forgive me, I knew the answer.

25

ODETTE

I did not know what he did to get us off this island; I did not want to know. All I could say was I was grateful to be sailing away from the plush jungle forest that was Aeaea.

The ludicrous thought made bubbles of laughter want to escape my throat.

Would I have ever imagined saying such a thing a year ago when we were stuck at sea?

No.

But beauty like that of Aeaea was as much a prison as being a woman. No wonder Circe was so bitter, trapped in a gilded prison of her own design. Nothing could truly get in and nothing could get out. The ecological system on the outside was no match for what went on within a woman, particularly one like Circe.

No wonder Gaia was the birther of the gods.

As the island grew smaller on the horizon, the wind, which had once carried us so rapidly away, now seemed to hesitate. I stood at the edge of the ship, as I had only a year ago, gripping the rusted railing as the waves rolled beneath us, the sea shimmering with a promise of something else to come, something always just out of reach, no matter how far we sailed.

Suddenly, I felt the warmth of Odysseus' body press against mine. He wrapped his arms around me from behind, his hands settling on my waist as he pulled me close. The roughness of his tunic brushed against my back, and his breath was hot against my ear as he leaned in.

"We're finally free," he whispered, his voice low and intimate, a private murmur meant only for me. "Aeaea is behind us, and soon Ithaca will be before us."

His words were meant to comfort, to assure me that this was what I had wanted, what I had fought for. But they felt like a weight pressing down on my chest, making it hard to breathe. The island was behind us, but the memories, the scars, the vows still clung to us, trailing like shadows we could never outrun.

I remained silent, staring out at the darkening sea as his arms tightened around me, his hold possessive yet gentle. "Odette," he murmured, his voice softer now, as if coaxing a response from me, trying to pull me from the depths of my own mind. "It's over. We're going home."

Home. The word hung between us, heavy with meaning. Ithaca might be his home, but to me it would become just another place of entrapment, another cage under a different guise, all thanks to that foolish vow I would never be free of.

I felt him nuzzle into the curve of my neck, sending a shiver down my spine. "You won't be Penelope's maid," he said, as if sensing the direction of my thoughts. "Not after the year we've had. I would not see you again become the shell of who you once were. Once we reach Ithaca, I'll make sure you're free."

Free. The word sounded hollow, like a distant echo of something that might have once been true, but was now out of reach. What did freedom even mean anymore? What more could it be other than an elaborate curtain of illusion the gods placed before us?

When I didn't answer, Odysseus went quiet and still behind me. For a moment, I thought he might release me, let me go. But then his arms tightened, and he buried his face in my hair, inhaling deeply as if trying to memorise the scent of me, to hold on to whatever part of me he could. Then, he turned me in his arms, his eyes searching mine, as if looking for something – understanding, forgiveness, maybe even hope. But I had none of those left to give.

"I don't want to let you go, Odette," he whispered, his voice breaking, raw with a vulnerability I had never heard before. "But I will, if I must."

His words were just another set of chains binding me to him, tightening around my heart with every syllable. I could feel the desperation in his hold, in the way he clung to me, as if I were the anchor keeping him from being swept away.

He had promised me freedom.

The ship creaked beneath us, the wind picking up again, urging us forward. I closed my eyes, the salt of the sea mingling with tears that threatened to spill over as Odysseus held me, whispering promises I could not trust. I wanted to believe him, to let myself be comforted by his words. But all I felt was the weight of his love, heavier than the weight of the vow, and I knew no matter how far we sailed, I would not escape one without breaking the other.

There was no true escape. It would have been better if I had just stayed on the island.

WHAT WAS freedom worth when my soul had been chained so tightly to his? That was what I kept thinking of as the wind tugged at my hair, and the salty spray of the waves kissed my cheeks.

Odysseus was at the helm of the ship now, his hands steady on the rudder, guiding us through an ocean that felt like an eternity. The men, those who had survived, moved about the deck with a quiet efficiency, their eyes darting nervously between the sea and the sky, as if expecting the gods to curse us now that we were back on their chessboard.

The past year had left its mark on all of us, but none more so than me. My body felt foreign, weakened by the long months of hunger, toil, and the weight of despair that had settled deep in my bones. I was a hollow shell, worn down by the months of servitude.

I had been naive to think that war would be the worst of it. The aftermath, by comparison, was a masterclass in sinister cruelty. At least war was in your face, brash; it couldn't hide what it was, nor did it attempt to. Ares did not hide his art. But what came afterwards – the torment, the unease in one's own skin, the *hatred* that could no longer be disguised as survival – was a merciless brutality that pounded and raged beneath my skin every day. One I had never expected.

We continued to sail on through the night, the stars above us as cold and distant as the gods.

The days passed in a blur of grey skies and churning waves, the wind driving us ever onward. It didn't take long for the men to grow restless once again, so when whispers began to circulate that we were approaching the island of

Helios – an island where sacred cattle roamed, untouched by time, watched over by the god himself – I knew what to expect. The promise of fresh meat would be too much for them to resist.

Hunger gnawed in my own belly, a dull ache that reminded me that Circe was a witch gifted with a godlike heritage. She had filled our stores with food she thought would last gods and goddesses, not mortals. Our constitutions were not the same. Where they could survive off mere morsels of delectability, we craved a volume of averages. We had been starving within three days compared to what she had fed us on the island.

Perhaps that was her way of getting Odysseus to return.

So, when we landed on Helios' island under a sky thick with clouds, I was not surprised to hear the men's urgent whispers in low tones: "... the need to survive, to fill empty stomachs, to hell with the gods ..." They were eager to hunt, their desperation palpable as they moved like wolves, eyes wild with hunger.

Odysseus gathered the men before they could scatter farther, forcing them to listen. "Men, heed my words," he began. "These are no ordinary cattle. They belong to Helios, the Sun God himself. If we harm them, we will bring his wrath upon us. Remember, the gods do not forgive lightly."

The men exchanged uneasy glances, and I swore only I could see it for what it was. They were *driven*, desperate to cling to life. Somehow, the detachment of this thought allowed me to realise I was slipping further from it; from life. I would not eat this cattle, but their hunger made them restless, and reckless.

Eurylochus, his face gaunt and eyes hollow, stepped forward. "We've faced the wrath of gods before, Odysseus.

We've survived war, storms, monsters, even the witch herself. But what good is survival if we're too weak to stand? We'll die if we don't eat."

I looked at him, at all of them, seeing the toll this journey had taken. They were mere shadows of the men who had left Ithaca so long ago – skin stretched tight over bones, eyes sunken with despair. I could see that their loyalty to Odysseus was not in question, but their endurance was nearly spent.

"I understand your hunger," Odysseus said, his voice softening as he tried to reach them. "But there are other ways to survive. We can fish, forage – anything but this. Promise me."

I watched the men turn to one another, questioning. Eventually they grumbled their agreement, but I could see it in their eyes. They had no intention of keeping the oaths they now swore before the gods. Their words were shallow, spoken only to appease their leader in the moment, but the truth was plain. It was only a matter of time before they gave in, before their starvation overwhelmed what little reason they had left. Hunger had a way of silencing reason, of drowning out the voice of caution.

Odysseus seemed satisfied, though. Or perhaps it was the weight of his responsibility that wore him down, for soon after, he lay beside me in a meadow, not unlike one I had lain in with Alcander once. I watched as he settled onto the hard ground, his body relaxing bit by bit, until the tension eased from his limbs and his breathing slowed. He fought sleep at first, his eyes fluttering open now and then as if he were trying to keep vigilant, but eventually, weariness claimed him. His eyelids grew heavy, and with a final exhale, he succumbed to the pull of sleep.

I leaned on my elbows and watched him, then turned to watch the men, now breaking their vow. I listened to the sound of Odysseus' breathing, steady and deep, and felt an ache in my chest. I thought about waking him, about warning him of the men's intentions, but the thought passed as quickly as it came. What difference would it make? Men always came out on top, didn't they? Even when they broke the sacred laws, even when they defied the gods. Somehow, they always found a way to survive.

I used to care about surviving. Back when I had a reason to live, a reason to fight.

But what did I have now?

A life that was no longer mine. The woman I had been when I left Troy was gone, and in her place was someone I barely recognised. Someone shaped by the hands of a goddess, by the cruelty of the Fates, by the choices that had been made for me and by me.

The night wore on and I was eventually sucked under, to the usual chorus of cicadas and distant waves. I swore I laid there for an eternity, staring into the darkness, listening for any sign of movement. But I must have fallen asleep, for when I woke, the smell of roasting meat was wafting through the air, mingled with the tang of salt and the earthy scent of the island. My stomach churned, and I realised, after consciousness hit me with the force of an ocean slap, that it was not with hunger but with dread.

The men had slaughtered the sacred cattle.

Helios would not let this go unpunished.

I glanced at Odysseus, still sleeping beside me, oblivious to the unfolding betrayal. What good would it do to wake him and tell him? The men were already lost, their fates sealed the moment they decided to take what wasn't theirs.

The night stretched on, and with each passing moment, the air grew heavier, charged with a strange energy that made the hairs on the back of my neck stand on end. The sky darkened, the night far from over, and an unnatural stillness settled over the island. Even the wind seemed to hold its breath, waiting for the inevitable.

A sudden crack of thunder split the sky, and I flinched, my heart leaping against my chest. The heavens opened up, and a torrential rain fell, drenching the island in a matter of seconds. The fire sputtered out, leaving us in complete darkness. I could hear the men's laughter in the distance, their voices high and wild as they feasted on the forbidden meat, completely unaware of the storm brewing above them.

But it wasn't just the rain. The very ground beneath us seemed to tremble, a low rumble that grew louder with each passing second. The sea, calm and gentle moments ago, now roared like a beast unleashed, waves crashing against the shore with a fury that matched the storm.

I tried to scream at them to stop, to beg them to listen, but my cries were swallowed by the howling wind. They were beyond saving, and so was I.

Odysseus stirred beside me, his eyes fluttering open, confusion etched on his face as he sat up, taking in the chaos around us. He got up quickly after that, his attention snapping to where the men had gone, realisation dawning across his face, like a sunrise that did not want to break.

He knew what this meant – what the gods would do in response.

But it was too late. The sky lit up with a blinding flash of lightning. The gods had been defied, and now someone would pay the price.

26

ODYSSEUS

The clouds tore apart, and an unnatural light flooded the sky, searing my vision. The golden glow that I had fallen asleep in now blazed with a ferocity that scorched the very air. The atmosphere thickened with an oppressive heat, the kind that presses against your chest until you can barely draw breath, and sweat beaded on my skin instantly. I wasn't alone. Around me, the air grew thick with the pungent stench of fear and body odour.

I tried to open my eyes against the blinding light, but it was useless. Helios himself had descended in fury, his form a smouldering silhouette behind my clenched eyelids. I could almost see his chariot of fire, drawn by four blazing horses, but I didn't need sight to feel his wrath. Instead, my eyes were torn to the earth beneath us as it shuddered in terror.

Before I could even comprehend what was happening, the grass and sand beneath the men bubbled and hiss, transforming into molten glass that clung to their feet. The air filled with their screams, inhuman, guttural wails of agony that pierced my skull and lodged deep within my soul. I knew, even in that moment, that those screams would haunt me for the rest of my days, echoing in the darkest corners of my mind. But it was the smell that truly marked this as a divine punishment – the nauseating stench of charred flesh, the same flesh that had greedily devoured Helios' sacred cattle, now roasted by the god's relentless fire.

The men flailed, their bodies writhing in torment as the divine flames consumed them, searing flesh from bone with an unceasing, unholy heat. Blind with pain, they staggered towards the ocean, driven mad by the agony that refused to relent. One by one, they plunged into the churning waves, their screams swallowed by saltwater. When the last head finally disappeared beneath the waves, leaving only the steaming surface of the ocean as a grim testament to their fate, I forced myself to look back at the island. The lush, vibrant glade that had teemed with life only hours before had been obliterated, scorched to a desolate wasteland.

And in that moment of silence, of utter devastation, I realised that there was no one left but myself and Odette.

Almost immediately, the wind died down to an eerie calm, the sea as still as glass. I watched Odette walk towards the ocean, her vision fixed on the horizon. There was something different in her posture, a tension that made me wary.

She wasn't doing what I thought she was doing, surely – we had just survived.

Only the two of us had survived.

I stood and approached her quietly, unsure of what to say, but as I reached her side, I heard her mutter something under her breath, soft enough for the wind to carry away, that made my blood run cold.

"I revoke my vow," she said, her voice trembling with resolve. "I revoke it, and I offer myself in its place, for nothing can be worse than what you have already put us through.”

My heart hammered against my ribcage. *What vow?*

Before I could ask, the sea beneath our feet churned once again until a whirlpool formed beneath us, its gaping maw widening with every passing second.

“Odette!”

My voice was swallowed by the roar of the water, but she turned to face me, her expression calm, almost serene. Our last remaining ship tilted dangerously, before there was a deafening crack and the boat was torn in two, the mast splintering as it was swallowed by the whirlpool.

I reached for Odette, who stood too close to the lip of the vortex, but she was already slipping from my grasp, her body pulled towards the ocean.

“NO!” I lunged forward, the force of the water dragging me down.

I caught one last glimpse of Odette, her now shoulder-length hair swirling around her like a dark halo, before the water closed over my head. The pressure was immense, crushing the air from my lungs as I was spun helplessly in the current. My vision blurred, and I fought to stay conscious, to keep my eyes on her.

I failed.

I FELT HANDS, cold and trembling, drag me onto a piece of drifting wood in my semi-conscious state, but my strength was nearly spent after surviving the violent currents. It was all I could do to hold on, to float, to be carried away to wher-ever the gods were sending me next.

WHEN I FINALLY CAME TO, I could feel something solid beneath my face; sand, I eventually recognised. Struggling, I blinked my eyes open to find Odette beside me. I had to concentrate all of my energy to focus on her form. Her hair was plastered to her face, her eyes closed, but she was breathing. It allowed me to hope, before exhaustion pulled me back under.

I have no idea how long we lay there. Days could have passed, it could have been hours, but eventually I stirred again when the warmth on my skin grew too much.

Groggily, I pried my eyes open to a sight unfamiliar, yet strangely comforting – an expanse of soft sand, a lush line of trees in the distance, and the steady murmur of the ocean behind me. For a moment, I lay still, letting the reality of the situation sink in. We had survived. Somehow, we had been spared.

Odette was already awake, sitting up beside me, her eyes fixed on the horizon. Her expression was unreadable, a mixture of exhaustion and something I couldn't quite place – resignation, perhaps, or relief.

I pushed myself up, my body stiff and aching. "Are you all right?" I asked, my voice hoarse from the saltwater and strain.

She nodded, but said nothing. Her sight remained on the distant line where the sea met the sky, as if she were searching for something far beyond our reach.

Had I truly heard her make that vow?

I replayed the moment in my mind, searching for certainty. The words had chilled me, but it was her voice – I was sure of that. Gods, had I imagined it? Perhaps it was thirst that had played tricks on me, that hollow dryness burning in my throat and filling my thoughts with spectres. Because, whatever she was, Odette was no fool. A vow that could destroy us both, if she had spoken such a thing, would surely have been laced with hatred, unmistakable in its intent. I would have felt it, wouldn't I?

I clenched my jaw and forced the thought away. It was nonsense, the fanciful imaginings of a man too long at sea, too worn by war and weariness.

Instead, we spent the day exploring the island in each other's quiet company, moving slowly, cautiously, as if afraid to disturb the peace that seemed to envelop the place. The land was bountiful. Fruit hung heavy on the trees, fresh-water streams flowed clear and cool, and the air was rich with the scent of flowers and earth. It was a paradise, untouched by the hands of men or gods.

As we walked, I could feel the tension in my shoulders begin to ease, the weight of our journey lifting ever so slightly. For the first time in what felt like an eternity, there was no immediate danger, no looming threat, no divine punishment to fear. The sun was gentle on our skin, the breeze a soft caress that carried with it the scent of salt and life.

Days passed in a blur of quiet routine. We built a shelter from palm fronds and driftwood, a simple structure that provided shade and a sense of security. We gathered food, drank from the streams, and washed away the remnants of the day's foraging in the cool waters of the island's pools. With each passing day, the island seemed to welcome us more, generously offering its resources.

Odette spoke little, her silence a constant companion that I had grown accustomed to. I watched her as she moved through our days with a calm efficiency, her hands never idle, her thoughts always elsewhere. She was still with me, but I could feel the distance between us growing.

One evening, as the sun dipped below the horizon, and we sat just close enough to the water's edge that the waves could lap at our feet, as had been our custom the last several nights, I found myself saying, "We could stay here," the words slipping out before I had fully considered them.

She turned to me, her eyes reflecting the fading light. "Stay?" she echoed, her voice soft, almost disbelieving.

"I would, with you," I replied, and I meant it. After everything we had been through, after all the losses and the pain, I was tired. Tired of fighting, tired of struggling to reach a home that had become more myth than reality in my mind. Here, with Odette, I could find a different kind of peace.

"We have everything we need here," I continued, the idea solidifying in my mind as I spoke. "Food, water, shelter. It's peaceful. We could build a life here, grow old here. Together."

Odette looked out at the sea, her expression unreadable once more. "And Ithaca?" she asked.

"Ithaca is a distant memory," I said, surprising even myself with the truth of it. "This place, it could be our Ithaca. We could find peace here, after everything."

She didn't say anything, but the way she leaned into me, the way her hand found mine, told me everything I needed to know. We were in this together, whatever 'this' was. For the first time in what felt like years, I allowed myself to dream of a future that didn't involve endless battles and impossible quests.

In the silence I watched her, noticing the way the fading light of the day played across her features, softening the edges of her worry. She must have felt me staring, for her eyes met mine, and for a moment something unspoken passed between us – a shared recognition of all that we had endured, and perhaps, a tentative hope for what might yet come.

Without a word, I reached over and with my other hand, pulled her hip towards me until she rolled onto my lap, the space between us closed in an instant. I reached out, my hand brushing against her cheek, feeling the warmth of her skin, the steady beat of her pulse beneath my fingers, until my thumb parted her lips and she let out a little breathy moan. I leant forward and captured it with my own mouth, my hand gripping her hair, pulling her deeper into me.

My other hand roamed over her body, memorising the spot between her neck and her shoulder, the heavy weight of her breast, the dip of her waist, and curve of her hip, as if trying to etch this moment into my very soul. Odette arched into me, her body willing as she moved on top of me, in that soft, urgent way of hers. I let myself get lost in her, in the rhythm of our bodies that was both familiar and yet entirely new, until the heat between us built to a burning intensity.

Unsheathing myself, Odette spread herself wider and then settled down onto me, both of us watching my cock fill her slowly. She moaned. I myself had to bite back a curse to stop from digging my fingers into her thick hips, pulling out and slamming myself back in or speeding it up.

I wanted to savour this sweet hell.

I took her mouth in another kiss. She tasted like the sweetest of ripe apples, her moans better than any symphony my mind could remember, the feel of her smooth skin against my calloused hands a balm I somehow knew I needed for the rest of my life.

She sunk down on me again, over and over, until my

head rolled back and she leaned to kiss the thick cord of my neck, and I couldn't have stopped myself if I tried, cupping her to me, her breasts crushed against my chest, as I pumped once, twice, three times, and came deep inside her.

Afterwards, with Odette snuggled into my chest, I leaned in to press a kiss against her forehead, her hair tickling me and smelling of crushed grass. This woman in my arms had become my home away from home, the one who could cajole me into a laugh or a tired smile, no matter my temperament, whose mind was so like mine. These past days, I had found myself craving to wake her just to hear her thoughts, though sparing but insightful during the day, or share my own with her.

I still loved my wife, and I'd fallen in love with the woman beside me.

As if the thought had conjured the divine, a strange sensation began to prickle along my arms. I lifted my head, scanning the treeline, then sat up, my arms braced on my knees.

"Odysseus? What is it?"

"We're not alone."

As soon as I said the words, the creature emerged, stepping gracefully from the jungle. Her skin was ochre while ebony dark waves of hair cascaded down her back wildly. Her eyes, the same colour as her skin, were round with curiosity, fixed on us with an intensity I didn't like.

She continued to approach us with an almost predatory grace, as if worried we would scarper. Yet, her attention never wavered, and for some reason my brain told me that if we ran, she would catch us, no matter how long it took.

"I've been watching you," she said, her voice lilting with a strange mix of innocence and power. "I do not understand this ... what you did." She gestured vaguely at our bodies, her expression a mixture of curiosity and confusion. "Show me," she demanded, her eyes locking onto mine with an earnestness that belied the command in her voice.

I felt Odette tense beside me, and I pushed myself up, wrapping my chiton around my hips as I did so. "No," I replied firmly, despite the unease crawling through me. "It's not something to be shown."

She tilted her head, as if pondering my refusal. For a moment, her gaze softened, and she looked almost human, almost vulnerable. But then, just as quickly, her expression hardened, and I knew that this was no ordinary woman. This was a goddess, ancient and powerful, and she did not like to be denied.

I expected her to condemn us, to banish us from this island, to do something Circe might have done. Instead, she giggled unnaturally. Then, with a voice as soft as a lullaby, she turned to Odette and posed the question that would shatter whatever illusions I had left.

"Should I tell him? Of the vow you made?

"Poseidon told me, for I am the Oceanid, Calypso, and this is my island. He said he does not release you from your vow. That the man," a curious look towards me, as if she was unfamiliar with the word, "has done too much damage. That your vow is the retribution."

Shock rippled through my body as I looked at Odette.

What had she done?

"But," the nymph continued, "I can find a way to help you."

"You can?" Odette breathed.

"I will give you the means to return home, to rebuild your life anew."

Already, Odette was shaking her head. "It won't work, I've already tried ..."

Calypso continued, summoning the sands until they took the form of a man and a little boy.

If I had anything to bet with the gods, I'd wager it was Odette's husband and son.

"I can give you peace in your heart, for as long as you want it."

"I'm not the same woman," Odette seemed to plead now, looking towards the sand and air sculptures of her old life ... and me.

"Don't you see?" Calypso asked, still in that childlike sing-song voice that was beginning to irritate me. "It is the loophole in the vow you spoke. You must be able to return home. That way, Poseidon will have no binding cause to keep Odysseus from Ithaca. I can grant him immortality for as long as he stays on this island with me, and once Poseidon's anger has cooled, he can make his way home again. Or, I'm afraid I will have to cast you both back into the ocean. I don't want to witness what you two do anymore, if I cannot try it for myself." She frowned, as if this were an obvious solution; as if she weren't threatening our very lives.

The decision was clear as day. Odette's old life, or together to the end.

I thought I knew what she would decide, after all we had been through. Ithaca had always been my goal, my driving force, the thing that had kept me going through all the trials and tribulations, and I had given that up. I had accepted my fate. I had chosen a life with Odette, however little of it was left.

And now I found that there was somehow a vow, that she had made, that had driven us here.

"Odette?"

But before I could voice the thoughts that tore at my heart, I saw it in Odette's eyes – the decision. I did not need to hear the words; I already knew. I had been played like a pawn in her game. She had plotted the very thing she had been accusing me of this whole time, and I, a damned fool, had ignored my instincts, ignored everything that had served me well in the past – for her.

"Did you really hate me so much you would not see me home to my wife? My family? Knowing how that would wound me? Have I really been so cruel to you that you would leave me here, with her?"

"At least you will be alive. You will have a chance to go home one day," she tried to reason. "If we leave together now, what hope do we have of surviving Poseidon's domain?"

"A god's wrath can last decades, centuries! You know this!" I threw my hands up in the air. "Do not leave me alone on this island, Odette. Do not leave me in this prison of your making, a *slave*, as you have abhorred. I have accepted my fate. I have chosen you over Ithaca. If you leave me here, I would rather die at sea anyway."

"And I would see you live long enough that you may return to your family once more. I no longer wish to take that from you," she whispered, trying to break away.

Instead, I pulled her closer, until our faces were mere inches apart, while Calypso watched on. "If you do this, I'll not be able to forgive you."

Tears pooled in her eyes, but she did not let them fall. "As is your right. I would still see you live."

Then, Odette turned away from me, and whatever fragile connection had entwined us for so long, snapped.

Calypso smiled at her, satisfied in her victory.

The older male sand body began walking towards a small boat that had risen from the depths of the ocean before my very eyes, while the small boyish figure ran forward, beckoning Odette to follow.

Calypso giggled as Odette almost broke into a run, just to see her son's form once again.

"Uh-uh, there are rules," Calypso sang, snapping out a hand with unnaturally fast reflexes, to capture Odette's arm and stop her in her tracks.

"What?" Odette impatiently brushed a tangled curl from her face, and there was a painful spike in my chest as I realised I would never get to do that for her again. That she was robbing us, me, of something I had come to treasure in those few and fleeting moments we'd had alone.

"One, you must return to your village by this boat. Alcander will lead the way. Two, should you change your mind, should you turn back to my island, the sands of time will take your boys as quickly as they appeared, and – poof – Poseidon will claim you as his own. The boat will be nothing but splinters floating on the sea, and you," – her focus darted over Odette, as if already seeing her drowned and broken body – "will end up shipwrecked, dead, with nothing to show for your sacrifice. We both know how that went for you last time."

Odette's jaw clenched ever so slightly. The moment dragged for what felt like an eternity, and then, at last, her chin dipped. A nod so small it could have been imagined, but Calypso saw it, and her cold smile stretched unnaturally. She had what she wanted – an agreement, unspoken but under-stood – that the broken shell of the man I now was would remain in her possession.

As she led Odette away, towards the conjured boat, the sand statues of Odette's loved ones already sitting in it, I stood there, muttering a vow of my own.

"Lady Athena, hear my words. May Odette spend the rest of her days with my cool breath on the back of her neck like the wind, forever watching over her shoulder, awaiting my retribution. And when the time is right, by your good graces, may I bury her myself beneath Poseidon's keep where the water is coldest, so that she may feel the cold she has placed upon my heart, forever in her death."

Ash, the same grey as Lady Athena's eyes, plumed from the volcano on the island.

My Lady had heard me.

Pre-order Book Two: Odysseus' Promise to find out what happens next.

About the Author

Gwyneth Lesley loves to write modern-day Greek myth retellings with heartbreaking, steamy romances. Her first series, Femme Fatale, is a mixture of standalone books, following the archetypes of seven different women with fictional ties to Greek mythology.

You can read the first three in the series here:

Prometheus' Priestess
A Lifetime Kind of Love
Madonna: Medusa's retelling

She also has a Greek Mythology cozy fantasy series you can delve into here:

The Urban Underworld Omnibus: Serving Up Bite-Sized Cozy Fantasy Based in Greek Mythology
(The Underworld Novellas 1-6)

WHAT GWEN IS WORKING ON NEXT

Apollo's Oracle
(Femme Fatale #4)

Odysseus' Promise
(Vows of the Lost Epics: Book Two)

As reviewers say, her work is: "Definitely recommend[ed] to people who have never read any Greek mythology and are looking to expand their reading palette."

Learn more at https://www.gwynethlesley.com

ACKNOWLEDGMENTS

There are a few people without whom I would never have finished writing this book.

Firstly, to G, who patiently read through my work and called me out on crafting a plot with more structure. Your guidance helped me make my writing infinitely better – even if I hated the process. This book would not have been the same, nor as easy to write, without that push. Thank you for all the nights you picked up the cooking or the dishes, or left me in my writing bubble so I could get this done and into the hands of readers.

To Aleena, who devoured this book in two weeks and showed me that the story really did have bones. And for all of you who appreciated the pining between Odysseus and Odette, you can thank her – she requested it.

To Erin, whose meticulousness makes all my work stronger. I love our late-night manuscript editing sessions, the little love notes you leave for the characters (and me), and how I can implicitly trust you with every word in this book.

To Taylor, who has patiently waited for this book for over a year.

To Shamera, who has done the same.

To Jo, who has supported all my work from the very beginning.

And to you, the readers, who make the process of writing a book so worth it. Thank you.